Praise for *Expecting*

"Ann Lewis Hamilton is a comic genius. Along with capturing the absurdity of everyday life, her astute observations pack an emotional wallop. *Expecting*, her refreshingly honest novel, is the first book about infertility that made me laugh. Then it made me cry. A charming, big-hearted novel, *Expecting* is an exuberant celebration of contemporary families in all their insane, messy beauty."

—Jillian Medoff, bestselling author of *I Couldn't Love You More* and *Hunger Point*

"Ripe with conflict and controversy, *Expecting* is a perfect book club pick. Ann Lewis Hamilton takes a serious subject matter—infertility—and layers it with havoc, heart, and humor. *Expecting* will lure you in with its fresh premise and sharply drawn characters. A remarkable debut, *Expecting* is a beautiful reminder of the resilience of love and the elasticity of family ties."

—Lori Nelson Spielman, author of *The Life List*

"Every once in a while that truly special book comes along that you just cannot put down, that you just cannot stop thinking about. That's *Expecting*. At once hysterical and heartbreaking, sweet and wise, Ann Hamilton's breakout debut is simply brilliant. With expertly drawn characters, complex and authentic as our closest friends, *Expecting* is an unexpected joy—a beautiful ode to relationships and love and all the things that really matter, rendered by a master storyteller. Book clubs grab this now!"

—Jeffrey Stepakoff, bestselling author of *Fireworks Over Toccoa*

"It's been twenty years since my last pregnancy, but Ann Lewis Hamilton's *Expecting* brought back every detail, from the queasiness to the sexed-up mood swings, with a hilarious yet poignant twist. This novel is the literary equivalent of 'easy on the eyes.' It's a pleasure to read—so much so that its message about what makes a real family sneaks up on you. You will miss every one of *Expecting*'s sweet, mordant, and slightly zany characters when you close the book."

—Ann Bauer, author of *The Forever Marriage*

Expecting

A Novel

Ann Lewis Hamilton

Published by Sourcebooks Landmark, an imprint of Sourcebooks, Inc.
P.O. Box 4410, Naperville, Illinois 60567-4410
(630) 961-3900
Fax: (630) 961-2168
www.sourcebooks.com

Library of Congress Cataloging-in-Publication data is on file with the publisher.

Printed and bound in the United States of America.
VP 10 9 8 7 6 5 4 3 2 1

For Max, my birth child
For Lucy, my heart child

Expect nothing. Live frugally
On surprise.

—Alice Walker

The worst place your water could break.

The Hollywood Bowl. During an especially quiet part of a classical concert, not Darth Vader's theme from the "Star Wars Suite." You're in a center box seat, close enough to see the sweat on the cello player's forehead, and the space is crowded tight with four people, so an inconspicuous exit will be impossible. Your husband notices the concrete floor of the box is suddenly slick and wet and whispers, "Did you spill your wine?" And you'd like to believe him—it could be wine, but you know it's amniotic fluid. Vintage, nine months.

There are several problems with this scenario, one of them being you're not drinking wine these days. Pregnancy requires Martinelli's Sparkling Cider, nothing alcoholic.

And two, it's been weeks since your husband moved out of the house and into an apartment. So what would you be doing together at the Hollywood Bowl?

Another bad place for your water to break—a plane. Flying to the most remote spot on earth, over the ocean, four hours from any airport.

Or alone on a desert island. No doctors, no midwives. You always meant to watch the YouTube video that explains how "Anyone Can Deliver Their Own Baby." Too late now.

At Grace's house, sitting on her new Roche Bobois white leather sofa. "It cost more than a car," she tells you. "The leather feels like butter."

So the parking lot at the Trader Joe's in Sherman Oaks isn't the worst place; it's not even top ten bad. Laurie is loading her bags in the trunk and thinking about how she caught the clerks winking at each other when they saw the crazy pregnant lady buying seven bags of dark-chocolate-covered pretzels. "The pretzels aren't for me," she told them. "I'm having a party. For my book club."

Inside the car, she opens a pretzel bag—just to make sure they're fresh—and feels something moist in her panties. Not a great rush of fluid, but the sensation is a shock all the same. The baby isn't due for another week. At home, she goes to the bathroom, and when she looks in the toilet, the water is pink. She calls Dr. Liu and he tells her to head to the hospital.

Laurie's mother is at home in Reno and still on crutches because of her broken knee. Calling will only make her worry.

Grace is in Napa, annoyed at Laurie because she hasn't been asked to be the birth coach. Grace is a wonderful person, Laurie's best friend, but her alarmist personality ("Do you know the *real* probability of an asteroid striking the earth?") is not the support Laurie needs in a delivery room.

Alan isn't answering his phone. She could leave a message. Or not.

Laurie walks down the hall to the guest room. The door is

closed so she knocks. She can hear the creak of the bed and Jack appears. His hair is messed up and he rubs at his eyes.

"I was studying," he says. He fights a yawn. "I wasn't asleep." He yawns again.

Laurie considers. Maybe she should call Alan back and leave a message.

Instead she nods at Jack. "I think it's time."

On *The Flintstones*, pregnant Wilma tells Fred, "I'm ready," and Fred gets so excited he hops in the car and drives off with Barney instead. Wilma remains calm, not worrying about how they haven't invented Pitocin or epidurals yet. She's a *cavewoman*; she probably has to butcher her own T-Rex if Fred wants steak for dinner. And she knows, even though he's Fred, he'll remember eventually and come back for her.

At the hospital, Fred paces and waits with Barney. He's not allowed in the delivery room with Wilma.

Who's going to be in the delivery room with Laurie? She closes her eyes.

Yabba dabba doo.

"Bring the notes for your final and I'll quiz you between contractions," Laurie tells Jack.

He frowns, his eyes wary. He's changed his clothes, and he's wearing a baseball cap—backward—to hide his bed hair.

"That's a joke," Laurie says.

Jack smiles, *oh right*, as if he knew that's what she meant all along, and Laurie considers saying the word *dilation* just to watch his face go pale. But that would be cruel and things are crazy enough already, and this isn't the way it's supposed to be and goddamn it, Alan is her *husband*; he should be here instead of Jack, her houseguest, although that's probably not the best way to explain her relationship to Jack, which is only *insanely* complicated and where the hell *is* Alan anyway? Jack takes a step closer and says, very gently, "Do you have everything?" Jack is sometimes surprisingly wise and perceptive for a twenty-one-year-old.

Everything except my husband. "I hope so," Laurie says. She packed her birthing bag weeks ago and has only repacked it three times. She tries Alan's cell again and leaves a message. "I'm on my way to the hospital."

On the drive over the hill to Cedars-Sinai, she times the contractions. Every twenty minutes. Good; little chance of Jack having to pull over to the side of Coldwater Canyon so he can deliver the baby himself. The air-conditioning in Jack's car is broken, so the vent above her knees blows out arctic air and Jack reaches in the backseat for a blanket. "Sorry," he says, and she's not sure if he's sorry about the broken air conditioner or the fact the blanket is a tiger-stripe Snuggie, but it's warm enough and keeps her knees from aching.

"Is there any music you want to hear?" Jack asks her.

"I have a labor mix on my iPod."

Laurie plugs her iPod into Jack's adaptor. Hits shuffle. Frank Sinatra begins to sing "I've Got the World on a String."

Jack makes a face. "This is your labor mix?"

"What would you pick?"

Jack shrugs. "I don't know. Something not as old-fashioned."

"Old-fashioned? It's Frank Sinatra. It's classic. Some songs, some voices, never go out of style."

"I guess. If you say so." Jack doesn't sound convinced.

Alan likes Frank Sinatra. Is that why she picked this song? She will try not to think about Alan. *Sing to me, Frank. About rainbows, about how life is a wonderful thing.*

Jack's hands clutch at the steering wheel. Is he dreading what's about to happen? *None of us signed up for this, Jack.* She leans against the headrest. It makes a snapping sound and pops back a few inches.

"Sorry. I keep meaning to fix that," Jack says.

The admissions nurse is young, not much older than Jack. Her nameplate says "Constance" and Laurie thinks that's a good sign, a name you'd like to see when you arrive at the hospital in labor. Nothing as upsetting as "Cruella" or "Maleficent." Why is Laurie thinking about cartoon characters? Is it some symptom of early labor? They didn't mention that in Lamaze.

Constance is smiling at Jack. "Your first?"

Jack's mouth opens, but he doesn't say anything.

Constance nods at Laurie. "First time fathers, you can always tell."

"I think it's my first," Jack says finally. "But there could be more. Lots more."

Laurie pats Jack on the arm. "TMI."

Constance flips through Laurie's file. "Super, you've already done your preregistration. You'd be surprised how many people put it off." Another smile at Jack. "Do you know what you're having?"

"I hope it's a baby," Jack says.

Constance laughs as if Jack's onstage at the Comedy Store. Laurie clears her throat. Shouldn't Constance be sending her off to a room?

Laurie hears a burst of music from Jack's pocket—"Cry of the Black Birds" from Jack's current favorite metal band, Amon Amarth. "Cry of the Black Birds" is ringtone code for Jack's parents. Jack pulls out his phone and moves away from the desk.

"Don't worry. He'll be fine," Constance says to Laurie.

"I know, thank you." Laurie hopes Jack is fine, but why are his parents calling? The timing is terrible; he's worried enough about his final and now she's in labor—she shouldn't have made him come with her. When he's off the phone, she'll send him back to the house, insist his final is the most important thing in his life right now. She'll be okay on her own. Alan will get her message and show up.

Unless he doesn't. The contractions are coming closer together now, and she realizes she'd like to lie down.

Jack walks over to Laurie; he turns his cap forward. Then back again.

"Everything okay?" Laurie says.

"Not really. My parents are here. *Here* here. In L.A. On their way to the hospital."

Laurie tries to take that in. "You told them?"

"My sister did. Blabbermouth."

Laurie exhales. "Okay. So they know. But don't worry about your parents. Or me. Think about your final. You need to study."

"I can't study *now*. I have to deal with this." He points at Laurie's stomach.

"This." A tsunami-sized wave of guilt washes over Laurie.

Her head feels fuzzy; the lights of the admissions desk are too bright. Like spotlights.

"I'm sorry," Jack says. "I don't mean to sound like an asshole."

Constance leans over the desk, waving a form at Jack. "Mr. Gaines? I need your signature on this."

Jack looks at Laurie, at Constance. "I'm not Mr. Gaines."

The lights around Laurie multiply. She has to squint and her fuzzy head grows fuzzier.

"Will you call Alan?" she asks Jack. "Maybe he'll pick up this time." Why are the lights so hot? And why does Jack have two faces? With four eyes, two noses? Is this another sign? Will the baby be born like that? Everything is supposed to happen for a reason, that's what people say. What people? Who would come up with a stupid saying like that?

"Laurie? You look kind of..." Two-headed Jack is moving toward her. And the admissions nurse, Cruella or Constance... Laurie can't remember her name, but she has two heads as well—no, *three* heads, a hydra-headed nurse. That can't be good. And she's moving quickly from behind the desk and motioning at someone.

"Tell Alan we'll name the baby Bamm-Bamm," Laurie says to Jack before she passes out in his arms.

Conception

Laurie

"Congratulations," says Dr. Liu. "You're pregnant." Laurie notices Dr. Liu has dimples on either side of his mouth, and she hopes her baby will have dimples. But not Dr. Liu's early male pattern baldness. Thank God Alan's father has a full set of hair. Or is it Laurie's father? Laurie frowns. Damn, why did she sleep through most of high school biology? When she gets home, she'll go on the Internet and research genetics. Unless the baby is born bald and *stays* bald. Does that ever happen? When will Dr. Liu tell her about all the things that can go wrong?

Dr. Liu taps her hand and gives her a reassuring doctor smile. "There's nothing to worry about. Women have been giving birth for thousands of years."

On her way home from the doctor's office, Laurie stops at a Barnes and Noble and heads for the pregnancy/childbirth books. Just walking into the section makes her feel special, as if she's got a secret. When she pulls out a pregnancy book, she considers showing it out to the first person she sees. "Yep," she'll say. "That's me. Having a baby." Instead, she flips through the book and glances at photos of pregnant women and infants. On one page, she sees a woman breast-feeding twins. Twins? She hasn't considered the possibility of multiples.

One will be plenty the first time around. The starter baby. The second pregnancy, twins will be okay. Because by then she'll be a pro. Unless maternal instinct kicks in the first time. Which it might; why wouldn't it? Laurie has always wanted to have a baby.

Growing up in Reno as an only child, her cousins and other family members scattered in Florida and Chicago, she'd begged her parents for a sibling. When that didn't happen, she invented a sibling of her own, an old G.I. Joe given to her by a friend who didn't want any boy dolls. G.I. Joe became her confidante. She'd tell him everything. About fights with her mother over stupid things like her messy room or getting in trouble at school for talking too much. Worries about her father when he got sick with cancer that would eventually kill him when she was sixteen.

"I'm going to having a hundred babies, Joe," she would tell him. "My house will be so filled with children I won't be able to keep track of them all."

Joe didn't answer back, of course. He stared at her with his scarred G.I. Joe face and she wondered, *How did he get that scar? What happened to the man who gave it to him? G.I. Joe probably killed him with his bare hands.*

In the bookstore she looks down at her still-flat belly. What is her baby doing right now? *Baby?* More like a clump of cells. Is he/she able to think yet? Of course not. What is the definition of life? Is it something only sustainable outside a womb? Does a SeaMonkey count as life? Laurie feels tears in her eyes. Is this what being pregnant is about—crying over SeaMonkeys?

The Barnes and Noble has a small music section, so Laurie looks at classical CDs. She pulls out Mendelssohn's Violin Concerto in E Minor op. 64.

The first movement is Allegro molto appassionato. She doesn't know what *allegro* or *molto* mean. Her musical knowledge is limited to five years of piano lessons and occasional trips to concerts or ballets. *Appassionato* might be about passion. Like sex. Is that what Mendelssohn was thinking when he was writing his violin concerto?

She takes out her iPhone and goes to her Dictionary.com app and searches for *allegro*. "Cheerful, or brisk." *Molto* means "very." Passionate, very cheerful, very brisk. A little like sex with Alan when he's preoccupied with work. Sometimes she sees a look in his eye as if he's wondering why he left his BlackBerry in the kitchen.

The last movement is Allegro non troppo–Allegro molto vivace. Laurie rolls the words around in her mouth. What a great word, *troppo*. A potential baby name? *Troppo* means "too much, excessively." Okay, she'll buy the Mendelssohn CD and play it later. It's good for the baby's growing brain.

Unless he/she can't hear yet. It's too confusing to refer to the baby as he/she. If she keeps doing that, the baby will be born with both male *and* female genitalia. She'll think of the baby as he. Not that she'd prefer a boy. Either one will be fine, just not both.

Back at home, Laurie goes into the office/baby's room and looks around. What color should they paint the walls? Is the room too small? Will it fit a crib, a changing table? Should they have bought a bigger house? She won't worry about that now; instead, she opens one of her new books to a fertilization illustration. With her finger she tracks the journey of hearty sperm making their way through the tubes in search of a friendly egg.

> *The fertilized egg divides into two cells, then four, and continues dividing as it floats down the fallopian tube to the uterus, by which time there are roughly thirty cells. This cell bundle is called a morula—Latin for mulberry, which it resembles.*

Laurie puts her hands on her stomach and imagines cells multiplying. Sees Troppo changing from zygote to morula to blastocyst, hundreds of cells creating an embryo.

"Yoo-hoo, Troppo. You can't hear me yet," she whispers to her baby-to-be. "But you will soon."

When Alan comes home from work, Laurie surprises him with a bottle of champagne and a homemade chocolate cake—a "welcome baby" cake, she calls it. Alan kisses her and they eat cake before dinner and Laurie has one tiny (very tiny) sip of champagne to celebrate.

"Wow. Pretty overwhelming," Alan says to Laurie.

Laurie nods. "I still can't believe it. Do you think Dr. Liu was kidding? Maybe he's not really a doctor; he's just a guy who sneaks into an ob-gyn office and puts on a white lab coat."

"And sees you naked?" Alan says. "I'll have to kill him."

Troppo will have a goofy sense of humor like Alan. He will be tall and handsome and blond and green-eyed like

Alan, smart and kind and, except for too-light eyebrows, perfect genetic material.

"Why are you staring at me?" he asks.

"I'm hoping the baby looks like you."

"Be as good-looking as me? There's not enough room on the planet. I want him to look exactly like you. Only masculine. No offense. You know what I mean."

She laughs, imagines Troppo split in half—half Alan, half Laurie, like someone in a circus sideshow. Will the baby be semineurotic and addicted to chocolate like Laurie? Set in his ways and almost OCD organized like Alan? Sometimes Alan refers to himself as "retro." That explains why he still carries a BlackBerry and wears Brooks Brothers oxford shirts and deck shoes. Laurie can't decide which decade Alan belongs in—the '50s? A member of the establishment in the '60s? On one of their early dates, he showed up wearing a light blue seersucker jacket.

"My grandfather had a jacket like that," she told him, trying hard not to make a face.

"I'm fashionably unfashionable," Alan said. And how could you not fall in love with a man crazy enough to own and *wear* a seersucker jacket? Even though after their wedding it mysteriously disappeared.

Alan finishes his champagne. "Pregnancy's already made you prettier."

"That pregnancy glow they talk about? Am I illuminating the room?" she says.

"I better get my sunglasses." He pours himself another glass of champagne. "So now I guess we make a list." Alan takes out his BlackBerry. "What do we do first?"

Laurie thinks. "Gather wood. Build a shelter. We've got that covered. Unless our house isn't big enough."

"Our house is fine. It's a baby; they're small. At least for a while." Alan frowns. "I'm a newbie at this. I need instructions."

"It's like riding a bike," Laurie says.

"You're sure?"

"No, beats me. I'm a newbie too, remember?" She sits in his lap and leans her head against his shoulder. "But how hard can it be?"

They tell everyone. Laurie calls her mother in Reno, Alan calls his parents in Virginia. Grace takes Laurie out for lunch to celebrate. Laurie has been helping set up Grace's new blog. Grace's husband, Hal, works in commercial real estate, but he's taking a sabbatical year to stay home with Emilie, their two-year-old daughter. Hal has given Grace workspace at his office in Van Nuys, a beautiful old building from the '20s that was scheduled for demolition until a group of preservationists fought to save it. Grace worked in the print magazine business for years and is anxious to take a leap into cyberworld. Her blog will be a guide to finding unknown treasures (cheap day spas, unusual museums, etc.) in the San Fernando Valley. Grace wants to call it Valley Gems.

"Sounds like a jewelry store," Laurie says. They are eating in a small Italian café on a busy street just off Van Nuys Boulevard near Hal's office. The food is good, but Grace hasn't decided if the restaurant will make it on the site. "Too much traffic," Grace complains.

"But the pesto's amazing," Laurie says, winding linguine around her fork.

"Enjoy it now. Because once morning sickness kicks in, you'll want to die. When I was pregnant with Emilie, I was sick for nine months."

"I don't believe you." Laurie's linguine is covered with olive oil, garlic, and basil. How could that ever taste bad?

"Remember your worst hangover in college? Sick like that. Puking, dry heaves. That 'by the second trimester you'll be fine' thing? Total crap. Wait and see. Are you sure you don't like Valley Gems?"

"Hate it."

"You could work with me full time," Grace says.

"Part time." Since college, Laurie has worked in PR but was transitioned (about to be laid off) from her last job a year ago. Since then she's done freelance travel writing, and she's not ready for nine to five again, especially with a baby on the way.

"Hidden Valley," Grace announces. "Better than Valley Gems?"

"Hidden Valley is a salad dressing."

"I like Hidden Valley," Grace says. "Because that's what it's about—places you might drive by every day, but you've never noticed them before. Like this restaurant. Which is great, except for the honking cars and exhaust fumes."

Grace hands Laurie a gift bag wrapped with a gauzy ribbon. "It's really more of a present for *after* the baby." Laurie pulls out a pair of neon-colored margarita glasses.

"They're cute, thanks," Laurie says. "But how am I going to survive nine months without margaritas?"

"I'm not kidding about morning sickness. Even if it were medically safe to drink when you're pregnant, you won't want to. The *thought* of tequila will make you vomit."

Laurie wipes the bottom of the bowl with her bread to get the last bits of pesto. She's not worried. Grace exaggerates everything.

When morning sickness arrives, it's not Grace's violent vomiting dry heave scenario, but 24/7 nausea isn't Laurie's idea of a good time. One of her pregnancy books suggests eating saltine crackers as a possible solution.

At dinner, Alan presents her with crackers on a small plate. "Yum," he says. Laurie wants to punch him. She had to leave the kitchen last night when he microwaved leftover pizza. The smell of sausage and cheese made her woozy, and she could hear the acid bubbling in her stomach.

She picks up a cracker. It looks gigantic, although not as gigantic as the torpedo-sized prenatal vitamins Dr. Liu wants her to take. "They're not so bad," Alan says.

"Then you try one."

Alan shakes his head, as if taking a prenatal vitamin will make him grow breasts.

She is looking at the cracker in her palm.

"It smells," she says to Alan.

"Crackers don't smell."

Troppo is starving. If she doesn't eat this cracker, his brain won't develop and he'll never get into an Ivy League school.

She nibbles the corner. Her mouth feels full, as if it's stuffed with paper.

"Maybe I could put a little margarine on it," Alan says.

Laurie shakes her head. Margarine would push her over the edge. Half a cracker, she might be able to manage that. She'll do it for Troppo.

She takes another bite, more aggressively this time. The cracker sits on her tongue like fingernail clippings. She takes a sip of water. Even water tastes funny these days. In her mouth, the water turns the cracker to the consistency of spackle. She wills the muscles in her throat to do their job and the soggy, disgusting mess doesn't exactly slide down her esophagus, but it lurches as it begins the long journey to Laurie's roiling stomach.

"Good girl, only two thirds of the cracker to go," says Alan.

Weeks pass, and on mornings when she doesn't feel like throwing up, Laurie goes into Grace's office. Grace tacks a pregnancy calendar above Laurie's desk. "So you can mark off the days," she says. When Laurie stays home, Grace emails her pregnancy tips and things to watch out for. For example, if seafood is polluted with mercury, it can harm a baby's brain and nervous system. The coating on nonstick cookware might flake off and release toxic gasses.

As they're planning the Hidden Valley format ("Blog, Facebook, eventually print," is Grace's master plan), Laurie asks about Grace's pregnancy. "Emilie is a whoops baby," Grace says. "We thought we'd wait another year to start a family, but…whoops."

"So were you scared?" Laurie wants to know.

"It was a surprise, but a bigger surprise at how happy we were. And now Hal wanting to take a year off to be home with her. Isn't that outrageous? It's so good for them, father/daughter bonding. Alan will make a great dad too."

"Yeah." Laurie came home from the office the other day to find Alan had gotten Thai takeout and a DVD of *Dumbo*. They watched *Dumbo* after dinner and both of them cried when Dumbo's mother sings "Baby Mine" to her child while she's locked up behind bars. Alan says he isn't really crying—he has something in his eye. But Laurie doesn't believe him.

"We planned Troppo, so it's not a surprise," Laurie says to Grace.

"And is it what you thought it would be?"

"I don't love the nausea. But everything else...I don't know. I expected joy, but this is a *ridiculous* amount of joy." She laughs. "I sound insane."

"You sound like a new mom." Grace looks serious. "You're not going outside on smoggy days, are you? Check the pollution levels first."

Laurie talks to Troppo all the time. She's standing in his bedroom and facing the doorframe. "This is where we'll measure you on your birthday. Right here," she tells him. She sees herself carefully drawing a line and printing the date. "Look how big you are, Troppo. How did you get so big?"

"Growing like a weed," Alan will say, and Troppo will look up at his parents, grinning. The lines will grow higher and higher on the doorframe and one day—surprise!—he'll be taller than Laurie.

Even though she calls him Troppo, the baby's room has a unisex decor. The room needed a fresh coat of paint anyway, so Laurie chose a light lemon yellow color. And as long as they were painting, why not add a cute animal alphabet trim along the wall just below the ceiling? A is for Alligator. B is for Bird. The Python wrapped around the letter P seems vaguely sinister. "To make sure the baby won't grow up afraid of snakes," Alan says.

"Really? Suppose the baby gets some terrible snake phobia?"

"Then we'll buy *real* snakes. Isn't that what you do with phobias? Confront them?"

"But maybe we *don't* know how to have a baby," Laurie

says as she looks at the almost-assembled crib. Okay, it's not as if they were going to completely finish the baby's room, but the Juvenile Shop was having a sample sale and now that they've got the crib, she'll go back when the Juvenile Shop has another sale to check out changing tables. Except—why does her maternal confidence seem to come and go these days? A baby? What were they thinking? "Suppose it's not like riding a bike," she tells Alan. "Suppose it's more like building a particle accelerator. With Q-tips."

"No going back. We've waited long enough."

He's not wrong, Laurie thinks. They've been married for almost five years. No children right away—Laurie's job meant lots of travel and Alan traveled for his job too, including to help organize a new branch of his company, Palmer-Boone, in Sydney. Friends told them they should travel now, prechildren. They listened to the advice, took advantage of Laurie's job, enjoyed river cruises down the Volga, glacier trips in Alaska. Scuba diving in the Great Barrier Reef, courtesy of Palmer-Boone.

Alan, the ideal travel companion. They have fabulous adventures. And then one day, they looked at each other and that was it. Time for a baby.

Now they're decorating a baby's room and putting together a crib. Years from now, in this room, Laurie will tell fourteen-year-old Troppo to pick up his clothes and he'll roll his eyes and say, "Yeah, yeah. I'll get around to it, Mom."

Mom. That's who she is. Alan is right; there's no going back.

"You'll hear the heartbeat for the first time," Grace tells her. "Alan should go with you, it's very cool." But Palmer-Boone is having a "power breakfast" to welcome visiting

VIPs from Palmer-Boone Great Britain, so Laurie arrives solo at her doctor's appointment.

Dr. Liu is in a good mood, very chatty, and Laurie wonders what it's like for Mrs. Liu, thinking about her husband rubbing gel on women's stomachs and looking in their vaginas all day.

"We should hear the heartbeat, right?" Laurie asks Dr. Liu as he slides the ultrasound paddle across her tummy.

"Who's the doctor, you or me?" He's grinning as he maneuvers the paddle. The machine makes a *thunk thunk* sound, slightly wet.

"I vote for you. I'd make a horrible doctor. And I look terrible in white," says Laurie. Dr. Liu moves the paddle to another spot. *Thunk thunk.* How loud will the heartbeat be?

Dr. Liu frowns, taps the end of the paddle. "Let me try another one, this one's acting a little funky."

Of course ultrasound machines go funky. So it's not unusual for Dr. Liu to leave the room to bring in another machine. It must happen all the time.

Only Laurie knows, deep down, not even deep down, she knows right there on the surface that Dr. Liu won't find a heartbeat; it isn't a broken ultrasound machine. Something has gone wrong; it's bad news, the worst possible news.

And it is. A second machine confirms what Dr. Liu suspected—no heartbeat. A blighted ovum, Dr. Liu explains, his face serious. No dimples this time. The fertilized egg attached itself to the wall of the uterus and began to develop a placenta, but there is nothing inside. No embryo. No baby.

No Troppo.

Alan

One morning when Laurie leaves early for work, Alan dismantles the crib. He looks down at the crib pieces scattered on the floor, and he's tempted to throw everything away, but instead he gets a roll of masking tape and a Sharpie and a box of plastic bags and prints in clear handwriting where each piece should go. "Headboard, twelve six-inch screws, twelve matching washers and nuts." He tapes the plastic bags to the corresponding pieces and carries everything out to the back of the garage. When he's done, he covers the crib with an old beach towel with a picture of Kate Winslet and Leonardo DiCaprio on it.

The room looks empty without the crib. Afternoon sun makes the yellow walls almost too bright. He looks up at the alphabet border. *A is for anguish*, he thinks. *B is for bereavement. L is for loss. Longing. Laurie.*

Alan grew up as the youngest child in a noisy house in Virginia with three brothers and a sister, parents who spoiled them rotten and made up for it by making them wear matching red-and-green reindeer scarves and hats for their family

Christmas card photo. It was a middle-class, white picket fence, Wonder Bread life. When Alan left home, finished college, and got married, no question about it, of course he'd have kids. Probably make them do stupid Christmas cards too.

Having children only to replicate yourself seems ridiculously narcissistic. Alan doesn't need an Alan Lee Gaines Junior to feel complete. Or Alan Lee Gaines Junior who grows up to have Alan Lee Gaines III. And on and on until Alan Lee Gaines Infinity. Not that he dismisses genealogy. Alan's mother would never let him get away with that.

Alan's mother has always kept scrapbooks and researched family trees and has recently discovered (and become obsessed with) Ancestry.com. She follows various family members through different countries, tracks their trips on ocean liners, prints up obituaries. "Family means everything," she says. "It's the thing that's *left*."

His mother emails him black and white photos of men standing beside Model Ts, women in shorts and gingham-checked blouses sitting on picnic blankets. One woman with dark hair in a white bathing suit is so pretty she could be a pinup. He asks his mother about her when they talk on the phone.

"Bess, my mother's older sister, isn't she gorgeous? She never got married. Lived in Vermont with a woman named Catherine. They didn't visit Virginia much."

"Were they gay?"

"My mother said no. Not that she had anything against gay people. She just didn't want to think about it."

If it's unpleasant and you don't think about it, it goes away. Worrying if Bess and Catherine were gay might've made Alan's grandmother crazy. So she ignored it. And life went on.

If Alan doesn't think about Troppo, maybe he never existed. Of course, that's the irony; he never *did* exist. Not exactly a ha-ha funny kind of irony, but irony all the same.

Does it make things easier? The fact that Troppo wasn't close to being a real baby? From a medical point of view, he wasn't. The pregnancy didn't take, never got off the ground.

"It's very common," Dr. Liu tells Alan and Laurie in the office after the D & C. "Forty percent of pregnancies end in miscarriage. But you two are young, in your early thirties. You're healthy. And more good news—you know you're able to conceive."

Dr. Liu is so cheerful Alan expects him to say that miscarriage is terrific, a wonderful learning experience. As they're leaving his office, Dr. Liu mentions forty percent again, as if that will make them feel better. But Alan is only thinking one thing—why aren't *we* the sixty percent?

"I can do the dishes," Alan says to Laurie after dinner.

She shakes her head. "That's okay."

He feels guilty and he doesn't know why. Of course the miscarriage is harder for Laurie—she was the one who was pregnant. But he feels the loss too. Laurie understands that, doesn't she?

When the dishes are done, he sits beside Laurie on the sofa in the den. She's watching *Dancing with the Stars*. He knows she thinks it's stupid, but her eyes are locked on the screen. "Doesn't that dress make her legs look fat?" she says. He sees a heavy woman with too much makeup swirling in the arms of an orange-tan man with a shirt unbuttoned to his waist.

"Like sausages," she says. "Cankles, isn't that what they call fat ankles?" She puts her elbow on her knee and rests her chin on her fist. He should reach over and take her hand.

But he hesitates. Ever since the D & C, he's been afraid of doing the wrong thing. "It's going to be okay," she told him in Dr. Liu's office as they prepped her for the D & C. And when it was over, she said, "That wasn't so bad, was it?"

Yes, he wanted to say to her. *It was the worst thing I've ever experienced. Watching the person I love more than anything in the world have the remains of what was supposed to be our baby scraped out of her. Wondering what they do with the remains of the pregnancy. Do they call it remains?* He decides he never needs to know the answer.

Another hard part of the miscarriage has been letting people know what's happened, telling the story over and over. To his parents, Laurie's mother, their friends. "Laurie's doing fine," he said. "Yes, we're disappointed, but we'll try again."

He's not sure how word got out at Palmer-Boone, but when he comes in, his secretary, Wendy, tells him how sorry she is. "My sister had a miscarriage and now she's got three kids. And a fourth on the way."

He hears that from everybody at Palmer-Boone, as if they've gotten together to come up with the same story—it happened to my sister/cousin/mother/brother's wife and now they have a girl/boy/*oodles* of children.

Craig from accounting pops his head in Alan's office, says he's sorry but, "Hey, at least it wasn't a stillbirth."

Craig wears Ralph Lauren polo shirts, the version with the giant rider and polo pony, the one that announces, "My shirt is *really* expensive." Alan is holding a cup of hot coffee and he wonders if he splashes it against Craig's face if the burns will be first, second, or third degree.

"Yeah," he says to Craig. "We're pretty lucky."

When Craig is gone, Alan looks out his office window to the San Gabriel Mountains, a gorgeous view on unsmoggy days. All the Palmer-Boone VPs get corner offices with floor-to-ceiling windows, another Palmer-Boone perk, like a lifetime supply of three-ring binders.

The best Palmer-Boone perk turned out to be meeting Laurie. Seven years ago, he was standing in line at a Staples in Burbank and noticed a pretty woman in front of him. She was wearing shorts and had great legs. Leaning forward, he peeked into her basket. "Those are mine," he said.

"Excuse me?" She turned to him and frowned. Great legs, equally great big, gray-blue eyes.

"My company. Palmer-Boone. We make those. Pressure-sensitive materials."

She looked at him as if he'd escaped from a mental institution. "Pressure-sensitive materials? You mean *mailing labels*?"

"Palmer-Boone makes more than mailing labels. We're a multibillion-dollar company with offices all over the world. Office supplies, retail branding, automotive and industrial products—you can probably tell I get a little too into this." Shit, was he making a fool of himself?

"I've always wanted to know everything about pressure-sensitive materials," she said.

"I could tell you. But then I'd have to kill you."

She laughed when he said that, and he saw she had a slightly crooked, loopy smile and he thought, *That's a smile I'd never get tired of. She had that smile as a child; she'll have it when she's an old lady. When I'm an old man and we're growing old together.* Huh. Why was he thinking about growing old with a woman he just met in line at Staples?

She watched him—*oh no, is she reading my mind?* "Would you like to buy me a cup of coffee? My name's Laurie," she said.

Peter comes into his office and joins him at the window. "I heard the news. Sorry."

"Thanks." Peter is his closest friend at Palmer-Boone, probably his closest friend in L.A. They met playing company softball, colliding with each other in center field trying to catch a fly ball. Neither succeeded; the other team scored and won the game. Alan cut his lip; Peter sliced open his chin. Blood brothers.

"How's Laurie?" Peter asks.

"She's hanging in there."

"Good. Give her a hug from me. How about you?"

"I don't need a hug." Alan forces a grin. "I'm hanging in there too."

Peter nods. "Good. You know what helps? Beer. Lots and lots of beer." Peter starts out, turns back. "Did you see Craig's shirt? What an asshole."

After dinner Alan asks Laurie if she wants to get frozen yogurt. Their house in Sherman Oaks is walking distance to Ventura Boulevard, lined with dozens of shops and restaurants.

"I'm too sleepy," she says. "But you go. If you bring me a cup of cookies 'n' cream and put it in the freezer, I'll eat it tomorrow. Thanks."

When he joins her in bed later, she rolls away from him. She needs her space. Or is she acting like she needs her space hoping he'll come close, that he'll comfort her? They've been together forever and suddenly he can't read her signs.

He should roll over, bend his knees into hers, feel her body slide into his; his breathing will match hers, and everything will be like it was before.

Before the baby that never was. Thinking that makes him ache, a physical pain deep in his body, as if he's aware of his bones.

Should he ask her more questions? How she's feeling? He doesn't want her to feel worse. For a smart man, sometimes he feels clueless. Like how he'll make a joke instead of facing a problem directly. He knows Laurie gets annoyed, and when she calls him on it, he tends to make another joke. Which makes her more annoyed.

Not that they fight much. Their marriage is in a good place. Nine out of ten, ten being best. If you had to graph their marriage, he thinks it would compare to most marriages. Highs and lows. Troughs. Parts you slog through, like the miscarriage. A few years back, they had some money issues when some of their investments went south. And then the roof leaked and Alan's car needed a new transmission. "When it rains," Alan said. And Laurie didn't laugh. "Blue skies up ahead," Alan announced, and in retrospect he shouldn't have made so many jokes—it would have been better to simply say their finances were fucked and they'd have to spend less and borrow money from his parents to get through the next couple months.

But nine out of ten isn't bad—and it's always important to have data to back up your analysis. When they were dating, Alan listed Laurie's best and worst qualities and assigned values to each. He mentioned that to her but didn't go into specifics. He thought she'd think it was funny. She didn't. "You did some kind of *risk analysis* on our relationship? Do you have a spreadsheet on me somewhere?"

"Of course not," he told her, vowing to destroy the spreadsheet the minute he got back to his apartment.

"A guy who makes spreadsheets. And tells dumb jokes," Laurie said. "What am I doing going out with you?" She looked at him. "So? When you ran the numbers in your analysis…how did I do?"

He grinned at her. And shrugged. "You'll have to guess." And he realized: *My jokes are dumb?*

"It's freaky, thinking about getting fat," Laurie said to Alan back when she found out she was pregnant. "Do you think I'll get fat?"

"I'll love you anyway," he told her. "Blimpy."

"Funny. Why can't men get pregnant? If I got three wishes, that's what one of them would be." She checked her reflection in the mirror. "I hope I don't gain eighty pounds."

"Then can I call you Blimpy?"

"Sure, as long as you get used to being called One Ball. Because that's what'll happen if you make fun of my weight."

She sounded serious. Eighty pounds or eight hundred pounds, he would always love her. Well…eight hundred might be pushing it. When they started dating, he was in awe of her body. She'd been a swimmer in high school and college and still had wide swimmer shoulders and strong thighs that tapered to high, tight calves. She'd told him he was the first nonswimmer she'd gone out with. "So that's a little weird because all the other guys I dated, I already knew what they looked like practically naked."

She hung out with guys in Speedos. He tried not to panic. His body was okay—he played lacrosse in high school, still went running and spent time at the gym. But compared to a swimmer?

"Why don't we go to the beach next weekend?" she asked him.

She wanted to see him without his clothes on. He told her he had plans during the day. How about a movie?

Later she suggested he visit her at the Rose Bowl Aquatic Center, near his office, where she would swim laps sometimes in the afternoon. At this point they hadn't had sex yet—would the reveal of his body be a deal breaker?

"It's hard for me to get away," he said.

Bull by the horns, he decided. He'd invited her to his apartment for dinner. Midmeal he left the table and came out of his bedroom wearing his boxers. And nothing else. She'd just taken a big sip of wine and almost did a spit take.

"This is what you get," he told her as he pulled out the elastic of his boxers and let them snap back against his waist. "Does my body make you wild with desire?"

They didn't finish dinner. Instead, they went into his bedroom and made love for the first time.

The first time, then many times—years of having sex and trying *not* to get pregnant and then trying to get pregnant and—*boom*—pregnancy. "I promise to never call you Blimpy," he said to her. And then asked the more serious question, the harder question. "You're going to love me the same, won't you? After we bring home the baby?"

Laurie ran her finger across her upper lip. "Hmmm. I doubt it. The baby will always come first. Sorry."

She was kidding; he knew she was kidding. He hoped she

was kidding. But it scared him—he was used to being the person she loved most.

With no more pregnancy, no baby to bring home, has he lost his chance to learn how to share? He's never been good at sharing. After growing up as the youngest of five and a lifetime of hand-me-down toys and Levi's, now he likes things that are his. New, unused. Like his love for Laurie. He can't imagine loving someone as much as he loves her. Of course he'll love his baby, but does that happen right away? It's a *baby*. At least for a while. Not exactly a person, somebody you can have a conversation with. More like a puppy. No, that's not right. A baby isn't *anything* like a puppy; it's a human being, the product of love between two people, the history of life repeated over and over, like his mother says—the thing that's left.

He sounds like a dick. He's thinking about a puppy. Yeah, that's what he'll tell Laurie to cheer her up about the miscarriage: "Hey, it doesn't really matter. Why don't we get a puppy instead?"

"Thanks, hon," she'll say. "Now I'm all better."

He doesn't suggest a puppy; instead, he calls Laurie at the Hidden Valley office and suggests they drive up to Ojai for the weekend.

Ojai is exactly what they need. An hour and a half north of L.A., tucked into a small valley between mountains that glow pink in the sunset, the town is quiet and charming, with art galleries and great restaurants. No freeway sounds or smog, and they can smell jasmine outside their window. They have a wonderful time and even though their room at the B and B is tiny and the bed is old and creaky, they don't care and have sex before dinner. And then again in the morning before breakfast. They take long walks and eat dinner outside at a restaurant under a canopy of tiny white lights that look like stars.

As for birth control, they don't mention it. If it happens, it happens. If not, oh well—the weekend reminds them there's a reason they're together in the first place. And sex isn't only about procreation.

Life returns to normal. Weeks turn into months. Alan and Laurie go to Lake Arrowhead with friends, investigate yard sales, eat too many deviled eggs at a Palmer-Boone picnic. They paint their front door red after Laurie saw an article in *Real Simple* magazine that explains how your house needs to make a good first impression. When they are done, Alan nods and says, "Okay, but it looks like we live in a firehouse."

Laurie loves her job with Grace. "I'm like a Valley detective," she tells Alan. "Tracking down the old, the new, the bizarre. Grace calls me an urban explorer."

"Do you need a pith helmet?"

"Yuck, who wants pith helmet hair?"

"Matching pith helmets, that's what we need," Alan says. Laurie laughs and she is the girl in line from Staples, the woman he married. When she's not looking, Alan will go on Amazon and track down pith helmets. He can already hear her laugh when she opens the box.

Laurie's car is in the driveway when he comes home from work. He thought she'd told him she and Grace were going to meet a man who runs an accordion school in Atwater Village. When he walks inside the house, he smells onions and garlic and peppers. In the kitchen he sees a pot of chili on the stove. No Laurie.

He heads to the bedroom, but Laurie is sitting on the floor in the yellow room, surrounded by pieces of the crib.

"Chili for dinner tonight," Laurie says. "Before I'm felled by the curse of morning sickness."

Chili, morning sickness, crib pieces. It takes a few seconds for Alan to process everything.

"I know, crazy. Here we go again," she says. And looks down at a screw in her hand, as if she hasn't figured out where it goes yet. He sits on the floor beside her and pulls her into his arms.

Jack

He wishes he could remember her name. He thinks it's Megan. He watches her sleep. She's smiling, and he wonders what she's dreaming about. She makes little puff sounds and he's pretty sure her name is Megan.

Unless Megan was the girl in the bar wearing a tube top and dancing on a chair. No, that girl was Kerry. Jack closes his eyes and he's back at the bar in Westwood—loud and crowded and hot, and he's thinking of leaving until he notices tube-top girl. Naturally, Danny knows all about her.

"Scary Kerry," Danny tells Jack.

"She's hot," Jack says, watching as Scary Kerry dances and tugs at her tube top to keep it from falling off.

Danny makes a gagging sound. "You know that plant? The one that catches flies and looks amazing on the outside, but inside it's got like razor teeth."

"A Venus flytrap?"

Danny nods. "Scary Kerry's vagina."

Scary Kerry doesn't look like the kind of girl with a razor vagina. But you never know, so Jack decides to head off, and when he's almost at the door, he sees an attractive, dark-eyed girl sitting by herself at a table in the corner. "You get stood up?" he asks her.

"That's your pickup line?" she says.

"No. It was just a question."

She looks him over. He returns the favor: big brown eyes she's made darker by lining them in black, blond hair with deliberate black roots. He bets she has a single tattoo—a butterfly on the small of her back.

"Are you a smart-ass?" she asks him.

"Maybe." He wonders if he should sit down or if she's waiting for her boyfriend, a big guy who's going to show up and beat the shit out of him.

"Are those your friends?" She nods toward the clump of guys at the bar. Surfer-handsome Danny surrounded by drunk, flirty girls; heavy-eyed Carter is dangling a spoon off the end of his nose.

"Fraternity buddies." Jack nods.

"Oh, you're in a fraternity," the girl says. "I should've guessed. Which one? Phi Delt. No, that's not right. Sigma Nu? Wait, I got it. SAE. Hipsters."

Jack frowns. She says *hipsters* like she means *pussies*. "What do you mean, 'hipsters'?"

"I'm right?"

Jack doesn't want to give her the satisfaction—but what's the point of lying? "Yeah, SAE."

"Your rep's that you're super straight. You know, *bor*ing."

"Are you in a sorority?" he asks her. She doesn't look like a UCLA sorority girl.

"The whole Greek thing is overrated."

Jack grins. "You went through pledge week and didn't get a single bid."

"Fuck you," the girl says, but she's smiling. "I'm in the theater department; I don't have enough time. And that's fine, I'm happy."

"Except you got stood up."

The girl shakes her head. "Theater people are flaky. You get used to it."

They talk about UCLA, what they like (lots of different people, a beautiful campus, living in L.A.), what they hate (terrible parking, too many students, living in L.A.). He tells her he's a senior; right now he's majoring in history, but since that's his fourth major in three years, he won't have enough credits to graduate until next year.

"What's the big deal about graduating on time?" she asks him.

"My parents expect it."

"It's *your* life. Duh."

He doesn't want to talk about his parents. He's in a good mood. Why ruin it?

She tells Jack about the play she's doing, *Medea*. "It's an awesome story. This woman gets revenge on her cheating husband. Jason, the Golden Fleece guy, dumps Medea for Glauce, King Creon's daughter. So Medea decides she'll get even by killing Glauce and her father, and she has this genius idea of sending them golden robes covered with poison. And if that doesn't make Jason crazy enough, she'll kill her own children."

"Whoa," says Jack.

The girl nods. "The poisoned robes trick works; Jason shows up, gets pissed about Medea killing Glauce, and then he finds out she's killed the kids too—he goes *apeshit*. Medea tells him he's an asshole, you know, you reap what you sow; she curses him and takes off. The end."

"Kind of depressing," Jack tells her.

"But Medea's an amazing part for an actress."

"So you're Medea?"

"No, I'm the understudy."

"Why didn't you get the part?"

"I'm not that good. Plus, the girl who's Medea is sleeping with the director. You want another beer?"

They go back to his room at the SAE house; they listen to music and make out and she volunteers to do a scene from *Medea.* She wraps a sheet around her body, Greek style, and begins to speak.

"And if these ornaments she take and put them on, miserably shall she die, and likewise everyone who touches her; with such fell poisons will I smear my gifts. And here I quit this theme; but I shudder at the deed I must do next; for I will slay the children I have borne; there is none shall take them from my toils; and when I have utterly confounded Jason's house I will leave the land, escaping punishment for my dear children's murder, after my most unholy deed. For I cannot endure the taunts of enemies, kind friends; enough! what gain is life to me? I have no country, home, or refuge left."

The girl grins at Jack. "I love that part, 'miserably shall she die.' Do you want to have sex now?"

They have sex; she is eager and bold, but not too bold, and doesn't take it too seriously, which Jack likes. Sex is overrated, Jack thinks. It should be a good time, simple, and uncomplicated. Unlike idiotic Carter, who keeps a fuck journal in a drawer by his bed and makes notes. He made the mistake of mentioning his fuck journal on Tequila Shot Night and Danny went into Carter's room and got the journal when Carter was passed out, took it back in the common room, and read excerpts aloud.

"Kendra. Two and a half stars. Average tits. Good BJ.

"Hillary. Two stars. Said she came, totally faking. Said I was too hairy. Should I wax?"

Danny put the fuck journal back into the drawer, and Carter never knew anything about it, although he might've suspected something when bottles of Nair and Veet suddenly appeared in the bathroom.

Jack looks over at the girl. One leg is visible from under the sheet, like a dismembered limb. Was Medea the one who served her children to her husband for dinner, or did he mix that up with something else? A *Saw* movie maybe? He'll ask the girl in the morning.

If he can remember her name. Damn. He's living in a *Seinfeld* episode. Bovary. Mulva. Dolores.

He is genuinely fucked. Except...her purse is on the chair. How hard would it be to slip out of bed, walk over, pull out her wallet, and check her driver's license? He slides out from under the covers. Should he put his boxers back on? Might make too much noise. *This is a bad idea*, he tells himself, but he heads for the chair.

And steps on something sharp; it pierces the ball of his foot and he draws his breath in quickly. Looks down to see a high-heeled shoe. What are the chances she's written her name inside? Slim to none, unless her name is Madden.

Could it be Madden? He thought it was Megan. What makes him think it starts with an M?

"Your butt is cute," she says from the bed.

He turns around. She's sitting up and smiling.

"Bathroom," he says.

"I'll be here when you get back," she says.

Maybe some of the other guys know her name. He could ask them, realizes that's a huge mistake, as stupid as Carter telling people he kept a fuck journal.

Maybe she'd have a sense of humor about it. Honesty, the best policy.

Which is bullshit. He tried that once on a girl he went out with. It wasn't about her looks. Okay, it was sort of about her looks—fat ass, the hint of a mustache. After the date, he said he'd call. And he meant to but never got around to it. When he ran into her in his European history class, he thought he'd explain things—in a nice white lie kind of way.

"I know I said I'd call you," he said.

"Yeah." She looked at him, and he could see the mistrust in her eyes. And—this made it worse—a glimmer of hope. Was he going to ask her out again?

"But I didn't because the two of us, we're not…compatible."

"How exactly are we not compatible?"

He didn't think she was going to ask for specifics. *Oh, shit.* "You know, like…personality things."

"You don't think I'm good-looking enough."

"No, it's not about your looks." Except for the mustache. And your fat ass. "You're really pretty."

"Just not pretty enough to keep going out with." The glimmer of hope look was gone, replaced by loathing. "You're right. We're not compatible. Because I don't waste my time on *douche bags*."

For a minute he thought she was going to spit on him. But she walked away. She was wearing a short skirt, and he was surprised to see her ass looked good, not fat at all, but kind of sexy. He felt stupid.

So as far as honesty goes, it's never worth it.

He could call the girl in his bed another name by mistake.

She'll correct him with her right name; he'll laugh—*whoops, that was my* last *girlfriend.*

Why won't that work? She's seen the *Seinfeld* episode; everybody's seen it. She'll be pissed. *You had sex with me and you didn't know my name? That's* cold. Maybe she'll call him a douche bag too.

Or she's crazy. Although she couldn't be as crazy as the last girl he went out with. Heidi was Hall of Fame Crazy. Jack's friend Will was dating a girl at UCSB; her roommate, Heidi, loved the *Harold and Kumar* movies and Heidi had a major crush on Kal Penn. So when Heidi found out her roommate's boyfriend knew an Indian guy—when could Jack come up to Santa Barbara?

Jack should've said no. Yeah, he's Indian, but he doesn't look like Kal Penn. At least Heidi turned out to be cute. She's on the giggly side, loves beer pong and Kal Penn.

"That's not really his name, you know," she says to Jack when they're alone at the table in the restaurant. "It's Kalpen Suresh Modi. His parents are from India, but he was born in New Jersey."

"I was born in San Francisco. My parents are from Mumbai," Jack says.

"Kal worked for Obama. Have you ever met Kal?"

Jack shakes his head. *Heidi thinks everyone with an Indian heritage knows each other? What a moron.* But he'll let that slide because he can see the top of her bra peeking out from her tank top. And she has excellent boobs.

After dinner, Jack and Heidi head to her dorm room, where they watch some *24* episodes. Heidi explains that Kal Penn's character, Ahmed Amar, works with Fayed, an Islamic terrorist, and he has to deliver a package, but it gets screwed up, like stuff always does on *24*, and there's a gun battle and Ahmed is shot by Jack Bauer.

She begins to cry when Ahmed dies, and the next thing he knows, she's got his arms around him and she's kissing him, and what's Jack supposed to do? Tell her to stop?

Afterward, he looks up to see a bulletin board above her bed and there's a picture of Kal Penn—actually two or three pictures of Kal Penn, possibly more. He decides to stop counting.

When it's time to drive back to L.A. with Will, Heidi squeezes Jack's hand and leans close. "Bye, Kal," she says. "See you around like a doughnut." And she makes a little circle in the air with her finger. Then turns it into a gun and mock fires at Jack. "Look at me. I'm Jack Bauer and I'm killing you. Take that, Ahmed. Pow *pow*."

Jack forces a smile and slides into the passenger seat quickly. On the road, Will asks if Jack had a good time. "Heidi's wild," Will says. "She's a physics major and super smart. Talks all the time about how she almost built an atomic bomb in her basement when she was in seventh grade. Why did she call you Kal?"

Jack imagines asking his father about the situation with the girl in his bed. Except Jack's father, Rakesh, doesn't like to talk about feelings. "Do I look like Dr. Phil?" he's fond of saying. His comment on Jack's current dilemma? He'd blame Jack for being stupid. *How do you get yourself in situations like this? Your sister would never do something so foolish.*

Of course not, because his sister, Subhra, is the ideal child, unlike underachiever, un-ever-going-to-accomplish-anything Jack. He tries not to hate his sister. It's hard. Her nickname growing up was Princeton. Jack's parents didn't bother to give him a nickname.

The Girl With No Name is smiling at him again. GWNN. Gwnn, that's what he'll call her. "You talk in your sleep," she says.

"Really? What did I say?"

"You said *upma*. What's that?"

"It's like oatmeal. My mother makes it." Why did he say *upma* in his sleep? Was he thinking about his *mother*?

"Are you having *upma* for breakfast?"

"No," he says.

"Good. Because I know what I want for breakfast." And she kisses him.

Suppose the name thing never comes up? She'll mention her name in conversation. Don't people do that sometimes? Like they forget their keys and slap their foreheads and say, "Oh, Monica, how dopey was that?"

What are the chances Gwnn will suddenly slap her forehead and reveal her name? Slim. No, impossible. Jack's parents are right—he's an idiot. He didn't deserve to have a nickname.

Gwnn checks the clock and says she's got *Medea* rehearsal coming up. "Do you want to see it? It's pretty good, except the girl who's Medea sucks. But who knows? Maybe she'll slip into a poisoned robe one night and I'll get to go on." Gwnn grins at Jack and he grins back, hoping she's not serious.

"Yeah, I'd love to come."

"It starts Friday. Opening night's too crowded, so Saturday? I'll leave a ticket for you at the box office."

Another moment of hope. Maybe her name will be on it.

"Want my phone number, just in case?"

"Sure." He pulls out his phone, but the girl grabs it and begins to tap on the keys. A wave of relief washes over him. She's typing in her number herself. He won't have to ask for her name. Everything's fine; he's saved.

"Here you go," she says. "My turn." She hands him her phone and he adds his number.

After breakfast—no *upma*; they have stale Thomas's English muffins with peanut butter—he walks her out to her car.

"It was fun. See you next week. *Jack*." She winks, gives him a quick kiss on the lips.

"Yeah," he says. "Same here. See you next week."

Whatever your name is.

When she is gone, he goes into the den and notices Carter semiconscious on the sofa. He has a trail of vomit on his shirt. "Cute girl," Carter says, but Jack ignores him.

Jack pulls out his phone and goes to Megan. But it's not there. Oh no. He was *positive* her name was Megan. Suppose her name doesn't start with an M at all? He goes to the top and scrolls down.

Notices a new number in the Ms. Right beside a new name.

Medea.

Shit.

Laurie

According to Elisabeth Kübler-Ross, there are five stages of grief. Laurie wonders if Elisabeth Kübler-Ross invented stages for everything. For example, at a party, if someone asked her what drink she'd like, did Elisabeth Kübler-Ross reply, "There are five stages of a drink. Number one, select the beverage. Number two, pick the glass. Number three, put in the ice…" Laurie could ask Grace what she knows about Elisabeth Kübler-Ross, but she's out of breath from hiking up a steep path in the Santa Monica Mountains.

"No wonder nobody knows about this trail," Grace says, panting heavily. "You need a goddamn *machete*."

Stage one. Denial. Elisabeth Kübler-Ross got that right. "Wait a minute," Laurie wanted to tell Dr. Liu. "The first time was an anomaly. I couldn't possibly have *two* miscarriages in a row. There must be a mistake."

No mistake. A second blighted ovum, another pregnancy that didn't progress. As they were driving home after the D & C—a *second* D & C—Laurie told Alan not to worry, she'd be fine.

"Are you sure?"

"I didn't have as many expectations about this time, so it'll be easier." She's lying. She expects Alan to realize she's lying. It won't be easier; it will be as lousy as before. Why wouldn't it be?

But Alan didn't pick up on that. "Good," he said. Once they were in the house, he asked if she wanted him to stay or should he go to work, and she told him of course he should go to work. She *insisted*. Didn't she already tell him she was okay?

And naturally, when he left, she got into bed and wished he hadn't gone. Wished he was there to hold her, bring her a heating pad for her cramps, stroke her forehead. He should have *known* she needed him. Even though she sent him away.

But she can't blame Alan for the miscarriages. Unless… is there something wrong with his sperm? It isn't sticky enough, or he's got some freaky-ass chromosome that instead of dividing into cells, his *un*divides and causes blighted ovums. Ova?

No, not Alan. It's her stupid eggs. Stupid, badly functioning eggs. Why did Alan's sperm have to pick *that* particular one, an egg clearly better suited to being part of a period, ending up on the end of a tampon. Alan's sperm had to meet up with a *dysfunctional* egg. Laurie's probably got two ovaries filled with dysfunctional, flawed eggs.

Rotten eggs. Hilarious, maybe the name of the book she'll write about her miscarriages. Because nothing says bestseller like a funny book about miscarriages.

"I used to imagine Troppo growing inside me," she tells Alan later. They're sitting on the patio after dinner, occasionally looking over to watch the neighbors behind them who are working out on their second floor balcony to a Zumba dance DVD.

Alan refills Laurie's wineglass. Laurie puts her hands against her stomach. "I'd think how Troppo could feel the warmth of my palms. Idiotic."

"Not idiotic," he says.

"At least this one didn't have a name. That makes it better, doesn't it?"

Alan nods at her. "What do you want me to do with the crib?" he asks in a gentle voice. He is trying, she realizes. He wants to say the right thing.

"I've got an idea," Laurie says. "Let's put it in the backyard, douse it with gasoline, light a match—*whoosh*—all gone."

"Won't work. We'd need a permit or our Zumba neighbors will get pissed at us for burning something outside and there's probably a terrible fine."

"You're right," Laurie says. "Too bad."

The crib goes back into the garage. Neither of them talk about another pregnancy. Or a next time.

Grace and Laurie have reached the top of the trail, a loose-gravel spit of ridge with a view that looks down over a new housing development, a tiny slice of blue ocean in the distance.

"You're kidding," Grace says, popping open her water bottle. "We climbed Everest for this?"

Finding material for Hidden Valley is interesting work, but at least half the tips turn out to be duds, like this trail. "The article I saw online called it 'The Trail of Secrets,'"

Laurie says as she opens her own water bottle. The houses in the development are big, with red-tile roofs, but squeezed too close together.

"'Trail of Tears' is a better name. *Damn*, now we have to go down." Grace turns to Laurie. "How are you doing? With the miscarriages. Are you okay?"

Laurie shrugs. "I'm going through the stages of grief."

"How far are you?"

"Stuck between one and two, denial and anger."

"That sounds fun. How's Alan?"

"Fine." She corrects herself. "Probably fine."

"It's bad for him too. Maybe worse because it's harder for him to articulate how he's feeling. Hal would be the same way."

"I don't think so," Laurie says. "Hal is more open than Alan. Alan tends to retreat, go quiet."

"Alan needs some time to deal with this. Both of you lost babies, you know. How many more stages of grief are there?"

"Five total."

"Sheesh. Let's see if you can knock 'em off while we hike our sorry asses back down this canyon. Assuming we survive. Why didn't we hire Sherpas?"

Stage two. Anger. *Why me? What did I do to deserve this?* And if she can't blame Alan, how about God? Laurie is torn between her faith that wavers between God is responsible for everything around us—bad drivers, an especially good latte from Starbucks, a zit on the end of your nose—to God is *way* too busy to be concerned with every bad driver, latte, or zit, no matter how big or omnipotent he is.

She'd grown up going to church—her family was Methodist—but since moving to L.A., she'd sampled a few other churches: Presbyterian, Unitarian. On one of her early dates with Alan, he asked how she felt about religion. *Uh-oh*, she thought, *a trick question*. Some people get nervous when you talk about faith or God. Suppose Alan was an atheist?

"I go to church sometimes," she said. "One day I'd like my kids to go too. You know, so they have something—values, a moral center. But nothing freaky, like speaking in tongues."

She'd *really* blown it. Sweet, funny, sexy Alan, *not* an atheist, but now he was about to reveal he's a snake handler and speaking in tongues is his favorite thing in the world. She waited for his answer.

"I go to church sometimes too," he said. "I was raised Episcopalian. There's a great church in Pasadena, All Saints. I go there sometimes. You could come with me one Sunday if you want."

"I'd like that." Hooray, no tongues.

They'd gone to All Saints, married at an Episcopal church in Reno (Laurie's hometown), and, when they moved to Sherman Oaks, found another Episcopalian church close by. But these days Laurie's relationship with God is on serious hiatus. For how long? At least until she gets past the anger stage.

The only way she's found to avoid anger is by sleeping. Work for Grace, come home, nap. When she's asleep, she's pregnant again. Waking up is the worst time of the day, the slow slide of dream state to reality. Nope, not pregnant. A look at the clock. *How long before I can go back to sleep?*

Stage three. Bargaining. "If I get pregnant again, I'll be a better wife. And a better friend," Laurie tells Grace. "I won't say *fuck* anymore."

Grace nods. "You could join the Salvation Army, stand in front of a kettle, and ring a bell at Christmastime."

"Maybe." Laurie sighs. "If only there weren't so many children *lurking* out there. I hate that."

At the mall it must be Discount If You Bring a Stroller Day. Laurie hurries to Bloomingdale's, past the play structure. Mothers, nannies, a few dads, a *thousand* children. She watches a child sneeze on the nose of a plastic cow and another child runs over and gives the cow a kiss. *When I'm a mother, I won't let my children play in a germ-infested, unsanitary place like this*, she vows.

And she realizes, hallelujah, she's ready to move on to the next stage.

Stage Four is depression. Laurie doesn't like that; it seems like a step in the wrong direction. She could ask Alan what he thinks, but he's been spending a lot of time at his office. At his office so he can avoid coming home, Laurie suspects. Not that she's a joy to be around. She wears the same pair of jeans every day, thinks about touching up her highlights, decides there's no point.

When she sees Alan, she waits for him to say something. *A dumb joke would be okay*, she wants to tell him. But she doesn't say that. And he doesn't make a joke. And their lack of connection and communication, shared baby loss dance continues.

She reads constantly. As long as the books don't involve pregnancy. World War II novels about Anzio or Guadalcanal.

Nonfiction about the sinking of the *Andrea Doria*, the fire on the *Morro Castle*.

"Are you sure you want to go to Kristi's baby shower?" Grace asks Laurie.

"Yes," Laurie says. Grace and Kristi and Laurie met a few years ago in a book club that lasted three months when one of the women insisted on only reading Maeve Binchy. Kristi is Laurie's age. "Plump and proud," she calls herself. Her husband is as round as Kristi is. "Well-rounded," he says, patting his tummy.

Laurie thinks she'll be able to manage a baby shower; she's been okay around Grace and Emilie. Grace's husband, Hal, brings Emilie by the office sometimes, and Laurie only occasionally feels a catch in her throat, like when she watches Hal and Grace squeeze Emilie between them and make "an Emilie sandwich."

Kristi's baby shower is held at a house in the Hollywood Hills with views of downtown L.A. "On a clear day, you can see Catalina," a woman says to Laurie as she hands her a mimosa. There are dozens of blue balloons everywhere, a three-tiered cake with *Monsters, Inc.* characters on top and "It's a Boy Monster!" piped around the side. Kristi is hugely pregnant and squeals each time she unwraps another adorable, infant-sized sleeper or baby blanket. She oohs and ahhs over Laurie's gift: a matching sweater and hat set with a friendly bear print. "Ben is going to look like a little bear cub," Kristi says as she holds up the hat with tiny round ears.

Laurie smiles at Kristi and doesn't tell her the gift was sent to her by a Chicago cousin for her first pregnancy. Laurie couldn't stand having it around the house, and regifting doesn't count if you've had multiple miscarriages, right?

She makes it through silly shower games that involve sipping wine from baby bottles and trying to diaper dolls while blindfolded. But she's not unhappy when Grace announces it's time to leave.

"I think you handled that most impressively," Grace says in the car. "How many mimosas did you have? Eight?"

"Two. I'm not sure I can deal with another shower for a while."

"You were super brave to show up for this one." Grace nods at Laurie. "Unless...you could always go to a shower and give a wildly inappropriate gift." Grace thinks. "A grenade. Or a switchblade. Every baby needs a switchblade."

Laurie laughs. "A hot melt glue gun. A bow and arrow set—baby's first eye patch."

Grace is laughing too. "Razor wire. A big bag of buttons. Straight pins."

"A pit bull."

Laurie's feeling better. It helps to have a sense of humor about loss. *I can beat this*, she tells herself. She runs into a friend at the dry cleaner and Laurie's put on a clean pair of jeans today and made a hair appointment. Her friend asks if she's heard the news—their mutual friend Rachel is having twins. *Twins!* Can you imagine?

Laurie smiles, feels her lips sticking to her teeth, tells the friend she can't wait until the baby shower.

Lightning rods. Surgical scissors. A bottle of yummy antifreeze.

Stage Five. Acceptance. Not easy—acceptance feels remote, light years away, but she'll try. Look toward the future, not dwell on the past. She'll comfort herself with clichés, like toasty warm blankets on a cold stormy night. And sure enough, her depression begins to lift.

Alan is still quiet. Quiet at home, quiet at a visit to Dr. Liu's office where Dr. Liu talks about recurrent pregnancy loss and tells them they could keep trying the old-fashioned way—he smiles here—or they could see a fertility specialist.

"What do you think?" Laurie asks Alan when they get home.

He doesn't answer right away. "A test-tube baby?" he finally says. "Is that what we have to do?"

"I expect the fertility doctor will tell us. And I'd rather have a test-tube baby than no baby at all, wouldn't you?"

Alan hesitates. "Of course. Sure. But the idea that we're not in control of this anymore, that we have to depend on outside people, it's just..." He trails off.

"I know."

"I want it to be normal," Alan says.

"Fertility treatments are normal. We're lucky they have them now. What did they do thirty years ago?"

Alan doesn't say anything and Laurie wonders if Alan would be happier living thirty years ago. He wouldn't have to change his wardrobe.

He is looking at Laurie. "But is it okay if we keep trying the other way?"

"The other way?"

"A roll in the hay. Bouncy bouncy. A little meat injection—" Alan begins to grin. And Laurie realizes she hasn't seen him smile like that in weeks.

"Meat injection?" Laurie laughs out loud. "Okay," she says.

"So right now. We'll show 'em we don't need any stinking fertility doctors." Alan wiggles his eyebrows up and down.

"What? Right now? I have to make dinner."

"We'll order pizza. Come on, you'll be the appetizer." He grabs her hand and leads her to the bedroom.

At the office on Monday morning, Laurie is supposed to be searching online for bowling alleys in the Valley. "Something vintage. Or with a ghost," Grace suggests. Instead, Laurie is thinking about Elisabeth Kübler-Ross. What did she look like? Thick braids wrapped on either side of her head like Princess Leia? Laurie goes to Wikipedia and is surprised to see a photo of a tan, handsome woman with short hair. Born in Switzerland, one of triplets. Naturally her mother was fertile. Everyone is fertile and carries a child to term unless they're Laurie.

> *She moved to the United States in 1958 to work and continue her studies in New York. She had four miscarriages.*

Four? No wonder Elisabeth Kübler-Ross knew about stages of grief. After two she must've thought, *Uh-oh*. And how do you try again after three? Did people continue to tell her, "Don't worry, it'll work out next time"? Did Elisabeth Kübler-Ross snap back at them, "Yeah, what the hell? Maybe the *fifth* fucking time is the charm."

But she had two children. After all that, a boy and a girl.

Laurie touches the photo on her computer screen. That's the message Laurie is supposed to take from this. After all, not everybody died on the *Hindenburg* or the *Andrea Doria*. Some people are survivors. Like Elisabeth Kübler-Ross.

Like Laurie.

Alan

The fertility clinic is in Beverly Hills. The waiting room has lots of dark wood bookshelves and Alan whispers to Laurie he bets the books are fake and wants to pull them out, but Laurie tells him to sit down. She is nervous; he watches her twist the wedding ring around and around on her finger.

Dr. Julian's office is more dark wood, possibly more fake books. Dr. Julian leans against his desk. He has a Ralph Lauren tan and he's wearing Italian loafers with no socks; late forties, with short, silver hair and a jazz patch. He speaks softly and confidently about multiple miscarriages, possibly caused by uterine anomalies, fibroids. All are treatable.

"But you want to know *how* to have a baby. That's why you're here." Dr. Julian puts his hands together, making a little "here is the church" building with his fingers. "A diagnosis can be difficult. Sometimes we never find out the cause. But we'll do every test available." He nods at Laurie. "You and your partner."

We're not playing tennis, Alan wants to say. *I'm her husband, not her partner.*

"The sooner you start the testing, the better. And that's why you've come to me," Dr. Julian says. "Because I'm the one who can give you a baby."

His tan is fake, Alan decides, imagining Dr. Julian on a tanning bed. Flipping over when the timer goes off.

"You seemed grumpy in Dr. Julian's office," Laurie says when they get in the car. "Didn't you like him?"

"No. 'I can give you a baby.' Who says stuff like that?"

"Maybe he *can* give us a baby. That's why we went there, right?"

Alan sighs. "I suppose if Dr. God can deliver—no pun intended—we have to put up with him."

Laurie moves close and nuzzles into his neck. "I hope we have all boys. Who look just like you." She pauses. "Only sexier. More *buff.*"

"You don't get more buff than me." Alan flexes his bicep and Laurie giggles.

At dinner, Laurie runs her finger around the rim of her wineglass. "There's also adoption," she says carefully.

"I think adoption would be great. We've talked about it before." Before seems like centuries ago, back when they were dating and imaging their future—how they'd marry and their children would pop out, one after the other. No miscarriages or complications would be involved. Alan and Laurie, their charmed lives. Adoption was mentioned, but almost as a fallback. The thing you do "just in case" or once you have two or three of your own.

Alan realizes how shallow that sounds now. Shallow and stupid. "Your own." As if adopted children don't belong to you? Aren't part of your family? And yet… "But a stranger's baby?" Alan says to Laurie. "Suppose the mother is a meth addict, or we do an open adoption where we're always in contact with the birth parents. Is that what we want? Sharing a child?"

Laurie sips her wine. "There are risks in having biological children too. Who knows what'll happen? Babies don't come with a warranty."

Alan nods at Laurie. "Yeah. But shouldn't we let Dr. God try his Dr. God thing first? Haven't you always wanted to have somebody inject dye into your fallopian tubes?"

"No," she says. "My dream has been to jerk off in a doctor's office so people can examine my sperm."

She grins at him and he has to laugh.

And then he thinks about it. "So…how *exactly* are they going to examine my sperm?"

Laurie smiles at him again. He doesn't laugh this time.

Alan enjoys being married to Laurie because she's his best friend—and not in that fake what-they-say-on-eHarmony-ads way, but in a real way. Sometimes she reminds him of Matt, his best friend when he was growing up—the perfect hang out, share jokes, belch-the-national-anthem-with pal. His relationship with Laurie is like that. Minus the belching. Plus, he gets to have sex with her.

He told his parents when he was nine he was never getting married because if he did, he wouldn't see Matt anymore.

"Matt and me, we're going to visit every country. There are almost *two hundred*, isn't that incredible?"

"Incredible," his mother said.

She didn't believe him. But he was sure he'd never find a girl who was fearless, who'd eat bugs and sleep on floors with spiders crawling on her face. What girl would do that?

On their first date, a Dodgers game, Laurie told Alan one of her dreams was to visit every country in the world, even the hard to get into ones, like North Korea and Cuba. Alan had found his female Matt.

The night before Laurie has her first test, he has a nightmare. He dreamed he was in Cuba with Laurie and she was wearing a baby carrier, and when he bent over to look at the baby, inside the carrier he was surprised to see a large bottle of dark Cuban rum.

"A chip off the old block," Laurie said to him. "Not to mention one hundred proof." She pulled out her diaper bag to reveal it was stuffed with cocktail glasses and fresh limes. "Would you like a Cuban daiquiri? They're quite tasty."

When he wakes up, he thinks about telling Laurie the dream but reconsiders. He'll keep his freaked-out, rum-bottle dream to himself.

Laurie goes through her testing—ultrasound, X-rays, hysteroscopy, blood work. Nothing shows up. Alan does blood work as well, and when that's done, it's time for the sperm sample. They say he can come into the doctor's office or bring in a specimen from home.

"Specimen doesn't seem like the right word," he tells Laurie.

"What's better? Your 'bodily essence'?" Laurie suggests.

A clinician at the fertility clinic gives him a small plastic bottle and a paper bag and tells him morning semen is best. He imagines collecting his specimen, driving to Beverly Hills, and getting mugged by a kid who takes the bag, looks inside, and says, "Whoa, what's this? It looks like jiz."

"It's my bodily essence," he tells him before he's pistol-whipped into unconsciousness.

And how does he go about collecting his specimen at home? Laurie volunteers to buy a sexy French maid outfit.

"You think this is funny," he tells her.

"No," she says. "But we have to promise we'll laugh. Even at the lowest point."

"We haven't had the lowest point already?"

"I hope so. Are you sure about the sexy French maid outfit?" She winks at him. "Ooh la la."

The morning he's supposed to deliver the specimen, he goes into the bathroom with the plastic cup, sits on the side of the tub. Who should he think about? Laurie? He closes his eyes. He remembers watching her take a shower, unaware he's come into the bathroom. She rubs soap up and down her arms, across her chest, under her breasts. She's smiling, unselfconscious. She might be singing. He tries to hear the words, but he can't make them out. Smooth and white and soapy, her body is as attractive as it was when they met. Maybe more attractive.

He opens his eyes and remembers hearing Laurie crying in the bathroom after the first miscarriage. Or was it the second? He's not sure.

He doesn't want to do this, be alone in a bathroom with a vial and a ridiculous job to do. But there's no way around it. It might be easier if he doesn't think about Laurie—not that he doesn't find her desirable. She's the most desirable woman he knows. But if he thinks of her, he'll see the pain in her eyes. He needs someone more anonymous. Neutral. If he could track down a Victoria's Secret catalogue, that could work. There's probably one in the house. Or the *Sports Illustrated* swimsuit issue. He likes how they paint suits on the models. He imagines having a job like that, trying to carefully maneuver a brush around a nipple.

Just when he's considering going out to the den, something slides under the bathroom door. A *Maxim* magazine with Jessica Alba on the cover. When he looks more closely, he can see Laurie has stuck a photo of her own face on Jessica Alba's body. From behind the door, he can hear Laurie laughing.

"Not funny," he calls out to her. "I'm taking this seriously."

Her laughter trails off down the hallway.

It's good she's laughing now. But suppose they have a serious problem? He originally assumed the miscarriages were related to Laurie, but the problem could be his. What will they find in his sperm? He's got to have enough. Millions, right? And at least his sperm was okay before; it's not as if he's shooting blanks.

But there could be something *inside* his sperm that doesn't work or isn't compatible with Laurie. He's heard about complications with antibodies. Is that what this is about? And the solution will be something easy, like taking vitamins—or having more sex.

Suppose he has bad antibodies and needs to have some kind of penis surgery? Something involving a glass tube they stick up your dick. And pull-y things they put on your balls. And the worst part—to do it right, they can't use anesthesia.

What happens if he finds out his sperm count is *five*? And his motility is zero? There's no way he could have impregnated Laurie. So the first two pregnancies—Dr. God will shake his head at Alan and say like Maury Povich, "Clearly you were *not* the father."

A knock on the door. "Need another magazine?"

He looks down at the *Maxim* and realizes he's been reading an article on "Motorcycle Mayhem."

"No, I'm fine," he says.

"They're not going to find anything, you know," Laurie tells him. "But we still have to do it."

She's right. And he's a moron for letting his imagination run away to nutso land. Everything is going to work out. They're young; they have an excellent fertility doctor. Alan has Laurie, his best friend.

"I'm lucky to have you," he calls out to her.

"You bet you are."

He hopes she'll still love him when she finds out about his zero motility, bad antibody sperm.

Laurie taps on the door again. "Hey, Mr. Lucky," she says. "I could put on my sexy black corset. Maybe find a riding crop." She lowers her voice. Says in a husky whisper, "Have you been a naughty boy?"

"Go away," he tells her.

When she's gone and he's finished the motorcycle article, he looks around. He's in a bathroom. With pictures of Jessica Alba.

This isn't how you're supposed to make a baby. Sometimes old-fashioned ways are the most *kick-ass*. Jessica Alba? Who cares? Although she is gorgeous. *Really* gorgeous.

He hates being dependent on doctors and lab tests, and why does it have to be so damn difficult? And humiliating? He looks up to see his reflection in the mirror above the sink. Are those wrinkles around the corners of his eyes? He's sure they weren't there a year ago. Oh, man. By the time they have a child, he could be *sixty*.

But what else can he do? They have to keep going, push forward. They aren't quitters. So they'll try anything. Dance naked around a maypole, sacrifice animals (not really, unless slugs or cockroaches count), they'll do whatever they have to do.

He will be positive and supportive. He will *embrace* this fucktoid fertility technology. He loves his wife. They want a child—even if he's uncomfortable with the process, even if he despises it. And it could be worse. He looks down at the seminaked photos of Jessica Alba.

Because this time, dammit, *this* is the one that's going to work.

Jack

He has every intention of paying back the money. It's not as if anybody will notice it's missing; people have been stealing from the fraternity party fund for years, no big deal. "Stealing" sounds too harsh. Jack prefers to think of it as borrowing. Granted, he could have asked Danny to help him out—Danny, who gets a new leased BMW every fall and wears a TAG Heuer watch ("A Carrera," he says, "like the Porsche"), but he didn't want to tell him the truth, explain how his parents had slashed his allowance in half. ("Perhaps if you're forced to deal with the realities of life—you can't stay in school forever," Jack's father told him.) Even though his father was the one who made the hard-ass phone call, he thinks his mother was the one who went apeshit because he changed his major again, from history to South American studies.

And who knew they audited books at fraternity houses? Danny told the guys it was no big deal, but some big honcho from the National SAE board would be dropping by some time in the future to make sure everything was running okay.

Jack only borrowed a little over a thousand dollars, so he's got a couple months to put the money back. Only how's he going to work *and* get his degree at the same time?

He's already decided to not drive as much to save on gas, so hopefully he can find a job in Westwood, within walking distance. Except the pay at restaurant jobs is shit and he doesn't see himself as a busboy. He looks at the UCLA job board, and everything listed looks crappy or offers more busboy jobs. As a last resort, he checks out *The Daily Bruin*, and while no amazing jobs appear, an ad on the back page catches his eye. The Westside Cryobank.

Sperm donation. Why didn't he think about that before? He goes to the Westside Cryobank website—$40 to $100 for each semen sample. The potential to make up to $6,000 a year. And the work—do you really call it work?—it's something you do for fun anyway. Why not get paid for it?

He reads through the info. The screening process is extensive—a long form to fill out and interviews and your sperm and blood work are checked and double-checked for diseases. Still, better than bussing tables. He clicks on the box to begin the application process. Name, address, the usual. And then more specific questions:

Have you had West Nile virus, Creutzfeldt-Jakob disease? Did any of your sexual partners live in Cameroon, Chad, the Congo? Unexplained diarrhea, SARS, exposure to heavy metals?

Heavy metal? Yeah, he likes Metallica and Slayer and Seether. Should he put that in the application, let them know he has a sense of humor?

Probably a bad idea.

Physical characteristics. Height, weight, ethnic origin of parents. Talents.

Talent. He can drink a bottle of Captain Morgan without puking. He's a beer pong champion. He took violin lessons for five years but didn't practice much.

He writes, "Play the violin."

He played flag football in high school, some tennis, ran

cross-country one season (most of one season—okay, *half* of one season) until he realized he hated it as much as he hated violin. His mother despaired: *What will become of you? You quit everything.* He liked kickball. A bunch of his friends thought it would be cool to start a high school kickball team, but they never did.

He writes, "Athletic, likes kickball."

Professional aspirations.

Oh no. Maybe he should email this question to his mother, give her a good laugh. "My son is coasting through life," she'll write on the form. "Four years, almost *five* years at UCLA, and he changes his major once a week. Who would choose such low achieving sperm? Now, if you need eggs, our daughter, Subhra—she's in medical school at Johns Hopkins. Brilliant, beautiful, excels at sports, especially swimming and volleyball, fluent in five languages, plays the violin and cello."

Jack chooses to be vague. "I have so many aspirations, I haven't narrowed them down yet."

Personal reasons for becoming a sperm donor. He thinks. Well, he's got plenty of sperm. Why shouldn't he use it for good? Instead of just squirting it into mouths. Or other places.

He'll do that question later.

Can he provide a childhood photo? He has a couple old little league baseball photo cards in his desk. He looks okay in the photo—his teeth are slightly funky (preorthodontist), but probably most six-year-olds have funky teeth.

But his teeth might be the kiss of death. People are going to look at the picture and read his file. Is this sperm donor thing a waste of time? Maybe it's easier to ask Megan for money, except she has less than he does. It's funny how Gwnn's/Megan's name really turned out to be Megan. And it's been great dating her. Except for the inconvenience of the missing party fund money and his mother's occasional annoying emails, things are okay. Pretty close to excellent. And now the sperm donor idea—what's more genius than that? It's foolproof. His life is *golden*.

He's eating dinner at a fish place Carter told him about; in fact, Carter is supposed to be here having dinner with him, but he hasn't showed up yet. The fish tacos are good, very tasty with a cayenne kick. He's on his third taco when he realizes there's something hard in his mouth—a fish bone. He chokes a little and spits out the bone on his plate.

"Disgusting," says a voice beside him.

He looks over to see a small, cute girl watching him. She has short red-blond hair, with bangs. Her haircut looks precise and squared off, no loose pieces anywhere.

"Sorry," he says to her, but she's walking over to his table and looking at his plate.

"Not you. This place is disgusting to serve big hunks of bone in their fish tacos. Don't they double-check? You could sue them. Did you break a tooth? I smell lawsuit." This is how Jack meets Normandie. She's a junior at UCLA, prelaw, very focused. "It's not enough for me to win at life," she says later after she's joined him at his table. "My enemies must lose."

Normandie has always wanted to be an attorney. People ask her why: Are her parents attorneys? Did she read *To Kill a Mockingbird* and fall in love with Atticus Finch? She doesn't understand what they're talking about. She wants to be a shark, a killer. For three years in a row, she dressed up as an attorney for Halloween. "And what are you supposed to be, little girl?" a sweet old lady would ask. "You've got a crack in your sidewalk that could potentially cause you some serious litigation worries," Normandie would answer as she handed the lady a card with her name and email address on it.

On their first official date, at a café in Venice Beach that'd been triple-vetted by Normandie, she tells him how much she admires Gloria Allred.

"I won't be as brittle," Normandie says, tucking her hair behind her ear. "I'll be warmer—not a viper, but some kind of animal that seems gentle and cuddly on the outside until you realize they can—and *will*—kill you. Like the dilophosaurus in *Jurassic Park* who looks cute and friendly to the fat guy who's stolen the dinosaur eggs, only then it sprouts this creepy frill and opens its mouth to reveal giant, sharp teeth and spits venom. And that's the end of the fat guy."

Normandie spears a cherry tomato with her fork and pops it in her mouth. "Squish," she says.

Normandie's parents run a local radio station in Fresno. Cool, Jack said. Normandie shakes her head. "My parents are ex-hippies with MBAs who should be Silicon Valley billionaires, but instead they embraced an alternative lifestyle. If you want to drive around in a beat-up truck with pot in the glove compartment, that's fine, but one day, you're going to have kids and be role models. They never thought about that part."

"I think running a radio station sounds great. You can be your own boss, play your favorite music all day."

"There's a lot of corporate stuff involved and zero money," Normandie says. "They have to do these terrible promotions like tractor pulls and mini slot car races."

"They must hate that."

"No. That's the worst part—they think it's fantastic. They had a 'Guess the Weight of the Pig' contest and they had this gigantic pig, like out of *Charlotte's Web*, and the winner got to keep it. Only not as a pet, duh. 'Mr. Bacon.' That's what they named the pig. Disgusting."

"So you're a vegetarian?"

"Hell, no. They're animals, not people." She pokes at her salad again, looking for another cherry tomato.

"What about all the inhumane ways they're treated?" Jack is almost a vegetarian. He likes a steak every now and then, but that's only when he forces himself not to think about slaughterhouses.

"You mean like veal? Yeah, it's sick to keep them cooped up in tiny cages so they can't move and won't develop muscles and feed them milk and kill them when they're babies. But they're *cows*. It's not like they know what's going on—or care."

Jack thinks they probably *do* care about being dead versus being alive. And the thought of living your short life in a crate, always indoors, with zero contact with other calves—it's pretty ghastly.

"Don't you worship cows?" she asks him.

"Hindus believe animals have souls. So that includes cows. Krishna was a cowherd."

"The blue guy?"

Jack nods.

"So you're Hindu?" she asks.

"Presbyterian."

She frowns. "You're not as exotic as I thought."

"Is that a problem?"

"I always look at the long term. An Indian husband, that would stand out. Look good on my résumé. Not that I'd ever change my name."

She's talking about marriage. He should run. But she's cute. Will she have sex with him tonight? A good chance if she's already talking about marriage.

She sips her drink. "Change my *last* name, I mean. My first name I'm going to change soon. Normandie. What were my parents thinking? They were probably high. Normandy's a place in France, you know, D-Day. Which would be stupid enough, but they had to end it in *–ie*. Isn't that hideous? My brother's name is Merlot."

Jack laughs.

"Get this—because the night he was conceived, they were drinking Merlot. I suppose it could be worse; they could've been drinking absinthe. Or mint juleps."

They don't have sex that night. Or on the next date or the date after that. Jack thinks it's probably okay, since he's technically dating Megan, although she's busy in a production of *Guys and Dolls*, understudying Miss Adelaide. According to Megan, the girl playing Miss Adelaide, Jyll, got the part because she told the director her father had cancer and his dying wish was to see his daughter in a UCLA musical, and even though Jyll is tone-deaf and dance-challenged, she got the part anyway. And Megan has heard some of the Hot Box girls talking about how the stuff with her father having cancer is bullshit.

So Megan is busy with her play and whenever Jack talks to her, all she wants to do is complain about Jyll, and Jack has never liked musicals anyway and seeing this one sounds especially awful. *Medea* wasn't bad though; he was surprised he liked it. But musicals give him the creeps. People suddenly bursting into song for no reason. Who does that? Life isn't *Glee*.

Why won't Normandie have sex with him? Because she wants to be sure, she says. Is she seeing anybody else? No, of course not. Would she care if she knew about Megan? Maybe. Would she care if she knew about the money he's borrowed from the party fund? Would she loan him money? He's not willing to go that far. Potential sex outweighs a loan. At least for now.

After dinner, Carter comes in with a keg he's liberated from another fraternity and even though the beer tastes flat, "What's that expression about a gift horse?" Carter says, so they finish the keg, and when Jack goes back to his room, he's a little light-headed, but checks his email messages and sees an email from Westside Cryobank asking if he could come in for an interview next week. Ka-*ching*, he thinks. He might be a failure at graduating from college on time or picking a major. Dating two girls at the same time could be considered some kind of failure too. And being forced to borrow money from your fraternity—wait, he refuses to go to the dark-cloud-hovering-over-his-head place. Golden, that's what his life is now, isn't it?

Yeah, look on the bright side—somebody wants his sperm. Woo-hoo, he's finally good at something.

Laurie

Dr. Julian wasn't surprised when none of the tests revealed anything. "With a high percentage of miscarriages and infertility issues, we never find the exact problem," he tells Laurie and Alan.

Not especially reassuring. Laurie was hoping he'd say something like drinking iced green tea three times a day would do the trick.

Alan has some motility issues. "Slow swimmers," says Dr. Julian. Probably not directly related to the miscarriages, but Dr. Julian will monitor the next pregnancy closely, starting with the conception process. "To make sure you have the best chance of getting pregnant and *staying* pregnant, with no worries."

No worries. Laurie wants to laugh. *What would that be like?* she wonders.

"It's not as if we're moving into the heavy-duty stuff," Dr. Julian says. "No in vitro. At least not yet." *Is he making a joke?* Dr. Julian doesn't seem to have a great sense of humor. And he's too old for his jazz patch. You're only allowed to wear a jazz patch if you're under twenty-five or play an instrument. Dr. Julian gives them a booklet about "the next step." It's called "Everything You Want to Know About

IUI." Laurie isn't sure she wants to know anything about IUI (intrauterine insemination), especially after Alan starts making jokes about it.

"Insemination Under the Influence, ha-ha," Alan says. They're driving home from the doctor's office and Alan is chipper. He's been very chipper lately, and she wonders if he is covering up his anxiety about another potential pregnancy.

"Insanity Under the Influence." Alan grins at Laurie. She manages a small grin back.

"Do you want to have lunch?" Laurie asks him. "Grace found a Greek place near our office. They have great chicken souvlaki and grape leaves. We could go over everything Dr. Julian talked about."

"I'd love to. But I should get back to Palmer-Boone. Everything goes to hell when I'm not there. Rain check?"

She looks at him, imagines his face with a jazz patch. "Rain check," she says.

"Great." Alan frowns. "Okay, IUI. Hmmm, I can't think of another one. Come on, your turn."

At the Hidden Valley office, Grace flips through the IUI booklet and tosses it on the desk. "Yikes, this looks grim. But it's probably effective." Emilie has come with her today; she sits on the floor and plays with a Duplo zoo set. Hal is in the office checking over things with his partner, Ian. Grace gets down on the floor beside Emilie and makes a zebra bounce on Emilie's hand. Emilie giggles and Grace giggles back. Their matching copper-colored curls bounce on their heads and Laurie smiles. They are so clearly mother and daughter.

"There's nothing wrong with doing fertility stuff and looking into adoption at the same time," Grace says to Laurie.

"Yeah. Alan and I talked about adoption back when we were dating." She doesn't say anything about Alan's recent fear of meth-addicted birth mothers.

"It still might work out that way. I know an adoption attorney in West Hollywood. He's supposed to be very good. Or you could check out some online sites, see what's out there."

"I guess I could," Laurie says, hesitates. "IUI, in vitro—yuck. Does this mean I'm going to turn into Octomom?"

"I hope so. Then you could get a reality series. And I could be on it as your best friend. Tetramom, is that when you have ten?"

"I think ten would be dectuplets. But I'm not sure that's medically possible. *Ten*, can you imagine?"

Emilie gets up and runs over to Laurie, hands her a giraffe. "Meow," Emilie says.

Laurie pulls Emilie into her arms. "I don't know what a giraffe says. I think they snort or grunt."

Emilie thinks. "Grrr."

"I'm not sure that's right either." Laurie attempts a giraffe sound. Emilie looks at her, puzzled.

"Woof," Emilie says.

Alan has a late meeting at Palmer-Boone, so Laurie makes herself dinner, and after wasting time looking at sandals on Zappos, she finally decides to visit adoption sites. She's surprised to see so many; obviously there are plenty of people looking for children. She goes to one site and clicks on the section featuring "Parents Looking to Adopt." They contain photos and "pick me" letters to potential mothers-to-be.

She sees a photo of a young, fresh-faced couple, Brian

and Rachelle. "Our Midwestern roots and values will make family our priority. Thank you for considering us."

Brian talks about his wife: "Rachelle teaches preschool but will quit her job to be a stay-at-home mom. She loves cooking and Rollerblading and quilting."

Rachelle says Brian works as an EMT, likes camping, and is one of eleven children. "He *adores* big families," she says.

"We appreciate your selflessness and courage in making this decision. Blessings to you."

Laurie looks at Brian and Rachelle's photo again. *If I had an extra baby to go around, I would send him to you,* she thinks.

Mike and Melody. Mike teaches fourth grade; he enjoys working for Habitat for Humanity and playing with his dog, Whiskers. Melody teaches piano and the church youth choir. "Having a child would be a dream come true."

Other couples talk about their infertility journeys. Lost pregnancies. The sadness is carefully hidden behind the photos people choose to accompany their letters. Women dressed in sweater sets, men wearing crisp khakis, sitting close to their wives. Posed in front of fireplaces with Christmas stockings or outside on the deck. ("We've already babyproofed our pool!") Views of mountains, green backyards with swing sets ready to be used. Couples with giant sunny smiles. Pick us!

Laurie understands their desperation. *I bet after you took the photo, Rachelle and Melody, you crawled into bed and pulled the covers over your head. Because you think nobody is ever going to pick you. All the swing sets and church choirs in the world won't get you a baby.*

Laurie sees a photo of another couple. The woman is pretty but very overweight. In Ivy's personal statement, she talks of recently having gastric bypass: "I need to be as healthy as I can. To be a good mother."

Poor Ivy. What pregnant sixteen-year-old girl looking at

pictures on an adoption website would select an overweight woman? *I don't want my baby raised in a house of Ho-Hos. I want my baby to have model-thin,* People *magazine–beautiful parents.* Unless the young girl looks closely at the hope in Ivy's face—and if she keeps reading, she'll see that Ivy and her husband Andy have a house not far from Denver, three acres of land, and two dogs. Ivy is a nurse, Andy owns a small construction company, and they love music and nature and books. Ivy likes Shakespeare, especially *The Tempest.* She's put her favorite lines at the bottom of her letter:

How many goodly creatures are there here!
How beauteous mankind is! O brave new world,
That has such people in't.

She doesn't hear Alan come home. He bends over her shoulder and looks at the computer screen. "What are you doing?" he asks her.

"Adoption sites. Pick-me letters."

Alan frowns. "Pick-me letters?"

"People post letters and hope pregnant women will select them to raise their children."

Alan checks out a photo of a young, athletic couple standing beside triathlon bikes. "Do we have to buy triathlon bikes?"

Laurie taps the screen. "Allison and Reid love triathlons. They own a vineyard. He's a volunteer firefighter. She runs the local food bank."

"Huh," Alan says.

Laurie nods at him. They are both thinking the same thing. Alan speaks first. "Who would pick us?"

Laurie pretends to type. "Alan and I have been married for five years. Infertility has made us cranky with each other, and we might be too set in our ways to be good parents. I work for a local blog called Hidden Valley, which sounds much more exciting than it is. Would you like to visit a man who has a shoelace collection?"

"Shoelaces could be interesting." Alan takes over. "My job. VP at a large company, job security slightly questionable, downsizing can happen like that." He snaps his fingers, turns to Laurie.

She smiles at him. Pretends to continue to type. "We used to go to church, but we're a little pissed off at God these days."

"We'd make great Satanists though," Alan says. Then looks serious. "Should we buy a vineyard?"

"I don't want to write a pick-me letter, Alan."

"I don't want to do a triathlon. We would make great parents." He corrects himself. "We *will* make great parents." He heads for the kitchen. "Are there leftovers?"

"Yes." Laurie will look at Ivy's page again, think good thoughts. *You'll get your wish, Ivy. Hang in there.*

Alan crashes early and Laurie picks up Dr. Julian's IUI booklet. *Here goes.* She begins to read.

> *Artificial insemination, or AI, is the process by which sperm is placed into the reproductive tract of a female for the purpose of impregnating the female by using means other than sexual intercourse.*
>
> *A sperm sample will be provided by the male partner, obtained through masturbation or the use of an electrical stimulator.*

An electrical stimulator? Dr. Julian didn't say anything

about that. Unless he told Alan when Laurie wasn't around. Except Alan would have mentioned it to Laurie; something like that isn't the kind of thing Alan could keep secret. Is "electrical stimulator" some man code for "super hot hooker woman who works at the fertility clinic?" Maybe they hire women to come in and give hand jobs. When Alan and Laurie arrive for the IUI, the receptionist will ask Alan, "Will you be masturbating or using the electrical stimulator?" And she'll wink at Alan to let him know who's waiting for him in the special room.

> *When using intrauterine insemination (IUI), the sperm must have been "washed" in a laboratory and concentrated in Ham's F-10 medium without L-glutamine, warmed to 37°C.*

Ham's F-10 medium. WTF? Everything is technical—the spontaneity, the joy of getting pregnant is long gone. When Laurie and Alan first decided it was time for a baby, they'd performed a "burning of the diaphragm" ritual even though it didn't exactly burn up when they threw it in the fireplace—it smoked and shriveled up in an icky way. A bad omen?

Will IUI work? Or will they have to go back and do it again and again, and eventually they'll move on to in vitro where *both* of them are absent from the process? They won't even be in the room when the baby is conceived. And when that fails—it's time to take the picture by the fireplace and start writing their pick-me letter.

Laurie's mother arrives from Reno for the weekend and they

go to the beach because her mother says it's important to see the ocean at least once a year. "To remind you how big the world is," she explains, pointing to the horizon. "Practically infinite." Laurie's mother looks out at the ocean for a long time, as if she's recharging her batteries.

"Okay, we can walk now," she finally says. "Keep an eye out for good-looking men, older than forty, younger than seventy."

Laurie's father died when Laurie was in high school, and she's encouraged her mother to date, but her mother has been reluctant until recently.

"Forty?" Laurie says. Her mom is in her late fifties and looks good for her age. Very good. But *forty*?

"I waited a long time before getting back in the dating game." Her mother nods at a handsome blond man standing with his surfboard. "Check out that six-pack."

"*Mom.*" Is it better if her mother *doesn't* date again?

"So when's the IUI?"

"Next week. I'm not sure it's going to work."

"To dream the impossible dream…" Laurie's mother starts to sing and Laurie laughs. Her father used to play his *Man of La Mancha* record over and over, and he'd sing along, driving everyone crazy until Laurie's mom threw the record away.

"I still miss Daddy," Laurie says. "But not that song." She's sad her father never saw her graduate from high school or college. Or met Alan. Or got to be a grandparent.

"You could talk to somebody," her mother suggests. Her mother has worked as a social worker for most of her life and she's a big advocate of therapy.

"I can handle this."

"It's okay if you can't."

"I told you, I'm fine."

Her mother shakes her head. "You've always said that. My daughter, Miss Independent. Everything's fine, I can handle it."

"I can."

"Sometimes it's okay to lean on people."

"But I don't need to."

"You sound like your father."

"Don't worry about me, Mom."

"*That's* the impossible dream," her mother says. "When you're a mom—and I'm sure you will be—you'll worry *constantly*."

The night before the IUI, Alan has a screwdriver with dinner. "Vitamin C reduces sperm agglutination," Dr. Julian had told them. "Whoa, I'd hate to have agglutinated sperm." Alan waved his hands in the air in mock despair, and Dr. Julian gave him a look like he was an idiot. "That means your sperm sticks together, not good for fertility," Dr. Julian said.

Laurie gets Alan's favorite red velvet cupcakes from the bakery down the street and he has two—sugar is bound to super-*super*charge his sperm, right?

"Screwdrivers, cupcakes? Suppose I barf?" he says. "Does that mean when the baby's born we'll have to give him a barf-related name, like upchuck? Upchuck Gaines."

He's trying too hard, that's what's going on, Laurie decides. "Are you scared?" she asks him.

"Of what?"

"Of all this."

"There's nothing to worry about," Alan says.

Laurie remains unconvinced.

When the lab tech comes into the examining room with the syringe, Alan squeezes Laurie's hand and says, "Looks just like me." Laurie squeezes Alan's hand back but wishes he would shut up. She says a silent prayer. *Please don't let Alan say anything about Upchuck.* Then she thinks, *Yeah, that'll be the* one *request God grants.* Nothing about carrying a baby to term. All she's ever going to get from God is one lousy hunk of time where her husband doesn't make an Upchuck joke.

Dr. Julian instructs Laurie not to move for thirty minutes, let the supercharged semen do what it's supposed to do. Alan tells Laurie he can stay here with her, but she says he might as well get a cup of coffee, so he leaves and Laurie is left alone in the examining room. *Well, Upchuck*, she tells the possibly soon-to-be-conceived baby, *this is a special moment for you. One your father and I will always cherish. Nothing says special moment like looking around an examining room at Modigliani prints on the wall and out a window with a fantastic view of a parking lot.*

"I promise not to call you Upchuck," she whispers. "Just don't make me write pick-me letters. Grow and thrive, dammit. No 'blighted' business. Are you listening? You do your part, I'll do mine. Is that a deal?"

In the silence of the room, she can hear the *tap tap* of footsteps in the hallway. A woman's laugh. And at that moment, Laurie feels a rush, a wave, something light moving in her body, like an extra breath. Or a sigh.

Alan

He thought about Nancy Futterman the other day. He'd found one of Nancy's Christmas card photos in his desk drawer at work; she sends them every year along with a chatty letter describing the latest accomplishments of her two young children. "Trevor is musical!! He loves to bang on the piano. And sometimes Ava sings along!" Nancy was his first girlfriend who "could be the one." And it scared him back then because who thinks about marriage when they're in college, even though Nancy Futterman was pretty, with long legs that went on forever, great boobs, and thick blond hair she'd toss like a horse's mane. "Not a horse, dummy," she'd say. "I'm practicing to be a stripper. If graduate school doesn't work out."

They broke up after graduation when they moved to different cities, no hard feelings; he's sure she had the same ambivalence about marriage he did. Not that they'd ever discussed marriage—not out loud anyway. Nancy's husband, Bob, works in real estate, born and raised in Dallas, where they live now. A big Cowboys fan. That's a negative for Alan, raised in Virginia and in the religion of the Redskins.

Trevor and Ava look like a blend of Nancy and Bob, healthy and blond and happy. Nancy's family goes on cruises and safaris. Trevor and Ava already know how to ski and snorkel. Alan and Laurie will never catch up.

That's not a reason to have children, he tells himself. *To brag about their accomplishments in Christmas letters. Thank God Laurie and I aren't that shallow.*

And yet, he wonders about Bob and Nancy: When did they make the decision to get pregnant? Did they have any doubts, any problems? Fertility issues? No, that's stupid. He knows it's a waste of time to compare his life to anybody else's. Nobody's life is perfect. He examines Nancy's Christmas card. Notices Bob's eyes are too close together. And squinty. Probably wears glasses but is too vain to put them on for the photo.

Does Nancy ever think about Alan? Not that it matters. He knows he's better off with Laurie. Even though they've gotten slightly out of sync lately. It's not about blame or guilt with each other. Unless maybe it is. A year of miscarriages and now a fertility doctor. Trying to stay positive is exhausting. And masking disappointment? Equally exhausting. But how long does the friggin' disappointment have to go on? Why is it so easy for the Nancy Futtermans of the world?

"Knock knock."

Alan looks up and Laurie is standing in the doorway of his office. "Nice surprise," he says.

She walks over to his desk and kisses him on the cheek. "Good. I hope you're in the mood for surprises because I have another one."

He looks in her eyes and they're brighter than usual. Of course they are, because she's got that glow again, the pregnancy glow.

They walk outside to the Palmer-Boone patio and watch a group of Palmer-Boone employees play basketball in a corner of the parking lot.

"Did you call Dr. Julian?" Alan asks her.

"Not yet. I just took the home pregnancy test this morning. Let's hear it for your supercharged sperm."

"I suppose if it's a girl, we'll have to name her Jessica Alba."

"Jessica's a pretty name," Laurie says. She takes a deep breath. "We're doing this again."

"Yeah."

"I'm afraid."

"Me too," Alan says. "But don't worry. I promise I won't say the third time's the charm."

"Nuts. You jinxed it." Laurie's smacks Alan on the arm. A friendly smack. He hopes.

"Congratulations," he says, kissing her.

"Congratulations to you," she says.

And then they don't say anything. They don't know what to say. Alan is sure she is thinking the same thing he is. *Now what?*

After Laurie leaves, he goes back to his office and thinks about calling his parents. They've been concerned. Not in a bad way; they're very supportive. But should he tell them? Should he tell *anybody*? It didn't work out before when he told people. Oh no, is he going to be superstitious this time?

He opens a desk drawer and finds a package of peanut M&M's, shakes out a few: a red one and a green one. That's a good sign, right? It's not as if two brown ones came out. Everybody knows brown M&M's are unlucky. He pops them in his mouth and realizes the package has been in his desk drawer too long and the peanuts are stale. A bad sign?

He can't spend nine months worrying about what could go wrong. He grabs an M&M. Whew, a red one. A red M&M must mean everything will be *fantastic*.

He checks his email, considers going on Facebook. But Facebook is silly; he'd resisted it until Peter created a Palmer-Boone softball team page and insisted he join.

Nothing new at the softball group. Alan could tell Peter about Laurie. Peter is married with a ten-month-old baby; he was sympathetic after the first miscarriage. Could Alan explain to Peter how he has an uneasy feeling these days, how it started with Dr. Julian saying, "I can give you a baby"? *Shouldn't Laurie and I be able to get our* own *baby?* Of course he's excited at Laurie's news, but there's a touch of something else. Fear? A premonition of something terrible about to happen? What would Peter say to him? "Just chill."

No, he's not going to tell anybody. Not his parents, not Peter. He'll wait ten weeks, or fourteen weeks. Or until Laurie shows up at the Palmer-Boone Christmas party with a baby in her arms.

Alan goes to his Facebook profile page. His profile picture is from a softball game where he's sliding into home plate. It looks like he beat the tag, but he didn't. The umpire had something in his eye, the run counted, and they won the game.

"Cheater," Laurie said. "You were out by a mile."

"Sometimes things go your way," Alan told her. "It all evens out."

Does it? *When* do things even out? Why does the squeaky wheel get the grease? Why shouldn't the wheel that works the hardest, doesn't behave like an asshole, why shouldn't *that* wheel get the grease? *Laurie and I were made to be wonderful parents. Why do we have to go through this bullshit? We are* unsqueaky wheels. *And we want* our turn.

What would Laurie like for dinner? Alan likes to cook whenever he has a chance. He'll make dinner for Laurie tonight, something special. Pasta or steak. She brought home ribs the other night from yet another Hidden Valley find. "'Gen-U-Wine Texas Barb-E-Q,' that's on the sign in front," she told him. "Their spelling sucks, but their ribs kick butt."

Something Texan? He could make up his own batch of barbecue sauce. Hey, Nancy Futterman is in Texas—maybe she has a recipe. He could send her a message on Facebook. He goes to Search, types *Nancy Futt*...realizes she uses her married name now. Nancy Campbell. When the names pop up, he sees a "Nancy F. Campbell." He clicks on her name.

Nancy of the Christmas card photos; she's standing on a beach in a long, gauzy dress and sun hat, one hand shading her eyes. With her other hand she's waving at the photographer, as if she's telling him (Bob?) not to take the picture.

There's other information listed. Not much though.

Sports: Dallas Cowboys. Mavericks.

Basic Information: Married.

Gender: Female.

If he wants to know anything else, he'll have to add her as a friend.

Sure, why not? It's not as if he'll keep it a secret from Laurie. Laurie has a Facebook page; she's friends with at least one of her old boyfriends. Probably. It doesn't mean anything, Alan reconnecting with Nancy. He needs a barbecue recipe. Once they start talking on Facebook, it will be clear they don't have *anything* in common anymore. What brought them together in the past? Funny, neither of them can put their finger on it.

Nancy was great in bed. No, not great. Outstanding. Innovative. Like that cooking show *Chopped*, where the chefs are given strange ingredients to put together for a dish, like kale and Rice Krispies and sake. How do you make something harmonious out of that? Nancy could do it. Give her a deserted putting green, a chocolate milkshake, and a scrunchie, she'd come up with a sexual feast. Surprising, shocking. Always a good time.

Has Nancy ever had sex with her husband Bob on a putting green? In the Christmas photos, Bob looks like a Sex in a Bed with the Lights Off guy. That's probably where Trevor and Ava were conceived, in a king-sized four-poster, Bob's ancestral bed. Is that the problem with Alan and Laurie: neither of them brought an ancestral bed to the marriage?

He should click on the friend request. It's not a big deal. Nancy will be thrilled to hear from him.

Except why hasn't *she* sent *him* a friend request? Because the Christmas letters are enough. A photocopied letter with a scrawl at the bottom: "Hope you all are doing great! Come and visit us when you're in Texas! XOXOX, Nancy and Her Crew."

Alan and Laurie don't have a Crew. They have each other.

I'm not lonely, Alan wants to say. Even though he knows that's not completely true. He shouldn't feel lonely; he's happily married. Yes, the past year sucked big time, but look at the news today—Laurie is pregnant. He should be celebrating instead of eating old M&M's and thinking about an ex-girlfriend.

He could leave the office early, pick up flowers and fixings for dinner. Not barbecue. Pasta. And if it's not too cold, they can eat outside. Sparkling cider for Laurie, a Red Trolley ale for Alan.

He could tell Nancy the good news. "Guess what? We're having a baby! We'll start sending Christmas letters like you guys. What's Bob up to? He looks like he needs to loosen up. Take him to a putting green, ha-ha. Those were the days. I'd like to see you again sometime, Nancy. I remember your hair tasted good. Funny, who has hair that *tastes* good? But yours was fruity. Was it the shampoo you used? Thinking about you. XOXOX."

Alan doesn't type any of this. And when he gets to the XOXOX part, he reaches in the drawer again, finds another peanut M&M, and eats it.

He should be thinking about Laurie. Not Nancy Futterman. It's ridiculous to think about Nancy Futterman. So what if she has a fabulous life (even with Bob's squinty eyes)? His life will be *more* fabulous. Who needs stupid Nancy Futterman anyway? Alan is a good man and he'll be a good husband. He'll eventually be a good father—assuming it works this time. Which it will. *Booyah*.

Alan and Laurie eat on the patio and because it's chilly, they wear sweatshirts with the hoods up. Alan makes Giada "Look at My Boobs" De Laurentiis's fettuccine with asparagus and a fried egg on top.

"I'm eating this every day. Breakfast, lunch, dinner. Until morning sickness starts," Laurie says.

"Maybe it won't be as bad this time."

"I'll survive. Although it's hideously unfair how much

morning sickness I've accumulated for one baby." Laurie wipes her finger around the bottom of her bowl, catching the last yellow bits of yolk. "Tomorrow night will you make chocolate mousse?"

"Yes, whatever you want."

"Thanks." She looks at him, touches her stomach. "It feels different. This one. Do you think? Or am I crazy?"

"I think you're crazy. In a good way. But yeah, it does feel different." He leans across the table and kisses her. Tastes egg and asparagus and apple cider. Laurie.

Laurie goes to bed early and after Alan does the dishes, he sits down at his computer in the office. A few emails from work—he'll deal with those in the morning. Peter has sent a new softball practice schedule. He thinks about reading it over, then realizes he wants to get into bed with Laurie. Even though she's asleep, he can wrap his arms around her and listen to her breathe. Listen to her breathing for two.

Jack

How did Jack end up dating two girls at the same time? His life has turned into a dumb Jennifer Aniston movie. But it'll work out, he tells himself. Like replacing the fraternity party fund money. He's already put back five hundred dollars, courtesy of Westside Cryobank.

Only one close call with the missing money. The SAE auditor showed up; he seemed cool, especially when Danny made everybody G&Ts. But when the auditor checked the accounting books, he found some problems. Including possible embezzlement. Jack's heart practically stopped beating, but to his surprise, Carter stood up and admitted stealing money from the kitchen fund, only he'd paid it back. But he messed up the books trying to cover his tracks. Carter cried; he felt terrible and he said he'd understand if they kicked him out. The SAE guy was sympathetic (and a little drunk) and told him not to worry. "Honesty is the key, dude," he said.

For a moment Jack considered doing his own version of throwing himself on the mercy of the court, but since he hadn't paid back all the money yet, he kept his mouth shut. Maybe the SAE guy has only one pardon per visit and he's already used that up on Carter. So the next person who turns up dirty is going down. And Jack won't be that guy.

Once the SAE inspection is done, the house decides to celebrate with parties. Themes are popular, like Bring a Twin Night and Strip Beer Pong. Not that Jack has to worry about his social life—he's got more than enough going on with juggling Megan and Normandie. He tries to convince himself he feels guilty. They wouldn't care; they're probably cheating on him too. So he's justified.

It would be a bitch to pick one over the other. Megan enjoys shock value, doing things just because she can. Like she'll stop using deodorant. Or brushing her hair. "Suppose I don't ever shave my legs again, would you leave me?" she asks him. Jack likes her because she's never dull. And because Megan is the living, breathing version of everything his mother hates. Not Indian. A Catholic father and Jewish mother. Flirts with Wicca.

Megan ran out of eyeliner one night and used a Sharpie. "You look like Michael Jackson," Jack told her.

"Smart-ass," she said. When he fell asleep, she drew a curling Sharpie mustache under his nose and laughed when he couldn't get it off.

The thought of taking Megan to Northern California for Thanksgiving is appealing. He can imagine Megan dressing for the big meal—something leather or sheer.

Megan takes him to an Avenged Sevenfold concert. She is wearing black thigh-high boots with cutoff shorts. "Maybe I should pierce something," she says. "But it has to be something people wouldn't ordinarily pierce. What part of your body would be the most unexpected?"

"A bone through your nose?" Jack suggests.

"Too common. The whole gauge thing is intriguing, but I hate the idea of having huge empty holes in my ears. And earlobes touching your shoulders is *gross*."

Jack agrees. He doesn't like gauges—or snakebite

piercings below your lower lip. "You could split your tongue," he suggests.

She thinks that over. "I wonder how much it hurts. And it must be weird when it's healing. I'd think if you ate something like pretzels—" She shivers. "*Agony.*"

Jack has no desire to pierce his tongue.

"You should get a Prince Albert," Megan says.

Jack doesn't want to admit he doesn't know what that is. Megan knows he doesn't know. "Your penis. You pierce it. Like with a ring."

Ow.

Megan leans in close, raises her eyebrows, and smiles. "Or...if you want to go really weird...you could split it."

"Split what?"

"Your penis."

Yeah, he'll bring Megan home for Thanksgiving. "Hi, Mom, I'd like you to meet Megan."

"Hello, Mrs. Mulani. You have a lovely home. Did Jack tell you he's having his dick split in two so he'll have a two-headed penis? I know, he is *so* creative."

What would his mother say about Normandie? Normandie looks better on the surface, but her killer instinct might be too much. Normandie and his mother in the same room. It would be like a meeting of two alpha dogs. Only one would come out alive.

Normandie is studying for the LSAT. They're in her tiny single bed. Jack is wearing a T-shirt and boxers; Normandie is in sweat pants and a camisole. "Sleepy time clothes," she calls them. She allows him to spend the night, but no sex yet. He watches her with her LSAT notes. He's thinking about sex, and she's thinking about sample questions. "I'm good at analytical reasoning, and reading comprehension is a breeze," she says. "It's the logical reasoning I get screwed up on."

"Speaking of screwing," Jack says, but Normandie is deep into her sample question about dental research and bacteria that can induce preterm labor and Jack stops paying attention and doesn't really care who's high risk or not, but guesses C and Normandie tells him he's right and he should consider law school.

Great, another decision he can't make.

Sort of like not being able to choose between Normandie and Megan.

Jack has never met anyone as ambitious as Normandie. She has her life planned out. Law, politics on the side, she wants to be a mover and shaker. "I can't help it, Jack," she tells him. "I'm attracted to power."

Why is she attracted to Jack? It's a mystery. But a mystery he'll go along with. She's such a contrast to Megan…not that that's a reason to date somebody.

And he knows he shouldn't be dating two people at the same time. But he's not in love with Megan *or* Normandie. And he's sure they're not in love with him. Which doesn't make his behavior okay, but he sleeps at night. Besides, how are they going to find out about each other?

Megan's unpredictability is always so—unpredictable. He never knows which Megan is going to show up. Medea? Miss Adelaide? She's good at playing roles, but does he know what she's really like? He guesses that's part of the attraction.

Normandie is the opposite. Very organized—her life is a schedule. "Okay, tonight after dinner you can come to my apartment and we'll watch two episodes of *Game of Thrones* I TiVoed, but you can't spend the night because I have to get up early to meet with my Little Sister. Do you know how impressive the Big Sister program looks on your law school application?" When she undresses, she takes her clothes off slowly and folds them into neat piles.

Her body is perfect. She'll let him see her naked, but there's still no sex. "I have to maintain some degree of mystery, don't I?" she says to him. She would never use a Sharpie as eyeliner. Normandie thinks tattoos are pathetic, an obvious attempt at attention. "What kind of person wants to go through life having people look at them and interpret their body art? It's as desperate as a vanity plate."

Megan has one tattoo—not a butterfly on the small of her back, but a wolverine above her right hipbone. Because she thinks wolverines are fierce.

Sometimes Jack imagines Normandie and Megan in bed together. They remind him of salt and pepper shakers his mother has, shaped like tiny bears that fit together as if they're hugging. Would Normandie and Megan do that? No, if they knew about each other, there would be broken bones involved. Probably Jack's.

What would Jack's mother think of Normandie? "Pleased to meet you, Mrs. Mulani," Normandie would say with a firm handshake. "Jack's told me so much about you. Except he didn't say you look more like his sister than his mother." Exactly the kind of thing his mother would be impressed with. And if Normandie mentioned her SAT scores and ambitions—bingo, who cares if she's not from India? Test scores and a life plan trump *anything*.

Together, Normandie and his mother would turn on him. He imagines the family sitting around the table, his mother patting Normandie's hand and looking at Jack. "Isn't it a shame? All that talent, those brains, and he still doesn't know what he wants to do with his life."

Normandie will nod, agree. Jack's mother will sigh. "I'm sure Jack's told you about his sister, Subhra. Subhra got the overambitious genes and Jack got..." She'll trail off and Normandie will smile sympathetically.

"Jack has your eyes, Mrs. Mulani. And your kind heart."

Jack won't think about Normandie and Megan. He'll concentrate on his Western civ paper. He's sitting outside at Falafel King in Westwood and he checks what he's typed on his laptop so far. His name, the class, the name of the teacher, "Metaphor of the Sun in Plato's 'Allegory of the Cave.'" That's it.

"Hello, stranger," a voice says, and Jack looks up to see Normandie. She's wearing a skirt and blazer, practicing her courtroom wardrobe. Jack nods hello and she slips into the chair beside him. "My class got canceled so I thought I'd hang out around here until my next one."

"Want some lunch?"

"I ate already. Is that iced tea?"

Jack nods and pushes his drink over to her. She sips from his straw, looks up at him and nods at his computer.

"Western civ paper," he tells her.

"How's it going?"

"Great."

"Econ would be better for you. I think you've got an econ brain. You should get an MBA. Did you ever consider arts management? That's an interesting field. I could bring you some reading material."

Jack nods. Sometimes Normandie is overwhelming. Sometimes she reminds him too much of his mother.

"I could help you study for the GRE," she says. "I've

got standardized testing down. It's not just knowledge; it's how they figure out the questions, like the traps they put in to catch you. I should start my own standardized test prep service."

She'd make a fortune. Jack could put up the initial capital, invest in Normandie. His parents might go for that. Jack thinks if his mother met Normandie and had the opportunity, she'd divorce Jack from the family and adopt Normandie.

"Yeah, I'd love your help. I'm not sure about getting an MBA though," he says.

"You're right. I think you need to concentrate on graduating. This century."

Jack laughs. She's not wrong; he knows that. He pops a falafel ball in his mouth. But at least she's offering a plan. What's wrong with business school? Three more years of putting off a career decision? That sounds perfect.

"Fucking shit, you are *so* not going to believe this."

Megan has appeared at the table.

"She broke her leg in five places," Megan says to Jack. "Not that I'm glad because that would be cruel but—*five*. Pins, surgery, she is *fucked*."

Jack doesn't say anything. Normandie is looking at Megan. Megan is wearing fingerless gloves, a "Stop Shark Finning" T-shirt, leggings. And a sombrero. "Who broke her leg?" he finally asks.

"Jyll. Miss Adelaide. She's out of *Guys and Dolls*. And I'm in. Go *me*." Megan does a spin, crosses her arms in front of her chest, and sings, "I love you, a bushel and a peck. Bushel and a peck and a hug around the neck."

"*Guys and Dolls* is one of my favorite musicals," Normandie says.

Normandie is sitting beside Jack. Talking to Megan.

Megan nods at Normandie. "The guy who's Sky Masterson is incredible—gorgeous, gay, of course, and he's got this Josh Groban voice, only more fuckable, you know what I mean?"

"When is it?" Normandie says. "I'd love to go."

"Two weeks. Oh my God, I have so much to do, I'm going to be rehearsing all the time." Megan turns to Jack.

What's Megan going to say? Something about his potential Prince Albert? "How'd she break her leg?" he asks.

"Goofy," Megan says, leaning over and picking at Jack's potato chips. "Ski trip."

"That doesn't sound so goofy." Normandie is smiling at Megan.

"She fell on the steps outside her condo." Megan eats another chip and licks the salt off her fingers. "When do you want tickets? I can leave two for you at the box office," she tells Normandie. "Just name the day."

Normandie looks at Jack. Before she can open her mouth he speaks first. "I want to go opening night. Won't that be like the best performance?"

"Maybe, assuming I'm ready." Megan sighs. "Jyll's anorexic, so they'll have to let out her costumes." She checks her watch. "Damn, I'm supposed to be at rehearsal. Hope I don't break my leg." She starts off, looks back at Normandie. "Let me know about the tickets." And she's gone.

Jack exhales. Has he been holding his breath this whole time? He thinks so; that must be why he feels almost ready to pass out. Dodged that bullet, *whew*. He pops the last bit of his falafel into his mouth and takes a sip of iced tea.

"I think your friend will make a great Miss Adelaide," Normandie says. "She's got so much personality."

Jack nods, his mouth is full of falafel and tea.

Normandie tucks her hair behind her ears, smiles at Jack. "How long have you been sleeping with her?"

Laurie

Laurie holds the phone close to her head as if it will help the words she's hearing make more sense. Her other hand presses lightly, protectively across her stomach.

"We are completely available to you and your husband, Mrs. Gaines. We'd be happy to refer you to a counselor."

Laurie grips the phone tighter. "You're sure? About the results."

Dr. Julian hesitates. "Yes, there's no chance of an error."

Laurie looks around her kitchen—at the ceiling, at a chip in the plaster she's never noticed before.

"I know this is unpleasant news. I'm very sorry. We'll speak again soon. My best to your husband."

Laurie allows the phone to slip from her hand. *You bet we'll speak again, buster. You and me and a roomful of attorneys—hoo*-ray. *We'll get enough money to replaster the kitchen ceiling, remodel the master bath, buy the house next door, knock it down, and build a fucking compound.*

I need a glass of wine, Laurie thinks. *No, something stronger than wine. A Long Island Iced Tea. Forget all that crap about taking care of You and The Baby. Unless this isn't happening, Dr. Julian didn't call, it's some pregnancy-induced hallucination.* She pinches the skin between her thumb and index finger—*nope, that hurts*. She's awake.

When she yanks open the cabinet door beside the refrigerator, it opens an inch and smashes against her fingernail. Childproof locks on anything that could potentially harm the baby. Laurie pulls the door harder, snapping off the babyproof lock (so much for *that* guarantee), and looks at the liquor inside. Vodka, rum, a thirty-two-ounce bottle of Kahlua bought on a trip to Tijuana years ago. What's in a Long Island Iced Tea anyway? Bourbon and gin? No, vodka, rum, gin…something else Laurie can't remember. She lines up the liquor bottles on the counter. And Coke. *Is there any Coke in the fridge?* One Diet Coke. *That'll do.*

Laurie grabs an old Taco Bell plastic cup, fills it with ice, adds a little vodka, a little rum, a little gin. The smell nearly knocks her off her feet. She adds a healthy amount of Diet Coke. No diet drinks either, the doctors advise. Could be dangerous, why take a chance? Laurie laughs out loud. *Take a chance my* ass.

She watches the Diet Coke fizz in the cup. What will this do to the baby? Alcohol and diet soda. Maybe Laurie should run out and score some crack, really give the baby something to think about.

She is raising the cup to her lips when Alan walks in. He takes in the liquor bottles, the Taco Bell cup. Laurie smiles at him.

"Guess what? You're not the father of our child."

Alan didn't allow her to drink the pseudo-Long Island Iced Tea. Instead, he finished it off quickly and moved on to more vodka and Diet Coke.

"But Dr. Julian told us it was safe. Mistakes never happen with IUI." Alan's green eyes look lighter than usual today, pale beneath his almost invisible blond eyebrows. She'd hoped the baby wouldn't inherit Alan's eyebrows. Ha, the joke's on Laurie.

"One of the techs in Dr. Julian's clinic switched around specimens," Laurie says. "She'd asked for two extra vacation days and the clinic said no. When she complained, they gave her notice. And apparently that made her unhappy."

"What about my specimen?" Alan asks. "Where did I go?"

Laurie sighs. "They haven't found you yet."

Alan taps the Diet Coke can against the rim of the Taco Bell cup.

"Dr. Julian wants to sit down with us," Laurie says.

"Because he knows we'll take legal action." Alan splashes more vodka into the cup.

Laurie's brain is filled with noises and voices and thoughts she can't sort out. Like letters in a Scrabble game bag, she could reach in and pull out anything—a Look on the Bright Side tile. After the disappointments and false hopes, at least she's having a baby. But whose? Did they ever let Charles Manson donate sperm?

There's another tile in the bag. A terrible choice she could consider—she's twelve weeks into the pregnancy, only twelve weeks…but no, she can't think about that. She touches her belly, feels the small rise of flesh.

"Alan? What should we do?"

Alan sips his drink. "Let's hear our options."

"I'm sure you have questions," Dr. Julian says. He's seated behind his desk, as if he'd like to be as far away as possible from Laurie and Alan. "The good news, the technician has been arrested." His jazz patch dances on his chin, Laurie wants to reach over and pull it out by the roots.

"Actually good news would be me having my *husband's* baby. Since that was the plan," Laurie says. "Have you been able to figure out who the father is?"

A long pause. "A sperm donor."

"I want to know everything about him," says Laurie.

"Our attorneys have advised us not to release any information." Dr. Julian looks down at his hands.

"What happened to my sperm?" Alan asks.

"The missing specimens haven't been located yet. As you might imagine, it's a huge conundrum."

"Conundrum isn't the word I'd use," Alan says. "Clusterfuck seems more accurate."

Dr. Julian takes a deep breath. "It's a terrible situation. But we have to think about our clinic. And our other clients."

"We could tell them," Alan says. "Go out in the waiting room, let everybody know what's happened. Unless that would be bad for your practice." His voice sounds polite, but Laurie can detect quiet rage underneath.

"We need to protect the donor's anonymity."

"What about *us*? Don't we count?" Alan stands up. "My wife is having a *baby*. It's supposed to be *my* baby and now you're telling us it's *not*?"

Dr. Julian pushes a brass letter opener back and forth, trying to line it up with edge of his desk. "You could choose termination," he says to Laurie and Alan.

"So. Now what?" Laurie asks Alan at breakfast. They're both thinking about it. They've *been* thinking about it; what else is there to think about? Laurie didn't sleep last night and she's sure Alan didn't either.

"I'll know more after I talk with the attorney," Alan says. He has a morning appointment with an attorney, but Laurie isn't going with him because she's promised Grace she'll finish a piece on the best tiki bar in the San Fernando Valley (Tonga Hut) and she has to visit Lake Balboa to check out the "fishing scene." Besides, she doesn't see how meeting with an attorney will accomplish anything.

"He'll only explain what we can do *legally*. What about the rest of it?" Laurie asks.

"We'll figure it out." Alan gives Laurie a kiss. As if the kiss will solve all their problems.

When Alan is gone, Laurie sits out on the patio with her laptop. Is the most popular drink at Tonga Hut the Voodoo Juice or Squirrel of Paradise? Perhaps the "I'm Coco Loco for Tonga Hut's Big Brown Nut!"

She closes her laptop. She'll start with the trip to Lake Balboa. It will clear her head. Hopefully. And if not, there's always Voodoo Juice.

Grace raves about Laurie's Tonga Hut piece; it could be the perfect spot for Laurie's baby shower (nonalcoholic tropical drinks for Laurie, of course). "Great," Laurie says, wondering what Grace would say if she knew the goofy details of Laurie's pregnancy. She tells Grace she'll be in the office later, after her doctor's appointment.

A week has passed since Dr. Julian's bombshell. A week of Alan meeting with Dave, the attorney, a week of Laurie trying to pretend everything is exactly the same, even though she knows nothing will be the same again. She's lied to Grace; she doesn't have an appointment with Dr. Julian, but she walks into his office, sweeping past the receptionist who gets up from her chair only to retreat when Laurie waves her off. She opens his door without knocking. Dr. Julian is on the phone and frowns at Laurie.

"I want to see the donor paperwork," she says.

He doesn't answer right away but mumbles into the phone, "I have to call back," and clicks off.

The first time she met Dr. Julian she thought he was handsome. Now he looks weak and pathetic with his tiny hands, uneven nails, and shaggy cuticles. *I'd bite my nails too, if I were you*, she thinks. *Bite them down to bloody stumps.*

"Mrs. Gaines, on the advice of our attorneys—"

"I don't care. I want the information *now*."

Dr. Julian puts his index finger in his mouth. *That won't help those cuticles, Doc.* Maybe he'll have to put cream on his hands and sleep wearing white cotton gloves. The thought of that makes Laurie smile.

"Your husband isn't with you today."

"He's at work. He's been meeting with an attorney. Discussing the lawsuit."

The index finger is back in Dr. Julian's mouth. "I see. Well. If it's only a question of the report…"

"I'd like to take a copy home. To look over. And show Alan, of course."

Dr. Julian nods. "I'll have Sandra make a Xerox for you. Mrs. Gaines, I'm sure this is difficult, but have you given consideration to how you'll continue with your pregnancy? I only bring this up because…decisions have to be made."

"I'll let you know," Laurie says. She imagines Dr. Julian wearing puffy white gloves, like Mickey Mouse.

Laurie sits on the carpet in the yellow room and curls her bare feet under her legs. She looks up at the alphabet border, closes her eyes and says a quick prayer. *Please don't let him be a madman.* She pulls the donor profile out of the manila envelope very slowly, as if the information inside has a life of its own. Which in a way, it does.

At the top of the page she sees "Donor number 296. Limited supply." What does that mean? They're running out of number 296? Is he popular? So many women read his profile they're *clamoring* for number 296?

"Ethnicity. Asian Indian." That's the first surprise. Indian food pops into her head. Tandoori chicken, paratha, saag aloo.

Alan has never been a fan of Indian food. He likes Mexican and sushi, and he'll try anything—fried crickets or haggis—but not Indian. Last night Laurie made American cuisine, meat loaf and mashed potatoes. She'd watched him push the potatoes back and forth on his plate.

"Dave is convinced the case is a slam dunk," Alan says.

Put the potatoes in your mouth, thinks Laurie. But no, the potatoes glide away from the turkey meat loaf, to the side of the plate.

"Dave's talking serious damages," Alan says.

"It's not about money. Did you explain that to him?"

Alan has the potatoes on the fork; they're almost to his mouth.

"Honey, I want to do the right thing," he says.

Laurie wants to scream or laugh, or both. Or rip the fork from Alan's hand and feed him, like a baby, like the stranger alien baby she's carrying.

She's not sure she can keep reading the profile. Asian Indian is enough to know for now. She touches the pages, imagines the donor typing in his information. Who are you? she wants to ask him. Genetic material that should never be allowed to reproduce? Kim Jong-il? The guy who thought up all those TV reality shows? Or are you polite? Do you hold doors open for people, say thank you and please? Do you read books, watch NASCAR? Both? At the same time? Are you a raging syphilitic? Do you drink Everclear for breakfast, is your body is covered with hair, front and back, are you Sasquatch?

And she laughs out loud at the thought of Sasquatch filling out a sperm donation form and going into a clinic to leave a specimen. Why is she thinking like Grace? This is Grace behavior.

Laurie pats her tummy. "You're not Sasquatch," she says. "You're mine. Mine and Alan's. And I promise we'll love you. Even if you like NASCAR, although I hope you like books better. Did you hear me? We love you."

She'll finish reading the profile after running errands and a quick trip to the Hidden Valley office. As she's sliding the file into the envelope, she notices a photo stapled to the back page, a baseball card with a picture of a young boy. Small and skinny, with medium dark skin, wearing a red uniform that says "Cardinals." He's missing his front teeth, but the new ones have started to come in so his mouth looks snaggly.

Laurie wonders if you can hear the sound of your own

heart breaking. She flips the photo over and sees something written on the back.

Jack Mulani.

Alan

He's never liked Indian food. People go on and on about how tender chicken is when it's been cooked in a tandoori oven and he thinks that's ridiculous. It tastes like dry chicken. Or sometimes a dish has spices he can't identify and when he asks the waiter what they are, the waiter will smile and say, "Family secret."

Oh yeah. Let me tell you about family secrets. Somebody stole my sperm. *How's that for a family secret? One minute it was safe in some kind of secure cryobank refrigerated tank and the next thing you know it's being inserted into Mrs. Somebody or Other's vagina. We don't know who yet. Maybe we'll never know.*

He's grouchy at the Sunday afternoon Palmer-Boone softball game and makes so many errors at third base Peter sends him out to right field. He looks over at the bleachers, at the Palmer-Boone spouses and their children. Peter's wife is bouncing their baby on her lap. *That could be Laurie in a year,* he thinks. But whose baby will she be holding?

What's his biggest fear? The baby will look Indian, nothing like Alan. No, worse than that would be the baby never bonding with him. Naturally the baby will bond with Laurie because they share a genetic connection. But the baby will see Alan, burst into tears, and reach for his mother. His *real* mother.

He tells himself he's being ridiculous. Adopted parents don't feel like that. They bond with their children. The baby will bond with him. Things haven't changed that much.

No, now he *is* being ridiculous.

He sees Laurie appear beside the bleachers and he watches as she bends over to admire Peter's baby. For two months he has put his hand on Laurie's stomach and imagined the life developing beneath his fingers. *His* life.

"Do you think the baby knows we're here?" he asked Laurie.

"I bet the baby's aware of everything—music, sounds. The positive energy we're sending."

And now—he feels like a schmuck. Like when Laurie was pregnant the first time with Troppo, talking to him, thinking Troppo was aware of her. And then Troppo ended up not existing. This baby, naturally *this* will be the baby to thrive and grow and emerge healthy and strong, only it's half Laurie and not *any* part of Alan.

What happens to the family tree? Will his mother put an asterisk by his child's name, like Barry Bonds's 762nd home run in the Hall of Fame Museum?

"Hey, Gaines, get your head out of your ass," Peter yells, and Alan realizes someone on the other team has hit a ball that's gone over his head and he has to retrieve it, but the ball rolls to the fence and before he can throw to Peter, the other team has scored an inside the park home run.

When the inning is finally over, Alan walks over to Laurie and gives her a kiss.

"I brought Gatorade and chips," Laurie says. "You guys kind of stink today."

"We stink most of the time," Alan says. Peter is holding his son, who is wearing a spit bib that says, "Daddy's Little Tax Deduction." Alan goes to the bench and waits for his turn at bat.

Alan looks at Peter. Peter is lifting his Little Tax Deduction up in the air. Then down. Then up again. Shit. Alan finally has a chance to create something that's his. No sharing involved. Just his and Laurie's. And now that's been taken away. He's entitled to feel a little sorry for himself, isn't he?

On the way home from the game (Palmer-Boone almost came back, but lost when Alan misjudged a fly ball), Alan asks Laurie how much they really know about number 296.

"You could read the file," Laurie says.

"I will. Eventually." He's flipped through a couple pages, but it was too overwhelming—Asian Indian, kickball. *Kickball?*

"We could meet him," Laurie says.

Alan doesn't answer. He'll wait on that one too.

Laurie is in bed, watching the end of a true crime show where the husband killed his wife and the cops found info on the man's computer that showed he'd looked up, "How to kill your wife. How to kill your wife with poison. How to kill your wife and make it look like an accident."

"Sometimes people are stupid," Laurie says.

Alan gets into bed, and she slides her feet under his legs. On TV, the husband/murderer is explaining how it's a mistake—he loved his wife; he'd never hurt her.

"Dr. Julian talked about termination," Alan says.

Laurie is silent; she clicks the remote to a local news channel. A fire in an L.A. county canyon; the flames are orange and yellow in the black sky. She doesn't look at Alan, keeps her eyes on the TV.

"Is that what you want to do?" she asks.

"No. Of course I don't. But we should think about our options."

Laurie pulls her feet away, pushes the mute button.

Alan hesitates, dives in. "So we keep it and go on. Like we're doing."

Laurie nods. She still isn't looking at him. He realizes he said "it."

"Keep the *baby*, that's what I meant to say."

"Okay." Laurie nods again. "What else?"

"We could arrange for the baby to be adopted after the birth. But that sounds awful."

"As awful as termination?"

Alan pauses. "You want me to be honest. I don't know how comfortable I am. With not being the father."

"It's okay to say you're mad, you're pissed off." Laurie gives Alan a tiny smile.

"Aren't you?"

"Yes. What are you worried about most?"

"You want me to pick *one* thing? A *million* things. Two weeks ago, I was the birth father. Now I'm not. You're my wife; this is supposed to be our baby. Not your baby and somebody else's. And I'm sorry if I sound selfish—"

"You don't."

Alan turns to the TV. The flames are mesmerizing; they look as if they go on forever. Maybe that's the best solution of all; the flames will spread from the far away canyon, get closer and closer to Sherman Oaks, wipe out their neighborhood, their house, their baby. Laurie's baby. His baby. Somebody's baby.

Couldn't we get a do-over? That's what he'd like to say to her. *The next baby will belong to* both *of us. Instead of this, this—freak show baby.*

He doesn't mean freak show. He would never say "freak show" to Laurie. She's watching him, guessing he's thinking freak show.

"It's not like it was," he says.

"I know."

"At least the baby is *part* you; you're not the one who's the outsider."

"Is that what you feel like?"

Alan feels like he's five years old when on Christmas morning he saw a new bike under the tree with his name on it and he was thrilled until he realized it was his brother Patrick's old bike that had been repainted. Wasn't Santa supposed to bring you *new* things, he asked Patrick and Patrick said Alan was a moron and by the way, Santa's not even real.

"This isn't what Dr. Julian promised," Alan says.

"He promised us a baby. He got that part right. Suppose we'd done in vitro and they messed up the sperm and the eggs," Laurie says.

"But we *didn't* do in vitro and some psycho tech *didn't* switch the sperm and the eggs. It was just me, my sperm. My half."

Laurie looks back at the TV. "You think we should end this pregnancy?"

Admit it, Laurie. You want a do-over too.

"I want a child," he finally says.

"Good. Because termination was never an option. Not ever." She reaches for Alan's hand.

On TV the flames are burning dangerously close to a house on a hillside. Alan hopes the TV cameras don't cut away so he can watch it burn to the ground.

He gets out of bed and tells Laurie he needs to check on some work emails. He does some work, plays a game of Spades, goes on Facebook to see if anyone has posted something funny. Nancy Futterman has added new photos of Trevor and Ava. They're eating cotton candy at some sort of county fair. He clicks on Nancy's profile page and sees pictures of Trevor's preschool carnival where someone has come and twisted balloons into funny animal shapes. "Guess what this one is?" Nancy has written under a photo of Trevor holding a giant lump of misshapen balloons. Nancy's answered her own question. "An armadillo!!!"

Alan smiles. Texas, armadillo. *Good joke, Nancy.* He wonders again if she remembers him. If the memories are good or bad. He wonders what she would think about his situation, his situation he can't tell anyone about. Maybe an outside observer would know what to do, offer sensible advice. Not that he'd ever ask Nancy. Not that he'd ever make contact with her again.

He glances up at the friend request box at the top of the page. Probably a bad idea. She won't have any interest in connecting with an old boyfriend. And he would never tell her about the baby and the switched sperm, so there is no logical reason to make contact with Nancy again.

He clicks on friend request. Thinks about going back to bed, but instead plays one more game of Spades. He tells himself if he wins this game, everything will work out. The specimens didn't go missing after all! It was just a misunderstanding! When he loses the first game, he decides to play a second one. He wasn't concentrating hard enough. The second game, *this* will be the one to prove that everything will work out exactly the way it's meant to.

He loses the second game. He should go to bed. Or check on the fires. Rub Laurie's back. Tell her not to worry.

A ping on his computer announces he has a message. His friend request has been accepted. Well, that's some kind of good news. He's ready to shut down the computer when a small box pops open at the bottom of his screen. It's Nancy Futterman.

"Hello, stranger," the message says. "What a nice surprise. I was thinking about you the other day. Time FLIES."

Time flies. He looks around his office, wonders if he should reply, what he should say. Finally writes, "Good to hear from you. I like your Christmas cards. Your children sure are growing up."

And they look like you and Bob. Lucky you.

"What r u up 2?" Nancy types.

Why isn't Nancy using real words? Alan has never been comfortable with texting slang. It makes him nervous, like a fraud, like he's trying to sound cool.

"Not much," he types. Wondering what the slang would be for "not much" and will Nancy think he's unhip? "I don't use the chat feature on Facebook very often."

He sounds like an old man. Nancy is probably sitting in her 30,000-square-foot McMansion in her tony Dallas suburb laughing at him.

And isn't it late? If it's eleven in Los Angeles what time is it in Dallas? Why is Nancy awake? Almost as if she's reading his mind, her message appears: "Our AC's out, can you BELIEVE it? It must be 200 degrees in the house. I might have to sleep in the pool. Ha-HA."

Nancy Futterman had incredible breasts. At college when the frosh books came out and everybody in Alan's dorm went through them and circled pictures of the girls they'd like to go after, Nancy's breasts won in a landslide. Who would be the lucky guy to see/touch Nancy Futterman's breasts? Alan didn't think he had a chance; it took him three weeks to get the courage to talk to her and another three weeks before he asked her out, and amazingly enough, she agreed.

Laurie's breasts are great. Smallish, but a solid A if he had to rate them. It's not Laurie's fault Nancy Futterman's were better. A-plus. Just a little on the too big size, firm and round with standing-at-attention perky nipples. What do they look like now? Will Nancy put on a bathing suit to go outside and sleep on a float in the pool? Why isn't she saying anything about her husband? Maybe she's pissed because he's a real estate agent and don't they have contracts with electricians and AC guys? What is Bob waiting for? Nancy is hot; she's sweating; she can't sleep. It's an emergency, for God's sake.

What's she wearing right now? If it's so hot, maybe she's not wearing anything.

"Can't you get a fan?" Alan types.

She's naked. She's sitting in a dark room, she's kicked her husband to the curb, and she's IMing Alan on Facebook.

"Bob's moving fans around, he has the windows open. He talks about 'fan technology.' BULLSHIT, I say." She adds a smiley face.

"Sorry you're hot," he types. Reconsiders. Is that too much of a double entendre? Wait, it's not a double entendre—his former college girlfriend is sitting in a hot house with a broken air conditioner. She sent him a message that said, "Hi." And what is his reaction? To imagine her naked.

He should be in bed with Laurie. Is there anything you need, honey? We'll make this crazy baby thing work out. Whatever you decide, I'll go along with it. If you like this guy's sperm, we'll use him again. Have a whole *family* of number 296. I'll learn to love Indian food; we'll have lamb rogan josh twice a week, go to Bollywood movies.

Nancy has sent him another IM. "What's new in ur neck of the woods?"

Don't get me started, Nancy. Laurie and I have bigger issues than air-conditioning. We're a mess.

"Not much," he types. "Got 2 go."

When he gets back to the bedroom, Laurie is asleep. The TV is still on, the fire continues to burn. He slips in bed beside Laurie and rubs her back. She makes soft purring noises even though she's asleep. On the TV, flames creep slowly up a hillside, growing closer and closer to a gated community.

Jack

The best solution would be for Megan and Normandie to become best friends—not likely, but possible. They could find something in common (besides Jack), start to hang out, and realize—hey, we can *share* him.

It doesn't work out that way. Normandie tells Jack he's a shit and she never wants to see him again. And by the way, she was just about to have sex with him.

Megan figured it out too. "That girl at Falafel King, she gave off this 'Jack belongs to me' vibe. Which wouldn't worry me since she screams *virgin* so I don't think you're sleeping with her. But it's still douchey for you not to tell me about her. I told you about other guys I went out with."

"I didn't ask you to," Jack tells her.

"Doesn't make a difference. Why don't we take a vacay from each other?"

Plenty of fish in the sea, Carter says when he hears the story. Carter tells Jack how he dated sisters at the same time and how messed up that got, but Jack stops listening because like most of Carter's stories, you lose interest after the first five minutes.

He decides it's a sign. He's meant to buckle down, study, graduate. The world is telling him he's made things too complicated; he needs to readjust his focus. Women are a distraction. And he doesn't have time for distractions right now. He'll finish up his classes, graduate on schedule. (Almost on schedule.)

So what if he doesn't know what he wants to do with his life yet? Without distractions, he can figure it out. For example, how about religious studies? Not that he'd be a priest; he could be an academic. *Teach* religion. He can explore his Hindu past—he's always meant to. His parents celebrate a few Hindu holidays, like Diwali. But they also go to the local Presbyterian church.

Unless being a Hindu priest is cool. He wonders how long you have to train for it and does a degree from UCLA help? What would you do exactly? Do you have to shave your head? He's not sure how good he'd look without hair. Are Hindu priests allowed to drink beer? Would celibacy be an issue? That's a deal breaker.

He looks into the requirements for a religious studies minor. It's probably too late to change to a religious studies major. But he's pleased to discover he's already taken a lot of the required classes to meet a minor. Buddhism, Western civ, anthropology, plus an intro to religion class he took one summer. He checks out the classes he'd need, and most of them look interesting. Ancient Jewish History, Roots of Patriarchy: Ancient Goddesses and Heroines. He's a little skeptical (ha-ha) about Skepticism and Reality. And Medieval Literature of Devotion and Dissent could be a killer. Or not. It's a toss-up between that and Saint and Heretic: Joan of Arc and Gilles de Paris. Who the hell is Gilles de Paris? Is he some male version of Joan of Arc, like a guy kid who had creepy visions and then got to lead an army until he got captured and was burned at the stake? Cool.

And after graduation, graduate school. In religious studies. Because why not?

Unless it's a stupid idea. That's what his mother would say. "A South American studies major and a religious studies minor? What do you do with a degree like that? Visit the Incan pyramids? I suppose you could be a *tour guide.*" (Actually he'd love to learn about the Incan civilization. He should see if there are any classes available.)

He's riding his bike through a neighborhood near UCLA, looking at houses. What kinds of jobs do people have to afford these big homes? Did they worry about their majors when they were in college? He could ring a doorbell or two, ask. "Excuse me, what was your major in college?"

Why did his sister have to get all the super smart genes? *This isn't my fault,* he should say to his parents. *Your genes made me this way.*

He could get a doctorate in religious studies. Not be a medical doctor, but still have a PhD. Dr. Jack Mulani sounds *excellent.*

He passes a house with a vaguely Tudor exterior: white plaster walls trimmed with thick wood beams. The kind of house Martin Luther would like? Probably not. Too fancy for Martin Luther. *What kind of guy was Martin Luther?* Jack wonders. *An arrogant windbag? Did he have a sense of humor? When he tacked his Ninety-Five Theses to the church door in Wittenberg, did he use a hammer? What kind of nail?* Aha, Jack thinks he's found his thesis: "The Mechanics of Martin Luther Nailing His Ninety-Five Theses to the Church Door in Wittenberg." Jack knows a little about the Ninety-Five Theses, but he'll learn more, be able to toss around Martin Luther facts. "By the way, did you know that the ninety-first article in Martin Luther's Ninety-Five Theses is about the Holy Trinity?"

He'll talk to his UCLA advisor, sign up for religion classes, get information on the best graduate schools for religious studies. Where would he like to live after L.A.? Somewhere on the east coast, not too cold though. Does the University of Hawaii have a religious studies program? That could be perfect. Surfing, studying, drinking piña coladas on the beach.

He has a new life plan. The best thing that ever happened to him was Normandie and Megan breaking up with him.

Megan calls first. Says she's still mad at him, but she took a happiness survey online and it talked about forgiveness and life being too short and stuff like that, so maybe he should come see *Guys and Dolls*. Although it's a pretty strange production because the director has been inspired by the *Godfather* movies.

Normandie calls a couple days later. "Sorry I unfriended you on Facebook. That was petty," she says. "We can still hang out sometimes. On one condition."

"Sure," Jack says, wondering what the condition would be.

"We date each other exclusively. No Megan. What do you think?"

Jack's thinking he'd prefer to study so he can graduate and imagine his new life as Dr. Mulani. But he agrees.

"Great," Normandie says. "I'm serious about Megan though. It's just me. Because I think our relationship could have real depth."

Real depth? Jack's not sure how he feels about that. But at least there's a chance of finally having sex with Normandie.

"You want to come over tonight?" he asks her.

Megan is right about *Guys and Dolls*. It's an unusual production, sort of noir-y and humorless. And Jack is confused by the shootout between Nathan Detroit and Skye Masterson in the middle of the "Luck Be a Lady" number.

"The director added the shootout," Megan explains after the show. "He also wanted a horse's head at the end of act one, but they talked him out of it." Jack and Megan are in her bed and Jack has a flash of Normandie, but it's just a flash and what Normandie doesn't know won't hurt her.

Not that Normandie has had sex with him. She still insists on waiting, but promises it will be soon. "I want it to be extra special," she tells him. "Unforgettable. Something you'll remember for the rest of your life."

Megan sticks her bare legs straight up in the air and admires her freshly painted toenails—tiny black skulls against white. "I missed you," she tells Jack.

"Ditto," Jack says. He's glad he's back with Megan, and how good could sex be with Normandie? It couldn't be *that* amazing.

Or could it?

He's signed up for two religion classes even though his advisor told him his plan was "ambitious." She didn't say ambitious in a good way. Jack reassured her and said he felt he was finally on track.

He hasn't mentioned anything to his parents about his Master Plan yet; he wants the timing to be right. First step, see what his sister is up to because it would be just like her to go and win the Nobel Prize the minute he announces *his* big news.

Two girlfriends, a Master Plan, a new minor in religion, money in the bank (almost). He's anticipating other great things, so when he gets a phone call from a number he doesn't recognize, he figures he's won five million dollars in a lottery he forgot he entered.

"Is this Jack Mulani?" the voice asks.

"Yes," he says, thinking the first thing he'll do with the money is buy a house. With a killer ocean view. And a sports court. And an infinity pool. Nothing too ostentatious…not that you can be super ostentatious with only five mil to spend on a house in Los Angeles.

"My name is Laurie Gaines." She doesn't say anything for a few seconds and Jack gets a feeling in the pit of his stomach. *She isn't going to tell me I've won five million dollars. She's going to tell me something else.*

He hears her take a breath. "I'm having your baby," she says.

Gestation

Laurie

Laurie recognizes him at once. He looks like the boy in the baseball picture but grown up. Lean and handsome and needs a haircut. At least he's here; he didn't chicken out. That's something, she tells herself. And then she thinks about going back to her car and driving home because this is scarier than she thought, meeting the father of your child for the first time.

Last night, Alan told her it was a bad idea for her to have lunch with Jack. Or "296," as he refers to him.

"You could come too," she tells Alan.

"I don't think so."

"Are you sure? Don't you want to know what he's like?"

"You read the file."

"I want to see him. Talk to him. You aren't curious?"

"I'm curious you're so curious."

"We agreed—" Laurie says.

"To have the baby, I know. But I'm still having a hard time with this."

"I understand."

"Do you?"

Another silence. Even though they're moving forward, the reality of what's happening is settling in, and as days pass, instead of bringing them together, the pregnancy seems to be pushing against them, shoving them apart.

"I need to know who he is, not just words in a sperm donor application," Laurie says.

"He likes to play kickball. Doesn't that tell you everything you need to know?"

"You can't understand somebody's personality from a file. I want to hear his voice. His laugh. Make sure he's got a sense of humor."

"And if he doesn't?"

"We'll give the baby up for adoption."

Whoops, she's said that with too much edge in her voice. Alan frowns.

"Funny," he says.

"I wasn't trying to be funny. Or bitchy. I'm sorry if it came off that way." She pauses. "He's part of us now."

"But I don't want him to be. That's the problem. I'm sorry too."

Alan walks out of the room. Laurie listens to him open the refrigerator door. He's getting a beer. *We're turning into the house of alcohol. We could open a bar.* She puts her hands on her stomach. It feels round and full, an almost twenty-week pregnant belly. Is she just imagining it, is that a flutter? Like a butterfly, she imagines wings inside her body moving ever so lightly.

Laurie watches Jack; he's sitting at a table by himself at the Castle Park Café. Café is a generous way to describe the food court at the Castle Park arcade—a dozen tables, several wall-mounted flat-screen TVs blaring ESPN channels, adding to the din of arcade game sounds—machine gun fire, game show music, revving engines. Will Laurie have to shout for Jack to hear her? And yet it seems like a safe place to meet. Not too fancy or intimidating. Jack sips his Coke, looks down at the napkin in front of him and begins to shred it. He's wearing a faded blue polo shirt splotchy with bleach stains. His hair falls in front of his eyes.

Laurie takes a deep breath. It's time.

"Nice to meet you." Jack stands when Laurie joins him. Good manners. That wasn't in the file.

"Well. This is a little..." she says.

Jack smiles. "Weird." He looks down, realizes he's staring at Laurie's belly, sits quickly.

"I'm not sure what to say. I read your profile."

"So you know everything about me. That's weird. Oh, I said that already." Jack concentrates on his napkin.

He's young; he could be eighteen, not twenty-one. What should she say? Why didn't she plan something? "How's school?" she finally asks him.

"Okay. I'm a fifth year senior. But I'll finish up by spring."

"What's your major?"

Before he can answer, a girl in a T-shirt with a Castle Park logo appears. She yawns, ready to go home. "You can order at the window," she says, pointing to a menu sign above the counter. "Or I could bring you something." She looks like she'd rather clean the tables with her tongue.

Laurie checks out the menu—burgers, pizza, quesadillas. "Ah—I haven't decided yet." She can feel the girl checking her out, noticing the bulge in Laurie's shirt.

"You're pregnant, huh?" the girl says.

"Yes."

The girl turns to Jack. "Whoa, aren't you lucky?"

Jack almost knocks over his Coke. "It's not, it's sort of..." He clears his throat, turns to Laurie. *Help me out here.*

Laurie smiles back at the girl. "He's not the father. Well, he *is*. It's a little nutty. My husband's at work. You know what? I think we're ready to order."

The girl practically tosses their cheeseburgers on the table, she's so reluctant to make eye contact. Jack is still grinning (sense of humor, check); he likes that the girl is uncomfortable.

Laurie watches as Jack squirts ketchup and mustard on his cheeseburger. "I suppose you want to know more about me," he says.

Laurie nods.

"My parents were born in Mumbai. It used to be Bombay. They had an arranged marriage."

"Yuck," says Laurie.

"No, it was actually okay. They're perfect for each other. They came to the States to go to graduate school; now they're both professors at Stanford. He teaches chemistry and she teaches biology and bioinformatics."

"What's that?"

"You combine biology, computer science, and statistics."

"And you get a really smart frog who can use a calculator?"

Jack smiles. His teeth are perfect and white against his mocha skin. His eyes are large, deep brown, almost black. "So my parents had big expectations for me," he says.

"Oh. Not a fifth year senior? You never told me your major."

Jack looks down at his napkin. "That's another problem. I keep changing it. Right now I've got a South American studies major with a religious studies minor. But I'm not sure what I'll do after graduation. My parents—they're not exactly over the moon."

"They're parents. Go figure. At least they want what's best for you."

Jack makes a face, picks at a french fry. "Do you know what you're going to do with the baby?"

The question comes out of nowhere. It was safer talking about UCLA. Laurie is tempted to tell him everything. She hasn't told anyone else yet about the switched sperm. Not Grace, not her mother. She and Alan have decided to wait to tell people. For how long? They're not sure.

Laurie could use a confidante, like her old G.I. Joe doll. Someone to talk to about what her life is like now, how it's become a mixture of joy and confusion, how she's mostly thrilled, but sometimes overwhelmed by the strangeness of it all. She could explain how she and Alan lie in bed at night, not sleeping, sharing their wordless anxiety about what will happen when the baby arrives.

"I'd like to hear more about UCLA," Laurie says to Jack.

Jack tells Laurie he's considering graduate school and an advanced degree in religious studies.

"I took a comparative religion class in high school," Laurie says. "You must've taken lots of classes."

"Some," Jack says, and Laurie can tell he's not being entirely truthful. She already suspects he wasn't a hundred percent honest on the donor application, so she's not surprised. But she feels a small moment of panic. How many other things did he lie about?

"I think because I've taken such a variety of *other* classes, I'll be able to bring all that experience with me to a graduate program," Jack says.

"Practicing what you'll say to the interviewer?"

Jack looks caught. "Oh, I didn't mean—"

"I get it. I was a college kid too."

She likes him. Is he what she was expecting? She's not sure *what* she was expecting—a steroid-pumped frat boy who crushes beer cans against his head? Jack seems open, smart, friendly. Nervous—well, who wouldn't be?

How much of Jack will be in the baby? Will Jack and Laurie's genetic material combine in a good way? Will the baby look like him? Latte-colored skin and dark eyes? No invisible Alan eyebrows. There's a blessing. Jack seems to be kind and he has a sweet quality. That makes her feel better. Well, betterish.

After lunch Laurie asks if he'd like to play miniature golf. "This is one of the best mini golf/arcades in the Valley," she says. She's explained her job at Hidden Valley, and Jack thinks it sounds "awesome."

He'll take a pass on mini golf, but how about they check out some of the games? He's interested in The Vault, a laser maze challenge where you thread your way in the dark and try to make it to the end without touching glowing laser beams. Laurie begs off—the baby, you know—and Jack nods, yeah, probably not such a good idea. Instead Laurie buys ten dollars worth of arcade tokens and gives them to Jack.

"All four of my grandparents are still alive," Jack says after winning twenty prize tickets on Ninja Assassin. "No hidden relatives in mental institutions. At least none I know about."

Laurie laughs. "The truth is, you shake anybody's family tree and you'll find some nuts. Do you have a girlfriend?"

Jack hesitates. Uh oh, should Laurie have asked that question? And now that Jack isn't saying anything, Laurie wonders if he's gay. Not that she cares.

"Sort of," Jack says.

"I didn't mean to get too personal." Although she *is* having his child.

"Her name is Megan," he says. "I'm not sure what she'd think about this."

Laurie can tell he's left something out. Here's a quality she doesn't want Jack to pass along to the baby—the inability to lie. Unless that's a good thing, to have a face that's completely transparent.

"Are you going to tell her?" she asks him.

"I don't know."

"What about your parents?"

"Are you kidding? They'd flip. Did you tell anybody?"

"Not yet."

They don't say anything for a while. Laurie knows Jack has questions for her, but he stays quiet.

"You can ask me anything, Jack."

"Really?"

Laurie nods at him.

"It's just—I don't have a lot of money," he says. "I'm not sure I can pay child support."

"I don't need money from you," she says. "That's not why I wanted to have lunch."

The relief on his face is obvious. "Then how come?"

"To know what the baby will be like."

With the child support issue off his chest, Jack talks more openly about his sperm bank visits. "They said if a kid gets conceived by donor sperm, at age eighteen, they can contact the clinic and get information. About me. So I knew it could happen."

"Just not right now."

"Yeah. It seemed more—hypothetical. Nothing to do with a real live baby." Jack looks around at the arcade, lights flash against his face. Red, blue, purple. "What does your husband think?" he asks Laurie.

A complicated question. "He's confused."

"That makes sense. He thought it was his baby. Now it's mine." Jack looks flustered. "Not mine. I don't mean I think it's mine…"

"I understand. Don't worry."

Jack looks at her. "What about you?"

"I'm confused too. And scared. But I want a child. And now I'm pregnant, so there isn't a lot I can do. Except take care of myself. And have a baby."

Laurie watches Jack concentrate as he plays Skee-Ball. What happens now? Will she continue to talk to him? Will Alan ever meet Jack? Will Jack come to a baby shower? Will they shake hands at Castle Park and say good-bye? "Good luck with the baby," Jack will say to her. She's taking the first steps in a journey where she has no idea what the ending will be. She feels tears in her eyes. Damn, she didn't want to cry in front of Jack. It was absurd to meet him; the whole situation is absurd.

Jack turns around. "Hey," he says. "It's going to be okay." Deep inside the Skee-Ball machine, gears grind, and with a *click click click*, a stream of blue prize tickets begin to appear.

After Laurie's meeting with Jack, she drives to Alan's office and waits in the Palmer-Boone parking garage. She's brought along a Sheila Kitzinger pregnancy book and opens it to the chapter with illustrations of fetuses at various stages. Mid–second trimester and her baby is beginning to blink, grow tiny toenails. *Are you sucking your thumb? Developing a brain curious for science facts from your paternal grandparents? Can you hear the fights with Alan? Did you recognize Jack, your birth father's voice?*

The baby will be born, *her* baby, and the baby will know who she is at once—her smell, her voice. They've spent ninc months together. Switched sperm specimens, the baby doesn't care.

Laurie is crying when Alan approaches the car.

"Honey?"

He gets in, doesn't say anything for a while. Finally he asks, "Did you meet him?"

Laurie nods, not trusting herself to speak.

Alan examines the dials on the dashboard, the button that makes the seats go warm. A silly indulgence when you live in Southern California, but it was one of the options.

"Is he nice?" Alan says.

Laurie nods again.

"What's he like?"

Laurie's not sure how to begin. Does Alan really want to know? She and Jack have agreed to keep in touch. Maybe next time they'll try mini golf. Or the batting cages.

She says to her husband, "He's like you."

Alan

Laurie seems happier after meeting Jack. That's good, Alan tells himself. And she said, "He's like you." That's good too. At least he can feel a little better about the situation although he hasn't asked Laurie how *exactly* he and Jack are alike. Personality? Eating habits? It's a safe bet they don't look much like each other, which is too bad because then Alan and Laurie would never have to reveal the secret of the baby's paternity.

At dinner, Laurie talks about making an appointment with Dr. Liu. Originally Dr. Julian would have delivered the baby, but that won't work out now, will it? Alan volunteers to come along, and Laurie says it will be nice to have Alan with her.

"Do you want to hear anything else about Jack?" she asks. "You're comfortable with me talking about him, aren't you?"

"Sure," he says, almost meaning it. "You liked him."

"Yes. Enough to want him to be the father of our baby? No. But if it couldn't be you, Jack's a good runner-up."

"So if I weren't around, you'd choose Jack." *Uh-oh, did that come off as snippy?*

Laurie frowns, ready to protest.

"No, I'm sorry, that's not what I meant." He hesitates. "You're going to see him again? Keep in touch?"

"I think so."

"So this will be like some kind of open adoption?"

Laurie doesn't answer right away. "I don't know what it'll be like. I can't predict what's going to happen. Maybe we shouldn't talk about it now."

"We have to," Alan says, thinking he'd love to never talk about it again.

"When the child is eighteen." Laurie tries to smile. "Because we'll have to tell him or her the truth eventually, won't we?"

And then how will the child feel about Alan? Alan will have taught him (he's sure the baby is a boy) how to throw a football in a tight spiral pass. He will have helped him with algebra. "No need to get frustrated by linear equations, buddy. That's what dads are for."

So he's taught his son, his buddy—*Buddy* has learned about sports and math, and Alan has helped him navigate girl problems too. The high school girl who's broken his heart. "She wasn't good enough for you. Come on, let's go out on the patio and have a beer. Your mom won't be home till late; she doesn't have to know."

And then at eighteen, they'll drop the switched sperm bomb and Buddy will look straight into Alan's eyes and say, "You're not my *real* father." And Alan's heart will literally rip in two, cleave—how does something cleave anyway? Well, Alan will find out in eighteen years, won't he?

"This will work out," Laurie says. "It's not as terrible as you think."

Alan returns her smile. But eighteen-year-old Buddy's rejection of him burns in his brain.

Nancy F. plays a lot of CityVille. Alan is surprised to see how often she posts about raising rent and energy points. He goes to Google and reads about CityVille. It sounds like fun. He could learn how to play, impress Nancy with his CityVille skills. She'll IM him more.

Wait. Why does he want more IMs from Nancy? Because she helps take his mind off thinking about Laurie's pregnancy. Shit, it's his pregnancy too. Sort of. Shit again. He could tell Nancy about it.

"Hi, Nancy. I have this very unusual problem. No, I mean *really* unusual."

Is he being disloyal to Laurie? Disrespectful? He just wants someone to make him feel better about what's going on, tell him he's not a douche bag for having conflicted feelings. It's not as if he's contemplating an affair with Nancy Futterman Campbell. No. Of course he isn't.

He'll tell Nancy the funny story about what happened to his missing sperm. "We just heard the news the other day. It's hilarious."

Not so hilarious. Laurie got a call from Dr. Julian. When Alan came home from work, she told him they'd found the missing vials in a landfill in Long Beach. She thought that would make Alan feel better.

"To find out my missing sperm ended up in a landfill? In Long Beach?"

"At least you know what happened to it," Laurie says. "There's one silver lining."

"Some silver lining."

"Don't you get it? It's a good thing."

"Instead of my sperm ending up in some other woman's womb. Because then we'd be even."

"Even?" Laurie says. "How is that even?"

"Then *you'd* know what it's like."

"You think I don't know what it's like? Are you telling me I don't understand?"

"You couldn't possibly understand," Alan says. "How would you feel if you suddenly found out there was a woman out there, a *stranger*, and she was having my baby?"

Laurie thinks that over. "I don't know. I guess I was relieved when they told me they'd tracked down your sperm."

"Stop saying it like that. You sound like Hercule Poirot."

Silence.

"We have to think of this in terms of *better*," Laurie tells him. "And this is better, isn't it? If the ultimate goal is for us to have a child, to be parents—we have that now. It's not ideal what happened; it's *insane*. But at least only one of us got mixed up."

He can't think of anything to say.

He doesn't mention the discovery of his missing sperm to Nancy. Instead, he looks at the pictures Nancy has posted on her Facebook page. A shot of the family visiting the Grand Tetons. Trevor is the spitting image of Bob, which is mostly a good thing—he's a cute child, but with Bob's unfortunate piggy eyes. Is Nancy bothered by Bob's piggy eyes? At least you can tell he's the father of your child, that's what Alan would tell her. Trust me, be grateful for that.

A photo of Trevor and Ava standing with a horse. *Their* horse? Are they visiting a ranch? Does Bob have a ranch? Of course he does. He has a ranch, a giant house with a wine cellar, biological children, Nancy's big breasts—he has everything Alan ever wanted.

Trevor is missing a tooth. Isn't he too young to be losing teeth? A horseback riding accident? Trevor has bad teeth to match his eyes? Alan's teeth aren't great either. Too soft, the dentist told him when he was a kid.

Maybe Buddy will inherit 296's teeth. *Jack's* teeth. Laurie mentioned Jack's wonderful smile. Good, that'll save them a few bucks. *See, Laurie is right.* A silver lining. When God slams a door in your face, he spares you orthodontia.

When people see baby Buddy, will they assume Laurie cheated on him? Alan and Laurie could have fun with that. "Oh," people will say when they peek in the stroller. "He looks so…much like his mother."

"I think he looks like the guy who delivers the Arrowhead Water," Alan will say to Laurie with a wink. And she'll wink back. All the agonies of infertility and mixed-up sperm are forgotten. So what if Buddy's genealogy is a little wacky? *Lots of people have even stranger stories, I bet.*

I bet not.

He clicks on more photos of Trevor and Ava and feels tired. The ice cubes in his scotch have melted and his drink tastes like brown water. He could get up and refill his glass but doesn't have the energy.

I'm not sure I can ever post photos of Buddy on Facebook. Shitty McShitster. Why can't I have my own child? Is that too much to ask?

He shouldn't allow himself to get gloomy. Alan will love Buddy the moment he sees him. But suppose he doesn't? Will the doctor hand just-born baby Buddy to Alan and say, "You can cut the umbilical cord now, Mr. Gaines." And Alan will answer, "I'd rather not," or, "That's okay, you do it. I'll just stand over here and play a game of Word Mole on my BlackBerry."

Some of their friends and family know that Laurie's pregnant again. They waited to tell people until after she was showing. Only a few family members and friends knew about the second miscarriage. And no one knows the details about the switched sperm. Peter brought champagne to work one day and a couple of VPs met in Alan's office and finished off the bottle after work. For a moment it almost felt like a normal pregnancy, not a crazy fucked-up one. Alan's not exactly sure how they'd tell people the truth. Some sort of prebirth "oops" announcement? Jack will pop out of a cake at the baby shower?

Alan is looking at a photo of Nancy on a lanai in Hawaii, a drink in her hand. Is this how she copes with life, sips drinks with paper umbrellas? She doesn't look happy in the photo. More resigned than angry, but with a touch of sadness. Has Bob been unfaithful to Nancy? She's never mentioned anything about her marriage in the Christmas letters. Although Alan's not exactly sure how Nancy would phrase that.

"We had a fabulous time in Maui last spring. By the way, Bob admitted he was *banging* his secretary. Lucky she didn't come along on the trip!! I got the worst sunburn and we ate pig at a luau! ALOHA!"

Everyone has an uncomplicated life except for Alan and Laurie. Even as he thinks that, he knows it's not true. Tim, who he works with, has been married and divorced three times. Three times by age thirty-four. What's up with that? At an office party last year, one of Alan's project directors got slobbery drunk and told Alan the only way her husband could make love to her was if he was wearing a Jason hockey mask.

"Are you happy?" he's tempted to IM Nancy. What kind of question is that? What would she say? "Of COURSE I'm happy. You're looking at my FB pictures. You can see the happiness SPILLING out of me"?

Oh, shit. He's typed, "Are you happy?" and hit return by mistake. Maybe she's not online now and won't see it. Can he erase it? Fuck Facebook, they have the worst Help section on any site he's ever encountered, plus no email address where you can post questions.

He hears a soft *ping* and her photo appears in Chat.

"Not especially," is her reply.

Is she being ironic? Is there an emoticon for irony? If there is, Alan doesn't know what it looks like. Should he type, "Just kidding, sent that by mistake," with a smiley face attached?

Instead he types, "Me too." He watches the screen. Will she type a response right away? Is she looking at the screen like he is, trying to decide what to say? He thinks about typing something else like, "Happiness is overrated," but reconsiders. Her "not especially" sounds serious.

Ping. "Do you ever think you've made wrong choices?"

Wrong choices. Everybody makes wrong choices, don't they?

"Sometimes," he types.

She replies quickly, "I forgot, you ALWAYS make the right choice ☺."

"Yeah, I'm perfect," he says.

"Maybe you HAVE changed."

"Very funny. You know, if you ever need a shoulder to cry on…"

"I might," Nancy writes. "I'm glad you're doing okay."

"You look good."

"You've been checking out my photos on Facebook?"

"Just catching up. You don't do the same thing?"

"All the time. Every old boyfriend. Every old girlfriend for you?"

"Of course." *No, Nancy. You're the only one.*

"How do we look?"

"You look the best."

"That's because I pick the photos. ☺ You should see me in real life."

"I'd like to. Do you ever get out to L.A.?"

"Not really. What about you? Ever come to Dallas?"

"I haven't been in years."

"We'll have to arrange a reunion."

Silence.

He's the first one to type. "I'd like that."

"Me too. I better sign off."

"Nice chatting with you."

"Talk 2 u soon," she says.

The green light by her name blinks to gray. Alan looks at his computer screen. He should check out other old girlfriends on Facebook. Instead, he goes to "history" and erases the things he's been viewing. Not that he's paranoid or ashamed of what he's been doing.

Because he's not doing anything wrong. Is he?

Jack

She's old enough to be my mother. That was his first thought when he saw her. But when she told him she was thirty-two, he realized technically she could be his mother only if she'd been some kind of a child bride.

Face it, the whole thing is seriously messed up and what was he thinking, *donating sperm*, like there wasn't some kind of catch involved? If something is too good to be true, it is. There are consequences, a price to pay. Like suddenly finding out you're going to be a father. A father? He can't even be a responsible college student. Or be faithful to one girlfriend at a time.

Or keep borrowing money from the fraternity party fund. Sure he paid back the money the first time, but unfortunately Westside Cryobank told him that after the mix-up he should take some time off. "Time off" meaning they're scared of legal action, even though Laurie told him the problem happened at her fertility doctor's office and not at the sperm bank.

He could sue Westside. Get millions of dollars. To hell with college—he'll buy a big house in Mexico and fish and drink tequila all day. Except he has a sneaking suspicion that with all the paperwork he filled out at Westside, he probably signed something that prevents him from suing, like the legal version of, "The minute you give us your sperm, it's *ours* and we can do whatever the hell we want to do with it."

He'll figure out another way to make money; three hundred dollars isn't much. Win some poker tournaments at Indian casinos, that's an option. Find things in his room he can sell on eBay—Xbox games, a pair of vintage Nike Dunk high-tops he only wore once. He'll *never* ask Danny for a loan. Smug rich boy Danny who organized a trip to Cabo over spring break—too bad Jack couldn't make it. Fuck you, Danny. Jack will *run it up* at the Indian casino. Pay the money back, move on.

And he'll break up with Normandie and Megan, or at least one of them. Juggling two girlfriends at the same time isn't the way a religious studies student should behave.

As if. As if he's going to get into a graduate school for religious studies when they find out he's fathered a child. Even though he didn't set out to father a child. Except, on one hand he *did*. Well, in theory.

He definitely should sue Westside. They won't want the news to get out, so they'll settle out of court. Jack gets a fat check, everything goes away.

Except the baby. Laurie didn't say much about what happens after the baby is born. But no obligations, she told Jack. Is she sincere? She bought him lunch to see what he's like. Which makes sense. He'd probably do the same thing if he were in her shoes, which he's not, thank God.

"I'll call you," she said. And he told her the same thing. And now what? Should he call first? Wait for her? He has no idea.

He should be studying. It's not fair he has to think about this other stuff. Like why didn't Laurie's husband come to lunch?

Did Laurie invite him? Suppose he doesn't want to meet Jack? If Jack comes over to visit Laurie, will her husband be hostile? Will he narrow his eyes at Jack as if Jack had an affair with his wife, which he clearly didn't. *Dude, I wasn't even in the room.*

His bedroom door opens and Megan walks in. She's holding two cups. "These milkshakes are cold as fuck," she says as she hands him one. "Chocolate banana. Delish. What are you doing?"

"Homework." He could talk about his situation with Megan, she'd understand. Megan collects oddball things, tidbits about life—how many teeth a horse has, why fingers get wrinkly when they're in water for a long time.

"Aren't you supposed to be studying for the GRE?" he asks her. She's decided to take it, just for fun.

"I changed my mind." She plops on his bed beside him. "I'm thinking I'd make a good spook. You know, state department, CIA, one of those jobs where you can't tell anybody exactly what it is you do."

"You can't keep secrets at all," Jack tells her. "You're the worst."

"Maybe that's part of CIA training. They teach you how. Of course that's a bitch, that I won't be able to tell you *how* they teach me to keep secrets. Do you think I'd get to carry one of those briefcases where you push a button and a knife comes sticking out of it?"

"No offense, I don't think you have a chance."

Megan shakes her head. "I bet they love actresses."

"What about torture? That would suck."

"I'd be awesome," Megan says. "They'd never get anything out of me."

Jack grabs Megan's feet and begins to tickle her. She screams for him to stop. "Being ticklish is a big problem," Jack says. "It's probably one of the first things they check out."

Megan pulls away from Jack, sticks out her tongue at him. "I don't think spies from other countries tickle you. You're just jealous. I bet they give you a ring with cyanide in it. How cool would that be?"

After Megan leaves, Normandie calls and goes on and on about her plans for their big "sex night." Dinner at a restaurant with ocean views. She's still trying to decide on the perfect menu. Everything's been coordinated to her period schedule ("I can predict when my period will start *to the hour*"), is he sure he has enough condoms? The overkill factor is starting to make him crazy. It's just sex, he wants to tell her.

"There's a reason people wait," Normandie says to him. "To make it extraordinary. An Event."

If it's an extraordinary Event, he should be looking forward to it, shouldn't he?

But first, he has to survive a family reunion back home in Menlo Park. Auntie Neeta is turning ninety and Jack's mother expects everyone there to celebrate. ("No one thought she'd make it to *eighty*," Jack's mother said.) And the best news of all, *Subhra* is flying in. Jack wouldn't want to miss that, would he?

He can't think of anything he'd like less, watching his relatives gush over Subhra. Not that he doesn't love her; of course he does. But after a lifetime of every teacher he's ever had saying to him, "Oh, you're Subhra Mulani's little brother? *Subhra*, she was one of my *favorite* students..."

Sheesh, he's *done*, he's over that. Yeah, Subhra's a goddess. What. Ever.

At least she's not bringing her equally overachieving Indian boyfriend Sonny. Sonny is in medical school with Subhra at Johns Hopkins. Something (most everything) about Sonny annoys Jack. Sonny likes Donald Trump, One Direction, and refers to Subhra as "his sweet cupcake." Sonny and Jack's mother are always debating which field of medicine Subhra should specialize in.

"Medical research can be quite lucrative," Jack's mother says to Jack in an email. "Pediatric oncology? Sonny suggested radioactive medicine because it combines research, plus the hands-on experience Subhra craves."

Why does Jack's mother think he cares about Subhra's medical career? And does she think Jack gives a rat's ass about Sonny's opinion? Jack told her once, "You can stop with the Subhra updates, Mom," but she's ignored him. Most of the time he deletes her messages if they say "Subhra" in the subject line.

Jack's plane gets delayed at LAX, so by the time he arrives home, the party is already in progress. The house is filled with people; it's a casual party, but a few of the older women are wearing saris. As they move, the rhinestones in the fabric and gold bangles on their arms and ears sparkle. He doesn't see his parents but spots Subhra in the dining room, surrounded by people, the center of attention as usual. He could slip downstairs to the basement where he'll be sleeping—his mother informed him Uncle Prem is staying in Jack's room. Jack is tempted to ask who'll be in Subhra's room, but he knows the answer. Subhra.

Jack's father appears and greets Jack with a hug. "Hurry, eat quickly. Auntie Neeta's friends have big appetites." His father is slender, with a full, thick head of dark hair that always reminds Jack of shrubbery. When he smiles, his eyes crinkle at the corners. Jack wishes his mother would smile like that.

As Jack makes his way to the dining room, various relatives squeeze his arm or pat his face. "Too skinny," he hears. "A handsome boy, did he graduate yet?"

The dining room is crowded and the table is covered with food. Samosas and pakoras and gulab jamun and ras malai—so much food he's surprised the table legs can bear the weight. Subhra has disappeared, but Jack's mother appears with a platter; she's wearing a pale green pantsuit and earrings that dangle almost to her shoulders. She is small, with child-sized wrists and fingers, and Jack has always been surprised that such a delicate-looking woman has the ability to scare the shit out of him. "You couldn't get a haircut before you came up?" is the first thing she says to him.

"I didn't have time," Jack says. His mother kisses his cheek, finds a spot for the chicken biryani, and heads back toward the kitchen. "Sonny isn't here, what a shame. Subhra helped make the biryani, get some right away. It won't last long."

Jack is positive it's time to go to the basement. He smiles at several of his father's friends and one of the men asks what he's up to.

"About to graduate," Jack says. "And I've been accepted at dental school in the fall. At USC." The men nod at each other, they approve. They would; they're dentists.

When he goes out to the backyard, he sees a group of people on the new deck. His father is explaining how the Eternity deck is made of recycled plastic lumber. No splinters! It will last forever, he hears his father say.

There are multicolored lights hung in the trees, and music is playing. At first Jack thinks it might be something Indian, then he realizes it's a Billy Joel collection. Jack retreats to the far corner of the yard, to an old stone bench that's ugly, but it came with the house and was too heavy to move. The stone feels cool against his legs and he wishes he had a plate of chicken biryani, even though his sister helped make it.

"I knew you'd be antisocial," a voice says and he looks up to see Subhra. She's in a long dress and wearing cowboy boots—pretty, a taller, more sturdy version of their mother. "You need a haircut."

"I was thinking of growing a ponytail. Just to make Mom insane."

"Because she's not insane enough?" Subhra sits beside him. She has a plate of samosas on her lap. She nods at Jack and he takes one.

"Mom says you might do some radioactive medical research thing," Jack says. "That sounds interesting."

Subhra snorts. "Mom's crazy. It barely pays six figures. It would take me the rest of my life to pay off these ridiculous med school loans. Orthopedic surgery or cardiology pay the best."

"What about Sonny?"

"Are you kidding? Sonny wants to do family practice. Stupid because his loans are as bad as mine, but I love him anyway."

"Are you getting married soon?"

"I want to be further along in school. Sonny wants to get married like yesterday. But my luck, we'd get married and I'd be pregnant *instantly*. Which would make mom happy; all she talks about is grandchildren."

Jack doesn't say anything. "She wants grandchildren?" he finally says.

"Yeah. She says she can't wait."

Jack considers. What do you know?

Subhra crosses her heart; she *swears* she won't tell their parents about Jack being a father. "It's sort of cool," she says. "I mean, it's not as if you knocked up some girl you barely know. And it's not like the mother will want you in her life."

But will she? Is that the right answer, to never see Laurie again? Shouldn't he meet the baby? At least once?

"I feel sorry for her," Subhra says. "It must be a shock. Is her husband okay with it?"

"Laurie says he's fine."

"Really? His wife is having somebody else's baby."

"Both of them wanted a child."

"But yours?"

He knows she's not trying to be a bitch, but right now she sounds way too much like his mother.

"You know what I mean. It's pretty wild. Not to mention, who would think you'd have a child before me?"

"You're not going to tell anybody, you promised."

"Just Sonny, we share everything. Hey, I'm going to be an aunt." She looks inside the house. "Uh-oh, Mom's got the birthday cake. Come on, we better go inside. I hope Auntie Neeta doesn't croak before she blows out the candles."

That night, lying in the basement on the sofa bed with a mattress the thickness of plywood, Jack imagines life after

UCLA—his amazing career that includes traveling the world, marrying a supermodel, and having half a dozen children. And when he thinks about the baby, Laurie's baby, he smiles. He's positive his first child will have an incredible life.

He wonders what Laurie is doing right now. Is she sitting on the sofa with her husband? Is her husband bringing her herbal tea, pickles, and ice cream? Doing all those things husbands do when their wives are pregnant?

What about the baby? What does it look like now? Does it have hair? Are its eyes open or is Jack thinking about kittens? He'll ask Laurie. When he sees her again.

Laurie

Moving through the second trimester gets her past the "Oh, she's just fat" phase and into the "Oh, she's *pregnant*" phase. Much easier. And the more pregnant Laurie gets, the nicer people are to her. They open doors, let her cut in line at the market. The only creepy part comes when strangers want to touch her stomach. It makes sense in some primal, shared-existence desire to share new life way. Still creepy though.

Gaining weight feels odd for someone who has lived her life as a skinny girl, the girl who had extra portions of everything and never gained a pound. Now she looks at a slice of bread and is suddenly five pounds heavier.

"Maybe your body is making up for all those second helpings," Alan says.

"Ha-ha. It's odd. Like my identity's changing in front of me," she tells him.

"At least it's *your* identity," he says, and he's trying to be funny but regrets the comment immediately. "Sorry."

Laurie nods. How many more years of "your baby, not mine" comments can she put up with? Alan bends over to her stomach. "Sorry to you too, Buddy," he says.

"I don't want to name our baby Buddy. That sounds like

somebody who works at a job where his name is embroidered on his shirt."

"Think of all the famous Buddys in the world." Alan tries to think of one. "Buddy Hackett."

"The fat comedian with a squished-in face?" Laurie doesn't want the baby to grow up with a squished-in face. "And didn't he have a squeaky voice?"

"Buddy Ebsen," Alan announces. "He was a dancer and then on some TV shows."

"Wasn't he a *Beverly Hillbilly*?" Which is worse, a squeaky-voiced, squished-in face comedian or dancer hillbilly?

"Buddy Guy," Laurie says. "The blues guitarist. And Buddy Holly." She feels better. Alan calling the baby Buddy means he'll be musical. But hopefully not die in a plane crash when he's twenty-two.

Clothes don't fit the same way. Laurie knew pants would be tight around the waist. But it's as if the weight gain shows up in unexpected places. For example, why should her shirts feel tighter around the arms? It figures, Laurie's good luck/bad luck streak continues. She'll give birth to a healthy baby, but afterward, she'll have permanent Popeye arms.

It's a mental thing, Grace tells her. You think about weight so much you obsess about it. They're touring The Mystery House of Toluca Lake, supposedly a smaller version of the Winchester Mystery House in San Jose with staircases that lead nowhere and windows that look out to views of brick walls. So far the Toluca Lake house seems like an ordinary house built by exceptionally bad contractors.

"How's Alan?" Grace asks Laurie.

"Great," Laurie says. "A little distracted."

"Men are goofy around pregnancy. Like they can't show how excited they are so they go all introspective. But he's thrilled. He's going to be a daddy."

Laurie nods. She should tell Grace about Jack. Not yet though.

Grace tries to open a closet door, but it's stuck. The homeowner appears and nods at Grace. "See? That door sticks for *no reason at all.*"

Grace is unimpressed. "Sometimes a stuck door is just a stuck door."

When they are in front of the house, Grace crosses The Mystery House of Toluca Lake off her list.

"There's a Mystery House in Agoura Hills we could check out," Laurie says.

"Let's check out happy hours instead." Grace frowns at Laurie's stomach. "Damn. I'll be glad when you can drink again. You know, your baby is going to be gorgeous, don't you? The combo of you and Alan. I'm the godmother, right? Because I'm counting on it. No surprises."

"Yeah," Laurie says. "I hate surprises too."

"I'm pudgy," Laurie says to Alan as she's getting ready for bed.

"You're not pudgy. Pudgy is this face." He puffs out his cheeks.

"I knew a girl they called Pudge in elementary school. She wore shirts that were too short and you could see her round poochy stomach."

"Kids are cruel." Alan is looking through a six-month-old *New Yorker.*

"Suppose Buddy is fat. And kids tease him."

"Suppose Buddy is the one doing the bullying," Alan says. "And we get a call from the school office and the principal tells us he belongs in reform school."

Laurie imagines Buddy in reform school, learning to boost cars and roll joints.

"How much do you know about Jack's background?" Alan asks.

"Are you suggesting he has a criminal past? His parents are college professors," Laurie says.

"There are a lot of things we don't know about him. He can't put his whole life in a sperm donor application."

Laurie looks at her reflection in the mirror. If she watches closely, she's sure she'll see her thighs growing in front of her.

"We could talk to his parents. The 'college' professors." Alan makes air quotes with his fingers.

"He hasn't told his parents about the baby."

"Why?"

"The same reason we haven't told anybody."

"But they're going to be grandparents," Alan says. "Well, sort of."

Sort of grandparents. None of the grandparents (real or sort of) know yet. When is the right time to tell them? How will Alan's parents react? Laurie's mom? For all they know, Jack's parents might have the best reaction of all.

"We should hire a private detective," Alan says.

"Why?"

"To check him out. They have detectives who track down birth mothers and birth fathers for adopted children. It's almost the same thing."

"I'm going to have lunch with Jack again," Laurie says. "You could come, ask him questions. Think of the money you'll save. You won't have to hire your private detective."

"I'm not ready." He goes back to his magazine.

Laurie wonders what ever happened to Pudge. A group of boys chased her at recess one day and she fell in the playground and chipped a front tooth.

"Her real name was Julia," Laurie says.

"Who?"

"Pudge. The fat girl." Laurie puts her hands on her stomach. She doesn't care if she gains two hundred pounds. She'll put up with Popeye arms and being called Pudge. She will give up everything for Buddy.

"Do you wish I hadn't met him?" Laurie says.

"In a way. It might be easier if we never knew anything about him."

"How would that be easier?"

"I don't know. We could pretend."

Laurie frowns. "Pretend what?"

"He could be anything we want."

Laurie looks at Alan. "But he's not. He's Jack Mulani."

Alan shakes his head. "The information in the file was bad enough, but you meeting him—"

"You sound like I'm planning on running away with Jack."

"But he's the father of your baby."

"*Our* baby."

Alan looks at her. "Do you really think it still feels like that? Because I'm not sure it does. And I'm trying. I'm trying very hard."

Laurie doesn't say anything for a minute. "Why don't you write up some questions for Jack and I'll ask him the next time I see him?" she says.

Alan doesn't answer but nods and continues to read.

In the morning, Alan is gone before Laurie wakes up and she sees an envelope on the counter. He's written "Laurie" on the front as if he'd be leaving an envelope for someone else in the house. Inside he's typed a list of questions for Jack. Laurie knows that's what they are because at the top of the page he's written "A List of Questions for Jack."

When did he make this list? In the middle of the night? He's been spending a lot of time in the office lately. She assumes it's work-related, although he asked her a question the other day about CityVille.

"1. I realize this is hard for you, and I'm sure you're aware the situation is awkward for us as well, but we're delighted to get to know you and see what you can bring to our family."

It's not a question. "An awkward situation." That's one way to put it. "What you can bring to our family" seems dismissive and condescending. You're bringing something to our family, but it's not as if you'll ever be part of it.

She decides she can't read the rest of the questions—assuming Alan has decided to make some of the questions actual questions.

Jack is already at the restaurant when she gets there. "Sorry I'm late," she says.

"I just got here." Laurie looks at the empty breadbasket and sees crumbs on Jack's plate. How long has he been waiting? He smiles at Laurie. And she realizes—*oh, am I looking at* Buddy's *smile?*

They order lunch, and Laurie can tell Jack is more relaxed today. "How are you feeling?" he asks her.

"Great," she says. "I'm reading these books and they talk about how pregnant women feel more womanly and connected with nature and that sounds ridiculous, but suddenly I *do* feel this weird connection to the world I never had before. Scary, huh?"

"Very." He clears his throat. "Do you know, I mean, have you seen pictures or anything? Of what the baby looks like?"

Laurie nods. "I had an ultrasound a week ago. Don't worry, everything's fine. I have a photo."

Jack's mouth is open and he doesn't close it. "Really?"

Laurie nods and takes an envelope from her purse. Alan's envelope is there too, but she can't bring herself to pull that out yet.

"The moving image is amazing," Laurie says. "You can see the heartbeat. And he was sucking his thumb."

"He?"

Laurie shakes her head. "We asked not to know the sex. But we say 'he.' Or call him Buddy, as a joke name." She hands Jack the picture. He takes it carefully, as if he's afraid he'll damage it.

"It looks like a real baby," he says. "Wow."

At the ultrasound Alan made his usual bad jokes. "Is that a Bob Hope nose? I hope not," and everybody laughed.

Of course it was tough on Alan. The ultrasound tech didn't know about Jack and the switched sperm. He talked about the similarity of baby's profile to Alan's and how he can tell they have the same long fingers and toes.

Is Laurie living in a fantasy world, imagining that as the baby gets bigger, Alan will become more invested? It's almost as if he takes one step forward, then two back. On the ride home after the ultrasound, Laurie looked at the photo and said, "I need to start a scrapbook. Buddy's first photo."

"There's the ultrasound of his heartbeat picture."

"But you can barely see anything. It's blurry and the tech put a little X on where the heart is. It could be any baby."

She realized what she said. To Alan, this baby *is* almost any baby.

"Do all babies look the same at this age?" Jack asks her. He hasn't let go of the ultrasound picture.

"I don't know," Laurie says. "It would be interesting to put together a bunch of pictures and compare them. I bet your mother has an ultrasound picture of you."

"She probably threw mine away. My sister's is framed and hanging in the bedroom with the rest of her shrine." Jack's smile seems both happy and sad at the same time when he talks about his parents.

"She didn't throw it away. She probably keeps it in a safe place. That's what I'm going to do. Would you like me to make you a copy?"

"Could I take a picture of it?"

He has his phone out of his pocket before she can say anything.

"Sure," Laurie says.

Jack checks to make sure there's no glare and clicks a picture. What will Jack do with it? Show it to the guys at his fraternity? Post it online? He gives the photo back to her. "Thanks."

After lunch, they go to a nearby park and sit on swings. Laurie watches children playing. And she watches Jack watching the children.

"This must be crazy for you," Laurie says.

Jack nods. "Sometimes I think I'm being punked."

Laurie smiles. *Oh no*—she remembers Alan's list. "My husband has some questions for you. If that's okay."

Jack looks suspicious. "Like what?"

"No big deal. I think things that weren't in your profile." She doesn't want to make Jack paranoid just because Alan is paranoid. She pulls Alan's envelope out of her purse.

She won't read the first "question"; it's too insulting. "Alan's nervous. He hasn't met you yet." Yet. Like Alan will ever meet Jack. "Okay, here's one," she says. "'If you could be any superhero in the world, who would you be?'"

Oh my God. Why did Alan write that? He doesn't even like superheroes.

"Superheroes?" Jack looks puzzled. "Are you going to write down what I say?"

"I guess I should." Laurie takes out a pen, curses Alan in her head.

"Shape-shifter maybe."

Laurie shakes her head. *Who?*

"Hobgoblin, from X-Men. You can change who you look like, that'd be cool."

Laurie writes down, "Shape-shifter."

"Or Superman, Green Lantern, somebody who can fly."

Laurie writes, "Ability to fly."

"This is easy so far," Jack says. He's pushing himself on the swing, going higher and higher.

"Okay, next one. 'Dallas Cowboys or Washington Redskins?'"

"I like the 49ers," Jack says. "But I'd go with the Redskins over Cowboys because I hate that 'Texas is best and everybody else sucks' attitude."

Alan will approve of this answer, Laurie thinks. "Good, Alan is a Redskins fan."

Jack nods, ready for the next question.

"'Have you ever shoplifted?'" Laurie frowns as she reads that one—oh, the criminal element thing.

Jack thinks. "I took a six-pack once from a 7-Eleven, me and a bunch of buddies. It was a dare. That's probably the wrong answer."

"I don't think there's such a thing as a wrong answer." *Totally* the wrong answer. Laurie writes down, "No, never shoplifted."

Jack stops swinging. "He thinks I'm not good enough."

"It's not about being good enough. It's about you not being him."

Jack doesn't say anything.

"Alan wants to be a father," Laurie says. "And he wants to be genetically related to this baby. Of course he does. It's natural. But now—he feels distant, not as connected to the baby as he'd like to be."

"But he's going to be the father."

"I know. And he knows too."

"Maybe if he'd meet me." Jack looks up at Laurie, his eyes are wide. He looks young again. Scared. "Unless I'd disappoint him."

Laurie wants to reach over and wrap Jack in her arms, hold him close, like a mother holds a child. Even though he's the *father* of her child. Oh, brother. She's glad she doesn't have to try to explain this to anybody.

"You wouldn't disappoint him, Jack. Not at all. I think it's time the three of us got together." She folds up Alan's questions and puts them back in her purse, looks over, and sees an ice cream truck. "Do you want dessert? Let me guess—are you Popsicle or ice cream?"

Jack grins. "Popsicle. Firecrackers are the best, the red, white, and blue ones, shaped like rockets?"

"Those are my favorite too. Come on, I'm buying." She hops off the swing and Jack follows.

Alan

Nancy Futterman's husband travels frequently for business. She used to go with him, but not as much once the children were born. Or Bob doesn't like spending time with his family, Nancy jokes. Only she isn't joking. Alan can read behind her typed words. And emoticons; Nancy is fond of her emoticons. "Bored with his family ☺."

They IM each other at night, after Laurie falls asleep (earlier and earlier these days; once she's out, she's out for the night. Alan could bring in a bowling ball and pins and have a game in the bedroom and she'd sleep through nine frames). Nancy suffers from terrible insomnia, she tells Alan. She's tried everything—pills, self-help tapes, white noise machines. Nothing works. So she's embraced her sleeplessness. When she wakes up at two thirty a.m., she'll do laundry or watch infomercials.

So it's perfectly logical she's around to chat with Alan; they type back and forth, Nancy's emoticons splashing across the page.

"Why don't you have kids yet?" she asks him.

"Complicated," he types.

"Oooh, did I get TOO personal? Sorry. ☹"

"It's a long story."

"I'm not going anywhere. ☹."

He tells her about the miscarriages, but he leaves out the recent news—the pregnancy and switched sperm. She asks if they're still trying. He doesn't type anything for a few minutes, finally writes, "We're taking some time to figure things out. And considering our options."

Which is sort of true. Although he realizes the way he's phrased it isn't exactly right. And it sounds almost as if he and Laurie are separated, which they most definitely are not.

Nancy asks if they've thought about adoption and he says yes. A lot of people only want children who look like them, she types.

"Yeah."

"I hope you figure it out," she writes.

"Me too."

He imagines Nancy sitting on her patio, computer on her lap. He thinks about the softness of her hands, the way they'd feel stroking his face.

He gets into bed with Laurie. She's sound asleep; her mouth is slightly open and she's snoring softly, quick short breaths, as if she's running a sprint. He moves close and puts his hand on her belly. She rolls away from him, dead to the world.

He closes his eyes and thinks of Nancy Futterman walking through her big house in Dallas, sitting in front of the TV in the kitchen and watching an infomercial for the Ab Circle Pro.

He imagines seeing Nancy again. Her husband off on a business trip, Alan will come up with an out-of-town Palmer-Boone business meeting—he'll find a spot halfway between Los Angeles and Dallas where they can meet. He gets an atlas from the den, tracks an imaginary route from his home to Nancy's, and looks to see what will be in the middle.

Albuquerque, New Mexico. He's never been there, doesn't know much about it. All he can think of is Bugs Bunny saying, "Albuquerque," in his funny Bugs Bunny voice. "I knew I should've taken that left turn at Albuquerque." Only Bugs Bunny says "toin" and "Albuquoikey."

But I don't want to have an affair, Alan thinks. *I just want to get away from my life for a couple days. That's a big difference.*

He reads up on Albuquerque. It's the largest city in New Mexico, the Sandia Mountains run along the eastern side of the city and the Rio Grande flows through north to south. "*Sandía* is Spanish for 'watermelon' and is popularly believed to be a reference to the brilliant coloration of the mountains at sunset: bright pink (melon meat) and green (melon rind)."

See? He's not having an affair. He's learning how to say watermelon in Spanish. "*Sandía,*" he says out loud.

He'll tell this to Nancy when they see each other in Albuquerque—that's assuming she'll agree to meet him. Who sounds more unhappy in the IMs, Nancy or Alan? Right now he'd call it a tie. Although Nancy hasn't been specific—except for the time she called Bob an "uncaring *ass*hole."

Alan has never said anything negative about Laurie in his IMing. *I'm lucky she puts up with me,* he writes.

He shouldn't look for an Albuquerque hotel. But it's an imaginary affair, isn't it? He finds a Hard Rock Hotel and Casino conveniently located near the airport. Sees a Marriott, a Hilton, finally the Hotel Andaluz, the "only boutique hotel in Albuquerque's City Center."

"Perfect for a weekend getaway or an important meeting,

the mystique and beauty of Hotel Andaluz in downtown Albuquerque is something you'll not soon forget."

He wonders about rooms, clicks "Accommodations."

"Our sheets and pillowcases are made by the Italian company Frette. They are considered by many to be the world's finest linens. Your pillow and comforter are made of northern Canadian white goose down, usually reserved for only the premiere suites of five-star hotels."

For a moment, Alan forgets Nancy and his Albuquerque rendezvous and imagines sleeping in a Hotel Andaluz bed. Who needs Nancy Futterman? He'd be happy getting away from Sherman Oaks and "the sperm thing" to sleep in a bed with Frette linens, a dozen Canadian white goose down pillows and comforter. No one snoring beside him, kicking his legs the middle of the night. No guilty feelings of looking over at Laurie and wishing he could change everything—no, that sounds terrible. Of course he still loves her; she's his wife, the soon to be mother of their child (in theory)—he will say this over and over until he convinces himself he believes it.

Nancy, do you have problems like this? Do you ever look at Bob in the middle of the night and imagine yourself at the Hotel Andaluz surrounded by Frette linens and possibly me?

Which room should he get at the Hotel Andaluz?

> *The Classic offers timelessness, sophistication, functionality, and elegance. The ambiance created by our designers would deter any suspicion that this room provides our most humble square footage.*

The Classic is obviously the low-budget room. He doesn't

like the phrase "deter any suspicion." *Admit it, Hotel Andaluz, you've got a handful of tiny, shit hole rooms, the ones above the hot kitchen or next to the noisy elevators, you can call them "Classic," but I've got your number.*

No on the Classic. If he's going to have an affair, he's going to have it in style.

The Premier room "maximizes its space." Code for not much bigger than the Classic.

The King offers a "sensual bed" and Alan wonders what makes a bed sensual. Does a maid come in to turn down the bed, scatter the sheets with rose petals? Or does she undress and climb in the bed to wait for you? (Extra fee required.)

Which room should Alan pick? Or is the Hotel Andaluz the wrong place? Would he be better off in a big anonymous hotel near the airport? But he's found himself seduced by the magic and grandeur and Moroccan-Spanish elegance of the Hotel Andaluz. He can impress everyone with his knowledge of Spanish—yes and no and thank you and watermelon. (*Sí* and *mucho gracias* and *sandía*.) Nancy lives in Dallas. She's probably fluent in Spanish and uses it with her housekeeper—not that people don't do that in L.A. When Alan and Laurie bought their house, there was a sheet of paper taped to the utility room door with words in Spanish for broom and mop, washing machine, dryer, dishwasher. Please don't use furniture polish on the hardwood floors (*Por favor, no use cera para muebles en el piso de madera*). No words for *thank you* or *you did a good job, see you next week.*

He can't have an affair. It's ridiculous. If Laurie knew what he was thinking, she'd laugh. "You? Have an affair? When? After work? Before softball?"

True.

"Where?" she'd ask him. "Here in our house? Suppose the neighbors see you. You'd never get away with it, you're not sneaky enough."

"You can't keep a secret," she'd say. "At Christmas or my birthday, I always know what you're getting me because you give it away. I wanted a Bob Dylan CD collection and you walked around the house humming 'Blowin' in the Wind' and 'All Along the Watchtower.'"

"You're too afraid of getting caught."

True again.

"And the guilt would kill you. When you leave the wrong tip, you go back to the restaurant the next day to make sure the waiter gets the right amount."

That only happened one time. Okay, twice. But years ago he was a waiter, and it sucked when people didn't leave enough, that doesn't make him an idiot, does it?

"And you love me too much to have an affair," Laurie would say. "Our wedding vows, remember?"

Back when they got married, he understood it. "In sickness and health"—miscarriages and infertility fell into that bit, didn't they? And he's stuck by his wife; he's tried to be supportive. He knows he could have done a better job, and he didn't understand exactly what she was going through, but he felt the loss too. She thought he didn't because he's a man and doesn't experience emotions like she does. And maybe he doesn't *exactly*, but that doesn't mean he's a lunkhead. Laurie needs to give him a little credit, doesn't she?

However, if the priest had mentioned anything about switched sperm, he would've stopped the wedding cold and said, "Nope. I can handle everything else. But if years from now, when Laurie gets pregnant and we think it's my baby, only we find out it's not, then *all bets are off.*" Would anybody have a problem with that? Doubtful.

Except for those know-it-all people who are always saying things like, "Adversity makes you stronger." What a load of crap. Sometimes it's okay to be a quitter, throw your arms up in the air, and say, "You know what? Fuck adversity." He can't take it anymore. He tried. It didn't work. He's done.

Dammit. Alan is responsible. He tries to be a good husband. He works hard and, not that he's expecting a medal or sainthood, but shouldn't he be able to have a kid, *his kid*, without an insane amount of drama? Is that too much to wish for?

Apparently yes. So if someone asks him if he's to blame for this affair—that admittedly hasn't happened yet and most likely won't—he's not a weasel or a wimp or an asshole. But he is confused and lost, and he needs something to make himself feel better. For some guys that would be a new car. A Rolex. A trip to outer space to visit the International Space Station. But for Alan, at this particular shitty part of his shitty life, the only thing that will make him feel better is to be lying in a bed on Frette sheets in the Hotel Andaluz King room with Nancy Futterman.

He would never have an affair. For a million reasons. Like how would he explain to Laurie he's going out of town for a business meeting in Albuquerque? "Albuquerque?" she'll ask. "That's weird, you've never had business there before." "Palmer-Boone is opening up a new branch," he'll tell her, turning beet red and revealing the secret before he's even had a chance to get in his car and drive to the airport.

Laurie is so distracted these days, she won't know if there's a new Albuquerque branch or not. She's busy working on Hidden Valley and taking pregnancy yoga classes and researching lead-free baby toys and organic crib linens. He'll come back from his weekend with Nancy and tell stories of boring meetings and dull conferences. "They stuck me in this hideous room; it was a joke. And they called it the Classic." They'll laugh about that together and he'll describe the rooftop bar and the excellent Manhattan made with some special kind of cherry—not bright red like the usual ones, but smaller and darker, so delicious you want to eat them by the handful.

And when Laurie kisses him, she'll know. It's not about finding a pair of Nancy's panties in his suitcase or Nancy's lipstick on his collar; it's about the kiss—the faint taste of Nancy that hasn't gone away and won't go away no matter how many times he's brushed his teeth. All the showers in the world can't erase the scent of Nancy in his skin.

She won't ask it as a question; it will be a statement. Short, sweet, to the point. "You slept with someone else."

And what can he say? He could try to massage the lie. "Me? I was in meetings the whole weekend." That sounds lame. As lame as, "Who would I have an affair with?"

He could get angry, pull out his cell. "How *dare* you accuse me of having an affair. Here, call my boss. Ask him if I had an affair this weekend. Or if we were doing business at the five-star-rated Hotel Andaluz in downtown Albuquerque. I have deadlines too, you know."

Or do the sad big puppy-eye thing. "You know me better than that. Betray our love and trust? Do you think I could ever do something like that? To *us*?"

No, she'd smell the bullshit on that one instantly.

Honesty? "You're right. I said I went to Albuquerque

on business and that was a lie. I went there to meet an old college girlfriend and we had sex. We stayed in the lovely Hotel Andaluz King room—so many pillows you wouldn't believe it."

She will slap him, burst into tears, walk away from him in silence. He'll stay in the hallway, wondering what she's doing. Crying? Packing a suitcase? Will she leave the house, suitcase in hand, get in her car and drive away? He could go talk to her. Apologize again. What can he do to make her feel better? Encourage her to have an affair? "Hey, our two affairs will cancel each other's out. Who knew this would end up being a good thing?"

Worst idea yet.

She will appear with a gun he didn't know she had and shoot him. The bullet will hit him square in the chest and he'll be dead before his body hits the floor. He won't hear her whisper above his dead body, "Justifiable homicide."

He looks at his computer. The green dot is blinking. Nancy Futterman has signed on to Facebook. He could walk away from the computer.

All he wanted was a baby of his own. No complications. Nothing funky. Nothing *Good Morning America* would want to feature. Just a quiet, simple, inconspicuous pregnancy. Was that asking too much?

He looks at the computer again. He could say, "Hey." Just "hey." Nothing wrong with saying "hey."

Jack

Jack never thought Danny would be such a douche bag. Sure, he's a rich-boy snob, but they'd always gotten along. Picked up girls together, almost got tattoos at the same time—they wanted something cool. Danny suggested words like "perseverance" or "$ucce$$." Jack considered getting the St. Pauli girl on his shoulder. They made it all the way to a tattoo place in Hollywood before they chickened out.

So when Danny came into his room and said, "We need to talk," Jack assumed it was about tattoos or going to the party at a beach house in Malibu on Friday night.

But Danny looks serious, and for a minute Jack thinks Danny is going to tell him one of their SAE brothers crashed his car or fell off the roof, but instead Danny sits on the edge of Jack's bed and says, "We know about the money. If you leave tomorrow, we won't say anything about it."

Just like that. After all the years at the house—and isn't the fraternity supposed to be about bonding and friendship and loyalty, *perseverance* for fuck's sake? Sure, Jack borrowed money from the party fund, but he paid it back. The first time. And he was going to pay it back the second time too.

Although he's not sure saying that is his best defensive move. I did it once; I fixed it. I did it twice; I'll fix it again.

"I was going to pay back the money," he says. "But you know…the recession."

Yeah, blame the recession. That's what everybody else does. Well, not Danny. Danny never has to worry about money. He'll get his degree in economics, then an MBA, clear six figures easy the first year after graduation.

"You could've come to me." Jack realizes there's a good chance Danny has highlights put in his hair at a salon. That beachy look thing is fake. He probably doesn't even know how to surf.

"I didn't think it would be a big deal. Carter borrowed money."

"Carter's situation was different. He confessed. You didn't. Your case violates the SAE honor code."

The what? SAE has an honor code? Jack vaguely remembers the first night of initiation years ago and the then-president talking about what it means to be an SAE Gentleman. The pledges nodded and agreed with him. Naturally, since they were naked and about to be covered with peanut butter and jelly and made to roll around the floor with each other as human PB&J sandwiches.

"I talked it over with some of the other guys and we agreed," Danny says. "You leaving is the best solution."

Jack's *friends* know about this? And nobody said anything? "But I'm about to graduate. This is going to fuck up everything."

Danny nods. "You should have thought about that before you became an embezzler."

Jack imagines at least a dozen revenge fantasies for Danny and the rest of the guys. Burning down the house is too extreme. But how about an anonymous call to the UCLA Greek Council about Carter selling pot out of his bedroom?

What's the point? His immediate concern is finding a place to live. Megan shares a duplex with a handful of roommates. If he asks to move in with her, suppose Normandie finds out? Normandie lives in a tiny one-room guesthouse in Santa Monica. And what happens if Megan finds out he's living with Normandie?

He's a terrible person. An embezzler, like Danny says. He's dating two women at the same time. He's about to graduate from UCLA in five years instead of four. His parents have practically disowned him.

Oh, and he's about to be a father. There's *that*.

A guy in his Zionism class has talked about his basement apartment and how much room he has, so Jack sends him a text and tells him he needs a place to crash for a couple days and the guy, Ringer—Jack doesn't know his first name, or maybe Ringer *is* his first name—says, "Cool, come on over." After he's packed up, he sees Carter in the living room, drinking orange juice out of the carton. "They like guys with pretty mouths in prison," Carter says. He laughs and takes another chug of orange juice.

"Check the date on that. It expired at least three weeks ago," Jack says to him.

Carter sprays juice all over himself, the sofa, the carpet. By the time he sees Jack has made up the expiration date story, Jack'll be long gone.

Ringer lives in Mar Vista, south of Westwood. He has dark hair, cut close to his scalp. And one time, Jack thought he was wearing silver nail polish. But that might have been the light. The house is on a quiet street, in the middle of a row of bungalows with well-tended lawns. Quiet, except for the occasional roar of a jet taking off from LAX.

He walks up the driveway toward a pink house. Ringer's directions say to go around to the back. Three cement stairs lead to a faded blue door. Jack knocks and Ringer appears, holding a beer in one hand. "Welcome," he says.

Ringer gives Jack a tour. It's a big space but dark, like being in a cave. "I don't see any windows," Jack says.

"Yeah," Ringer nods. "That's sort of a drag. But you get used to it after a while."

Where does the ventilation come from? Jack wonders. Is that why the place smells like urine and dirty socks?

"Your room," Ringer says, pointing out a dark bedroom. When he clicks on the overhead light, a dim bulb sputters and glows an orangish yellow. "A bug light," Ringer explains. "Another thing about living in a basement. Sometimes you get critters."

Critters?

Jack looks around his room. The single bed feels comfortable, but there's an overwhelming sense of wet all around—the sheets feel moist, the knobs on the dresser, the carpet. *I'm living in a science experiment on condensation*, Jack thinks.

That night he dreams about swamps and beautiful women in one-piece bathing suits being dragged into the water by college students wearing SAE T-shirts.

When he wakes up, Ringer is already gone, but he's left a note on the kitchen counter. "Eat what you want, just replace stuff, and we'll square up at the end of the week."

Jack sees a bag of bagels on the counter and takes one out of the package. It feels wet. Naturally.

He wonders about Ringer. There is something vaguely subterranean about him, like he's some kind of creature of the earth. And a basement apartment? Well, where else would a creature of the earth choose to live?

Ringer has left him a key on a key ring. When Jack picks it up, it slips out of his hand and he hears a *plop* when it hits the carpet. A plop? Of course. Because it's wet. Because he's living in a cave with a monster.

When he gets outside, he gulps air. It might be Mar Vista air tainted by jet fuel, but he's out of the basement.

Normandie calls around lunchtime when he's sitting out on the UCLA quad. There's something about needing to inhale as much fresh air as possible before going back into the Bat Cave. She's been calling for a couple days, but Jack is avoiding her. He's not sure how to explain his expulsion from the SAE house. But this time he picks up.

"Hey," he says, wondering if living in the Bat Cave is depleting his supply of vitamin D and if he should take supplements or not.

"Where have you been? I was going to call the campus police." Normandie sounds more annoyed than concerned. "I called your fraternity and they said you moved out. I knew it must be serious if you'd miss our sex date."

With all the SAE drama, he'd forgotten about the sex date. "Too many people around there," he says. "I need to concentrate. To study."

"Did they kick you out? They can't do that. You should sue them. Want me to look into it?"

"You're not in law school yet. There's nothing to sue them for."

"I can't believe I have to plan the sex date again—the restaurant, my period schedule. I should just break up with you."

"Fine," he says. One less potential crisis in his life. He hears Normandie gasp.

"Oh my God, you're cheating on me," she says.

"What are you talking about?"

Normandie's words come quickly. "*That's* why you didn't call me back. You moved in with your girlfriend."

"I didn't move in with a girlfriend. I'm staying with a guy."

Normandie snorts. "How attractive is she?"

"*He* isn't attractive at all. He's sort of like a character out of *Twilight*."

"You're living with a vampire?"

He's ashamed to admit it, but the thought crossed his mind. Why is Ringer so comfortable living in a dark, wet, underground bunker?

"Where's your new place?" Normandie asks.

That's the last thing he wants, for Normandie to see the Bat Cave. "On the west side," Jack says, hoping that's vague enough and yet offers enough information for Normandie to lose interest. He's wrong.

"Where on the west side? I could come by tonight."

"I don't want to start bringing people over. Not yet. We'll have a party soon and you can see the place."

See the place. Good luck, bring a flashlight. When Jack goes to sleep at night, he has a feeling he's not alone. That once the lights go out, hundreds of cave creatures appear and watch him sleep. He hears crackling and faint shuffling noises. They are watching him, getting ready to make their move.

"Are you there, Jack?" Normandie says. "I know you're lying."

"Why don't we have dinner one night? Okay?"

Silence from Normandie. "Okay. Sorry if I sounded bitchy. I was worried about you. You'll pick up when I call again?"

"Unless I'm in class." He looks up and sees Megan walking across the quad. She waves at him.

"Good. I miss you tons. Miss me?"

"Tons," Jack says as Megan puts down her backpack and does a cartwheel. It's not the best cartwheel in the world, but several students applaud and Megan takes a bow.

"Do I hear people clapping?" Normandie says.

"My phone. AT&T sucks. Got to go." He clicks off.

Megan comes up and kisses him on the end of his nose. "Was my cartwheel excellent or what?"

"Excellent," Jack says. Megan sits beside him and brushes grass off her jeans.

"Are you okay?" she asks. "You look sort of...pale."

Jack and Megan walk to class together and he tells her about his new place, how it's funky and dark and creepy, and naturally she wants to see it. "Maybe we can shoot a movie there, like *Paranormal Activity*? We could make a zillion dollars."

"It's probably too dark to photograph," Jack says.

He's told her how he left the fraternity, describing his departure as a mix-up over financial bullshit. Megan thinks it's fine he's gone. "Fraternities soften your edges; they take off the most interesting bits, you know?"

Jack doesn't disagree. He's never really thought of himself as a nonconformist, but maybe that's what he is after all.

He should tell his parents. There's a good chance they'll be impressed. Well...possibly impressed.

He owes them a call. They're excited about his upcoming graduation, although his mother has managed to get in a dig about "the five-year plan."

He owes his sister a call too. She texts him about "how the project is coming along," meaning the baby. They debate about telling Jack's parents. The debate is more on Subhra's side—Jack absolutely refuses to tell them. It would just be another example of his incredible ability of disappointing his parents.

"What were you thinking, donating *sperm*?" his mother would say. "Who would do something like that? Homeless people. People who use the money to buy drugs and prostitutes. People sell their sperm and their blood, what will you sell next?

"And why would prospective parents choose *your* sperm? They want smart boys, the ones who graduate in *three* years, who have advanced degrees. Rhodes scholars, MENSA members. Ask them at the sperm bank, how many people have requested your sperm, Jack. I bet it's none."

He should call Laurie to check in. They've talked a few times; she told him everything was fine, that Alan appreciated the answers to his questions. Jack knows she thought Alan's questions were stupid. "You don't have to call back," she said. But he wants to make sure she's taking care of herself.

Megan is rehearsing a play by Conor McPherson, an Irish playwright, and the director wants the actors to practice Irish accents, but all Megan has done so far is add "boyo" to the end of every sentence.

"That's kind of annoying," Jack tells her.

"Aye, it would be, listening to meself talking that way, boyo."

She finds an online site that teaches Irish accents. "It's about softening your vowels," she explains to Jack, "*O*s and *A*s, hardening your consonants, and inflection. You have to be lyrical."

"What's so lyrical about saying 'boyo' at the end of every sentence?" Jack wants to know, but she ignores him.

"They use these really cool words we don't, like *bollocks*. They say *cheers* all the time, kind of like aloha. Means hello or good-bye or whatever the hell you want it to mean."

"How do they say shut up?"

"Be careful, boyo, or I'll kick you in the bollocks. *Bastard*, only you use it like an adjective, 'Where's my bastard backpack?'"

"Do you want to see the Bat Cave or not?"

But Megan is on a roll. "Eejit. For idiot. You probably already know what wanker is because you're acting like one right now. Chips and crisps and bangers—" And Jack thinks she might talk about this forever, so he takes her by the hand and leads her to his car.

"This can't be good," Megan says as they pull up to the pink house in Mar Vista. Fire trucks and EMT vehicles line both sides of the street. Blue and white lights flash and Jack can see people silhouetted against smoke. Smoke? The Bat Cave is on fire? That seems impossible.

He parks at the end of the street and walks toward the Bat Cave, Megan right behind him. The firemen are rolling up their hoses. Shouldn't there be more rushing around? Don't they need to put out the fire?

Ringer is watching the firemen and there's a large dog at his side, some kind of shepherd lab mutt. "Hey," he says to Jack. "No worries, our stuff is fine."

"What happened?"

"A small electrical fire in the kitchen upstairs. The only damage was to the stove. And some water damage from the hoses. They say our place might be a little damp for a few weeks. This is Groucho."

Jack frowns. Who is Groucho? The large dog barks and Ringer laughs.

"He's really smart. I thought it would be fun to have a dog."

Megan is looking from the house to the firemen then back at Ringer and the dog. "Cheers," she says. "Seems as if someone is living with an eejit, boyo."

Ringer grins at Jack. "You didn't tell me your girlfriend was Irish."

Laurie

Childbirth Then and Now. In Europe in the late 1880s, superstition played a role in assisting difficult labor. The ringing of church bells was thought to hasten labor.

Laurie hates pregnancy clothes. "They're better than the crap our mothers had," Grace says. "My mother wore long Laura Ashley tiny floral print dresses. And acid-washed overalls." Grace shudders. Laurie and Grace are spending Sunday morning at the Studio City farmer's market. It's crowded and hot today, and the air smells like popcorn.

"But everything now squishes you in," Laurie says. "And it's designed for eating-impaired celebrities who love going out wearing skin-tight outfits—look at me, admire my pregnant belly. Yes, my navel would be an outie now, thanks for noticing."

Grace laughs. She pushes Emilie's stroller, filled with fresh tomatoes and lettuce and flowers. Emilie walks beside Grace and occasionally tugs at her hand.

"Stroller," Emilie says.

"Stroller is for Mommy's things," Grace tells her.

"I can pick you up." Laurie reaches for Emilie.

"No, you're too pregnant. Come on, Em." Emilie jumps into her mother's arms and Grace slides Emilie to her hip.

A perfect fit, Laurie thinks, imagines herself carrying Buddy like that, balancing his weight against hers.

"So when did you get boobs?" Grace says.

"It's crazy—after life as an A cup, now I'm buying sexy bras, bras with *underwire*. They won't shrink back after breast-feeding, will they?"

Grace shrugs. "Who knows? Embrace your bodacious boobage while you can."

> *Food Facts. If you're feeling hungry for something sweet and cold, opt for a 100 percent juice bar, sherbet, sorbet, or frozen yogurt instead of ice cream. If you're feeling hungry for something sweet and warm, consider low-fat, unprocessed versions of candied yams.*

Laurie is regretting coming home from the farmers' market and eating a slice of chocolate cake, a fistful of honey roasted peanuts, and a Milky Way bar.

Seriously. *Candied yams?*

"We need to sign up for a Lamaze class. It's almost time. Third trimester, ticktock," Laurie tells Alan. He is reading the *L.A. Times* sports section at breakfast.

"My work schedule's a little crazy," he says. "They've fast-tracked the Choc-O label. We need to have the design presentation six weeks earlier than we planned. The company is Belgian and they get anxious. Plus we're working with the beverage team, and you know what they're like. It's a minefield."

Laurie has a vague memory of Choc-O—it's some kind of chocolate-flavored water. Sounds terrible, but supposedly it's "huge" in Europe. "Just give me an idea," she says. "Grace knows somebody in Encino who's supposed to be fabulous. Once a week for six weeks."

"Do we sit in a circle and talk about our feelings?"

"After we make s'mores, sing 'Kumbaya,' and pass around a magical acorn and tell our deepest, darkest secrets."

Alan grins. "I'll check with Wendy about my schedule." He looks down at the paper. "And I might have to go out of town."

"I hope it's soon instead of closer to when the baby's coming."

"Yeah, it would be soon. I don't know where yet. Chicago. Or Albuquerque."

"I'll call the Lamaze lady and tell her we'll figure it out."

"Okay," Alan says.

> *Childbirth Then and Now. In colonial America, the pain of labor was thought to be relieved by leaving an ax by the bed with the blade up to "cut the pain," opening the windows, or setting the horses free from the stable.*

Alan is scared to death, she tells herself. A lot of men act this way when their wives are pregnant. Every baby book says the same thing: "Don't forget, they're pregnant too." Grace told Laurie when she was pregnant she caught her husband, Hal, crying one night watching *The Sound of Music* on TV. "All those children," he sobbed.

Alan stays up late and comes to bed after Laurie's asleep. Some mornings he's up and gone before she's out of bed. But he'll have made her breakfast and left a note beside her plate ("Hope the two of you slept well last night. XOXO").

The Lamaze class will help. He can meet some other

fathers; they can sit together and commiserate. "Wow, my wife's never been so moody before," they'll say to each other. "What the hell is life going to be like when the baby comes? Suppose I never get to watch football again?"

Should she tell Jack about Lamaze? No, she wants to take it easy with him. The last time they talked he sounded overwhelmed, complained about finishing his classes in order to graduate, and he's had some trouble with his living situation too—a zoning violation at his fraternity so a bunch of guys had to move out and he's been staying with friends. "I'm like a hobo," he told Laurie.

So she won't mention Lamaze. But she will insist to Alan it's time he meets Jack. Seeing Jack face to face will force Alan to accept the inevitable. He can only spend so much time working on the Choc-O project and hiding out in his office playing CityVille.

The Lamaze teacher is Kathy and she sounds sweet and practical, not at all Kumbaya crunchy. "My husband's busy at work," Laurie explains and Kathy tells her not to worry, suggests a Lamaze website for Laurie to check out and is pleased when Laurie says she's been doing yoga.

Laurie makes an appointment to meet Kathy at her studio to discuss expectations and goals. "Labor doesn't scare me," Laurie says. "But learning more about relaxation and breathing would be a good thing. I'm a little stressed these days."

She and Alan haven't had sex in weeks. She was the one who didn't want to have sex in the first trimester when she constantly felt like throwing up. But now in the third trimester, she's back and good to go. Only Alan is the one who doesn't seem engaged. "It'll hurt the baby," he says.

"Not true," Laurie tells him. "Dr. Liu says we can have sex as much as we want. Every hour on the hour, those were his exact words."

"His exact words?"

"Pretty close. Close enough."

Alan smiles. "Maybe tonight."

"It's a date." She kisses him.

But when Laurie goes to bed, Alan is still working on his computer. "I'll be in there in a minute, honey," he calls to her. She waits for him, but when he doesn't appear, she falls asleep.

At breakfast she mentions the missed sex date opportunity.

"Sorry," he says.

"Really?" She realizes she sounds grumpy. Oh, well. She hesitates. And decides to dive in. "You know, I'm thinking it's time we invited Jack to dinner."

"I'm not sure that's a good idea," Alan says.

"Why?"

"Does he need to know where we live?"

Laurie frowns. "How else is he going to case the house and eventually rob us?"

"He makes me uncomfortable."

"How can he make you uncomfortable when you won't meet him? He's not replacing you."

"I didn't say he was."

"That's what you're thinking."

Alan is silent. "I know he's not replacing me," he finally says. "It's knowing he's *there*. The baby was ours before. Nobody else's. And now—it sounds crazy to try and explain it." He kisses Laurie—on the lips and then on the end of her nose. "I've got to get to work. I love you."

When Alan is gone, Laurie sits in the yellow room in her new rocking chair, a gift from her mother. It's a glider and makes a *whoosh whoosh* sound when she moves back and forth.

Buddy begins to kick. *I hope you're a soccer player. Male or female. David Beckham. A kick-ass girl like Hope Solo. Strong and fast and fearless. That's what I want. And for your father to love you as much as I do.*

Father. Fathers.

Buddy has two.

> *The bladder is usually a convex organ, but is rendered concave from external pressure during pregnancy. Thus, its retention capacity is greatly reduced.*

Translation: Laurie has to pee all the time.

She is clearing out the yellow room. Alan has promised to put the crib together over the weekend. Laurie has packed up most of the office things in bankers boxes to put in the guest room/office for now. Laurie looks at the alphabet trim. She remembers how excited they were when they put it up. Happy and optimistic, preparing for the arrival of Troppo. It seems like yesterday. But it was a year and a half ago. And since then—everything has changed.

"It'll all be fine, Buddy," she says to her stomach. "I hope you like this room." She looks up at the Python P. "And I hope you like snakes."

Her mother calls and says she's coming for the shower Grace is planning. She can't wait—she's already bought way too many baby clothes and the cutest shoes. Does Laurie know they make baby Uggs? And of course she'll be there after the baby is born, but she doesn't want to get in the way, unless Laurie would like her to come now because she could do that too.

"I found an old christening gown. You're going to christen the baby, aren't you?" her mother says.

"Of course." Laurie's anger at God has faded and she's been to church a few times. She hasn't totally forgiven God for the miscarriages and the mixed-up sperm, but she's working on it.

"I'd like to tell you the christening gown has been in our family for generations, but the truth is I found it at a garage sale," her mother tells her. "Two dollars. It's darling."

"I can't wait to see it." Laurie hesitates. She could tell her mother about the baby. About Jack. Alan has told Laurie he's never saying anything to his parents even though Laurie points out they'll find out eventually.

"Laurie? What's wrong?"

That damn mother instinct. How does her mother know something is wrong?

"Oh—it's kind of a big deal. Sort of funny. Sort of not." And she realizes she'd love her mother's advice. "Remember when Alan and I were going to this fertility doctor..."

Laurie's mother understands their disappointment, but tells Laurie she needs to concentrate on the baby. "That's the most important thing," she says. "And I have another suggestion."

"I don't need a therapist."

"What about Alan? How's he handling it?"

"Okay."

"Really okay or fake okay?"

Laurie sighs. "Somewhere in the middle."

"It's a big thing for a male ego to wrap his head around. For *both* of you to wrap your heads around. The two of you should talk to somebody. Therapy's not a sign of weakness—"

"I know, I know. I promise, if things get bad—which they won't—we'll go see somebody."

"I don't believe you."

"You're my mother; you're supposed to trust me," Laurie says.

"That means I know you better than anybody else. That means don't even *try* to lie to your mother. Take care of yourself, be patient with Alan, and email me more pictures. You look good with boobs."

Being pregnant is like being in a club. Encountering other pregnant women, they nod at each other, compare notes. They speak the same language—how many weeks are you, who's your doctor, Lamaze or Bradley, do you know what you're having?

"Have you babyproofed your house?" a pretty pregnant woman asks Laurie in line at Starbucks one morning. "I know a great service where they come to your house and point out the dangers. Curtain cords strangle babies to death all the time. Toilet locks—do you know how many babies drown in toilets every year? A baby can drown in *one inch of water*," the woman says. She has crazy eyes.

Before Laurie can answer, the woman continues. "Cats suck the breath out of babies. People think that's a myth, but it's true. We should get together sometime. Like have coffee—except not caffeinated because that's bad for the baby. Messes up their genes, lowers their IQ score by at least ten points. My name's Melissa."

"I'm Sheila," says Laurie. "Give me your number and I'll call you."

When Alan comes home from work, he finds Laurie in the yellow room.

"I can't decide if we should paint again. What do you think?" she asks him.

He looks at the alphabet trim as if he's seeing it for the first time. "I think it's okay."

"Should we pull up the carpet?"

"I don't know. Isn't carpet better when he's crawling around? And learning to walk?"

They look down at the floor, both imagining a baby crawling there.

"The carpet's a little shabby," Laurie says.

"Think what it'll look like after a baby lives in it for a couple years."

Alan smiles. She can see the effort he's making—but at least it's a smile.

"Maybe new curtains," Laurie says. "No blinds. They're total baby killers."

"What?"

Alan has wine with dinner and they don't talk about the baby. Laurie tells Alan how the neighbor across the street has sold his house to a developer known for building houses too big for the lot and a group of neighbors are trying to organize something to stop the gigantic house.

"That's a sycamore in the front yard," Alan says. "They're

protected by the state, I think. So developers can't cut it down without some kind of variance. You and Grace should look into it. You could do a piece on McMansions for Hidden Valley."

"Great idea," Laurie says. "I'll call Grace after dinner. She's mad at me because I haven't signed up Buddy for preschool yet."

"What? Buddy's not born yet."

"If you wait until he's born, it's too late. Emilie is still on the waiting list for Grace's top choice and she's only two. We don't want Buddy to be left behind."

Alan thinks that over. "Buddy going to school. I can't imagine that."

"Can't you see him all dressed up? Carrying a little lunch box? We'll take tons of pictures of his first day," Laurie says.

Alan sips his wine and to Laurie's surprise says, "Why don't you invite Jack over for dinner sometime?"

It's a turning point, Laurie tells herself. He's finally coming around. Alan will realize Jack isn't a threat; he can be a mentor to Jack, help him figure out his career, offer suggestions about graduate schools. They'll end up friends.

She'll plan the dinner menu carefully. Chicken? Some kind of casserole? She can't decide now. Some of her pregnancy books have suggested menu options. She'll check them out later.

Childbirth in Other Cultures. By tradition, some new mothers in the Philippines are given a special meal after childbirth of boiled chicken, cold porridge, and a small amount of cooked placenta.

Delicious.

Alan

Who knew hot air ballooning was such a big deal in Albuquerque? The city has an international balloon museum and a balloon fiesta. Alan imagines himself walking with Nancy Futterman, looking up at multicolored, multishaped balloons, hearing the hiss of helium from vents, people chattering as they point to the sky.

Another Albuquerque tourist site suggests parachute jumps. Would Nancy go for that? Probably not. He hasn't sprung the hot air balloon idea on her either. In fact, he hasn't mentioned Albuquerque. They continue to chat on Facebook; Nancy talks about her children. Ava is the perfect child, sweet and good-natured. Trevor, on the other hand, is trouble. "He was born sneaky," Nancy writes. "Maybe that's a terrible thing to say about your own child. It must be something he inherited from *Bob's* side of the family. Ha-ha."

Ha-ha indeed. Let me tell you about the unknown side of my *unborn child, Nancy. Not that I can let anyone else know. Like my family. Especially my mother, the Ancestry.com queen. She can trace our family back to England and Ireland for generations. And that's just her side of the family, the Caffrey side. I can show you photocopies of birth announcements and obituaries. Ask me any question about a Caffrey or a Gaines, I'll be able to answer.*

But sperm donor number 296—what do we know about him? His parents were born in India. I guess my mother will be able to figure it out on Ancestry.com/India. Assuming they have Ancestry.com in India, which they probably do.

He doesn't say any of this to Nancy. He tells her he's sorry about Trevor. It's probably a phase and he'll grow out of it.

"Bob said the same thing. He says I worry too much. Like Bob would know. He's never around—*I'm* the one who gets stuck with the hard shit. Bob doesn't like to discipline the children, so guess who's the heavy? *Moi.* It sucks being the Nazi *all* the time. Sometimes I think children take *years* off your life."

"I bet," Alan types back.

Suppose Nancy is afraid of heights? He checks out other Albuquerque attractions. A botanical garden? Nancy might like that, but Alan would be bored to tears. He finds the perfect spot. The Trinity Site. Wow, he never thought you'd be able to see the place where the first atomic bomb was tested. Not that there's much left to see. Obviously.

Nancy has to like this, who wouldn't? He keeps reading the online information. Oh, this might not appeal to her:

> *A one-hour visit to the inner fenced area at the Trinity Site will result in a whole-body exposure of one-half to one milliroentgen. Although radiation levels are low, some feel any extra exposure should be avoided. The decision is yours.*

Nancy might wonder why Alan is offering her a choice between a hot air balloon ride and radiation poisoning. "Some kind of death wish for me, Alan?" She'll laugh. Or maybe she won't.

At ground zero, trinitite, the green, glassy substance found in the area, is still radioactive and must not be picked up.

They can stay in their room in the Hotel Andaluz; they never have to leave. No worries about falling out of a balloon or picking up radioactive trinitite.

He looks one last time for an attraction that Nancy would like.

The American International Rattlesnake Museum.

Talking to Nancy gives him something to look forward to. Talking to Laurie is tricky these days. He's afraid he'll say the wrong thing. He anticipates seeing her frown, hearing a nasty comment. He can't do anything right. If he asks how she's feeling, she snaps at him, "How do you think I'm doing? My back hurts." He could volunteer to rub it, but he hesitates. She'll only remind him that he *didn't* rub her back last night. And as for making jokes—he thinks that would only make things worse.

He's exaggerating. She's not that bad. Yes, she's short-tempered, but aren't most pregnant women? He can't blame her; she's running around, either working with Grace or getting things ready for the baby. And that's okay; everything seems almost normal—except the Jack part.

"Jack was so funny the other day," she'll say. And she'll tell a story about how Jack and his family got locked out of their car after a 49ers game and Jack's father held up a twenty-dollar bill in the parking lot at Candlestick and shouted, "First one to break into my car without smashing the glass gets this." And a bunch of guys jumped forward and had his car open in under a minute. And Laurie will laugh and Alan will wonder why he's jealous of a twenty-one-year-old college student. Yes, it's great that Laurie is getting to know Jack, but every story she tells, every clever Jack anecdote—it makes Alan dislike Jack a little more. And it shouldn't, he knows that, and when Laurie tells Alan she'd like Jack to come for dinner, the easiest thing in the world would be to say yes, of course Jack should come for dinner, I'll grill something on the barbecue. But instead Alan shakes his head and says no.

Why can't he meet Jack? Is it because Jack has his whole life ahead of him and Alan is settled into middle age and wants to be young again?

No, it's not about age. Alan is jealous because Jack has a part of Laurie's life that he doesn't. It reminds him of the James Joyce story, "The Dead." Laurie made him watch the movie on cable one night.

"That's Gabriel," Laurie points to the TV. "He's insanely in love with his wife."

In the film, Gabriel observes his wife listening to someone singing an Irish song. And the look on her face—she's remembering something: a different time, a person? Later when Gabriel asks his wife what she was thinking about, she talks about her life before she married Gabriel, how she was in love with a boy named Michael Furey. He got sick but came to see her anyway and stood outside in the rain. A week later, he died.

Gabriel is stunned. His wife loved another man before him? He had no idea. He thought their love was exclusive. But all this time, Michael Furey was there, part of his wife's past. Everything has changed for Gabriel—nothing is what he thought it was.

Jack is Laurie's Michael Furey. Jack will always have a piece of Laurie that doesn't belong to Alan. Not to mention the physical presence of Michael Furey/Jack. Every day the baby will remind Alan of someone else in Laurie's life. Jack and Laurie have created a human being together. Alan is only there to catch the football after it's thrown. He reconsiders, realizes that's a terrible analogy.

But this isn't Jack's fault. If Alan should be mad at anybody, it's the crazy fertility clinic tech who switched around the specimens. Jack is as innocent as Laurie. Or Alan. Or the baby.

Alan could give Jack money to disappear, leave the state, promise to never contact them again. Would that make him feel better, even though it's creepy and borderline criminal?

Or if he agrees to dinner that might put everything to rest. He'll reassure himself that Jack is a fine potential father/donor. And once he's reassured, he can let the ghost of Michael Furey go away. Hopefully for good.

Unless the giving Jack money thing works out.

Alan and Nancy Futterman talk about life in Texas versus life in California, their marriages. Nancy and Bob's marriage is going through a rough patch. Alan says he understands.

They haven't acknowledged their new relationship except when one of them types, "I'm so glad we made this connection again. ☺." That would be Nancy.

Does ☺ mean Nancy will meet him in Albuquerque? Alan isn't sure how to bring that up. Does he casually work it into a conversation about CityVille or Ava's new haircut? "You ever get out to Albuquerque?" Alan could say. "No, why are you asking?" Nancy will answer. And then Alan could tell her he has business there, and when he was looking it up on a map, he realized Albuquerque is almost *exactly* halfway between Los Angeles and Dallas, what an amazing coincidence.

There must be an easier way to suggest they get together in Albuquerque. *Hey, do you like balloon rides? How do you feel about atomic testing?*

He tells himself he doesn't want to have sex with Nancy. Yes, he liked having sex with her way back when, but that was way back when. Yes, he liked her breasts, not that he should compare them to Laurie's because Laurie's are excellent—and changing. At first it was exciting, watching them grow rounder and fuller, and when Laurie told him they tingled sometimes and her nipples felt more sensitive. "Let's see how sensitive," Alan said and touched his fingertip to her nipple. Laurie gave a little "ooh" of pleasure and Alan touched it again, this time with his tongue.

But that was weeks ago. The last time Alan reached for Laurie's breasts, she was getting dressed, putting on a lacy bra he's never seen before and he saw her breasts in the mirror—large, engorged, the areolas darker, the nipples pinker. He reached over and squeezed them, gently, the way she likes. But she pushed him away. "Sorry, ow. They're super tender today."

He knows she's not rejecting him. It's the pregnancy. Once the baby is born, their sex life will go back to what it was before—different time schedule, but mostly the same.

So he's not thinking about sex with Nancy Futterman; it's more about how he'd like to lie in bed with someone, have the imaginary someone put her arms around him. No one judging him or telling him his fear about having a baby that is only *part* his is unnatural and will go away. He won't have to think about the baby at all. He can bury his head in the crook of her neck and she won't push him away.

He won't have to think about anything unpleasant, like the pressure of the Choc-O presentation at Palmer-Boone—he's been told the presentation has to have wow factor. He won't worry how a new baby will change his life. Or how his feelings about the new baby are still complicated and possibly unresolvable.

Nancy will nod, say she appreciates him. She knows he works hard, she knows he always tries to do the right thing; he's a good man. Laurie should appreciate him more. She shouldn't take him for granted. "Poor Laurie," Nancy will sigh as she massages knots out of Alan's neck. "She doesn't know what she's missing."

"I don't want this to be complicated," he'll tell Nancy. "I can't leave my wife. Just like you can't leave Bob and your children." But suppose Nancy says her marriage is over? "Bob and I have decided it's time to move on. Nothing acrimonious. We'll share custody. Money's not an issue; we just don't want to live together anymore."

And she'll ask him to leave Laurie, tell him she doesn't like L.A. and could never live there. But she's not crazy about Dallas either. Albuquerque might be an interesting place to live; there's something soothing about the desert. She likes the vast horizons, the dry air. ("The humidity in Dallas is HELL on my hair," she says.) "We could get a little place in Albuquerque," she says. "Not too big, but big enough for when the kids come to stay. It'll be a nice spot for them. Halfway."

Halfway. You have a whole affair; you don't jump into it halfway. He's either going to have sex with Nancy Futterman or he's not.

He's standing at the end of a diving board. A high board, not a low one. The one where if you make a wrong move, the pain when you hit the water leads to unconsciousness.

And the sound, the *crack* when you hit—everyone will look over. Grimace. Feel your pain.

He loves his wife. He doesn't want to do anything to mess up his marriage. He should delete his Facebook account. After he tells Nancy Futterman his business requires him to be out of the country for a year. And in a place, strangely enough, with zero Internet or wireless connections. He is a man whose wife is having a baby. He needs to be there for her. One hundred percent. He is not the kind of man who has an affair—he is *better* than that. What is he thinking?

He'll have dinner with Jack. Step one of repairing the damage he almost did to his marriage. That will reassure Laurie and make her happy. He'll get to know Jack and who would have believed it? Jack will turn out to be a great guy. Maybe Alan will figure out a way to get Jack on the Palmer-Boone softball team. And the awkwardness with the baby—that'll be fine too. He'll be able to laugh about it with Jack. *Why were we thinking this would be such a big deal? Families are all kinds of different these days. We'll be all kinds of different too.*

Alan takes a deep breath and exhales. Okay, *now* he's ready to be a father. He flirted with the idea of running away, doing the cowardly thing, having a wild, semicelibate but possibly not weekend with an old girlfriend, but that's *over.* Even though he can't tell Laurie any of this because she would be majorly pissed off. But he's back and in a good place. There's nothing for Laurie to worry about.

This weekend he'll put the crib together.

Jack

Megan's duplex is Spanish-styled with arches everywhere, three bedrooms, and a kitchen that's not huge but has a cute, rounded breakfast nook on one side.

"This is great," Jack tells Megan as he's moving in.

"Yeah, it's brilliant." She's still working on her Irish accent. "Except the landlords live upstairs and stomp around and you can't complain. They're eejits."

His room will be the smallest of the three. Megan explains the current roommate, Florence, has moved in with her boyfriend. Megan is giving Florence's relationship a fifty-fifty shot.

When Megan told Jack he could stay at her place, she made it clear he wouldn't be sharing her bedroom. It's their apartment rule—no live-in boyfriends or girlfriends. "It changes the dynamic," Megan says. "Suddenly you get this *couple* vibe and the balance gets messed up. We get along brilliantly, why ruin that?"

They get along brilliantly, except for Jeff. He's in the graduate screenwriting program at UCLA and needs to finish a screenplay to get his degree, which doesn't sound hard, except he's been working on it for two years. Apparently the script hasn't been going well, and Jeff has decided to vent his frustration on his roommates. For example, he's stopped cleaning. When his roommates complained, he said his writer's block prevented him from getting his hands wet. Megan told him fine. But he's no longer allowed to share the communal dishes or silverware. Instead Jeff uses paper plates, cups, and plastic utensils, which is bad for the environment, but, "Hey, we're not his cleaning service," Megan says.

"Why don't you evict him?" Jack asks.

"We're trying. But tenants have all these crazy rights and even if somebody goes eejit batshit like Jeff, you can't just boot 'em."

Casey lives in the dining room. She hangs heavy floor-to-ceiling curtains to make her space more private. She's an accounting major—petite and pretty and only wears one color at a time. Like blue jeans. With a blue shirt. Blue socks, blue Converse. Sometimes a blue beret.

"What Jeff's screenplay about?" Jack asks one morning when they're eating breakfast in the breakfast nook.

"He asked us to read a rough draft." Casey keeps her voice low. "It's set in the future. Sort of *Catcher in the Rye* meets *Alien*."

"That doesn't make any sense," Jack says.

"Jeff said it's about the ultimate alienation—get it? Alien-ation. Don't ask to read it," Megan says. "I'm *so* not kidding."

Jack hasn't told Normandie where he's living. "You could at least check in with me," Normandie tells him. "Maybe I should get you a GPS device, so I'll always know where you are."

He laughs—and realizes she's serious. Her neediness is starting to freak him out. One night, driving to Megan's, he thinks he sees Normandie's car behind him. No, just his imagination. Hopefully.

He's happy in Megan's apartment. They have a good time, except for Jeff, who rarely appears. Jack tells himself it's much better than life in the SAE house—Megan and Casey walk around in their underwear, there's not nearly as much farting, and the kitchen doesn't smell like beer. Almost paradise.

The only big negative right now is his Medieval Literature of Devotion and Dissent class. It sounded cool in the course listing—life, death, the plague. How could that be boring? Unfortunately, he missed the part that explained how the readings would be in Middle English. Trying to translate stuff like, "And in pis he shewed me a lytil thing be qualitie of a hassyl nott..." What the *fuck*? He'd drop the class, but then he'd lose his minor, and how else is he going to get his religious studies masters and/or PhD?

He's failed two quizzes and made a D-plus on his *Piers Plowman* paper, possibly one of the most boring things he's ever read in his life. Written in unrhymed alliterative verse—oh, yeah, *that's* a good time—in his paper, Jack compared Piers Plowman to Frodo Baggins from *The Lord of the Rings*. His hard-ass, lard-ass professor Mr. Bryant wasn't amused. Jack can do a makeup paper, but he should know—unless he makes an A on the final, he'll flunk the class.

One class short of getting his degree? His parents will show up for graduation and wait for him to get his diploma and his name won't be called. "I knew you'd find a way to ruin everything," his mother will say.

At least Subhra is supportive, texting him, sending emails. She wants to come for graduation, but she doesn't think she'll be able to get away. She asks how Laurie's pregnancy is going, about things like incompetent cervixes and placenta previa. "I'm sure Mrs. Gaines is getting excellent medical care. I checked out her doctor, and he's highly rated. If she has any questions, she can email me."

Jack isn't sure that's a great idea. He talks to Laurie at least twice a week, and lately she's sounded cranky. Jack suspects her crankiness has to do with Alan, but he doesn't want to say anything that might upset her like, "Hey, my sister wonders if your cervix is incompetent or not."

"I know this is hard, Jack," Subhra writes. "But it'll work out. I have a good feeling." So there's one major positive thing that's come out of the baby business. He's feeling closer to his sister these days.

"Mom and Dad want the best for you, you know," she says to him one night on the phone.

Jack laughs. "You think? Then maybe they could say that to me. Instead of always making me feel like I suck at everything."

"Come on, when you're a parent, you'll act the same way." Silence on the phone. "When you're a parent," Subhra says. And laughs. "Whoa. And that's going to be sooner than later, baby bro."

Jack is going to be a parent. How will he feel if baby Buddy grows up to be a slacker? Suppose *Buddy* is a fifth year senior. Will Jack have to tell him to man up and get his shit together?

If Jack is part of Buddy's life. Buddy's real parents, Laurie and Alan, will be the ones saying to Buddy, "Man up and get your shit together."

There must be some sort of switch in your brain. It's turned off now, but the minute your child is born, it snaps on. The thing that gives you the ability to wake up in the middle of the night when you hear a child's cough, to touch a forehead and feel a fever. Jack remembers getting ready to throw up when he was little and how his mother rushed forward to catch his vomit in her hands. In *her hands.* Disgusting. But now—he gets it. Sort of.

He remembers his parents reading to him every night before he'd fall asleep. "Another Babar," he'd say, and his father would talk about growing up and seeing real tigers walking in the street and Jack believed him. It wasn't until years later that he realized tigers weren't strolling the streets of Mumbai.

His mother would tell him Indian tales—about a woman who had a snake instead of a baby, stories about crows and banyan trees. When Jack would ask what a banyan tree looked like, his father would take out a small notebook he always carried with him and draw a picture for Jack.

In a few lines, Jack's father could capture the exact expression on Jack's mother's impatient face when the family was late to dinner. Or Subhra checking her reflection in a mirror, her lips curled in an admiring smile. And Jack, his hair too long, bent over a Harry Potter book.

"I wanted to be an artist," his father said. "Cartoons especially, but my parents were practical. They told me I should make a good living. And they were right."

"But you loved art."

"I respected my parents to make the right decision for me. And they did. I have had a successful career. A successful life. I am blessed many times over. And I wish the same things for you."

It's harder to be a parent than he thought. If someone told him that years down the line Buddy would have a terrible life, Jack would be crushed. He wants Buddy to have all the things his parents want for him. Now that he understands this, he'll have more respect for his parents. This lasts two days—until he gets a text from his mother that says, "Let us know if you are truly graduating before we make our travel plans."

"Conor McPherson is a genius," Megan says. They're sitting in the living room and Jack is helping her run lines. It's cold, and there's a thunderstorm outside, rare for Los Angeles. Megan is thrilled with her part in *The Weir*. She's explained to Jack the play is about people who hang out in a rural bar in Ireland. Megan is Valerie, a young woman who's just moved from Dublin.

"So everybody's drinking and they start telling ghost stories," Megan says. "You don't know if the stories are true or not. Valerie talks about her husband and her little girl, Niamh. Niamh was always afraid of the dark." Megan goes into her Irish accent and Jack is surprised how real it sounds, not forced or boyoish at all. She talks as Valerie, about her daughter Niamh who won't go to sleep at night. But Valerie reassures Niamh and tells her if she's ever afraid, just pick up the phone and call. Anytime.

And then one day, Niamh's school has a swim meet, and when Valerie arrives to watch, she finds out there's been an accident, a terrible accident. Niamh's been hurt, so badly that she might not survive. And would Valerie like to say good-bye to her daughter?

"'And I gave her a little hug. She was freezing cold. And

I told her Mammy loved her very much. She just looked asleep but her lips were gone blue and she was dead.'"

Megan looks down at her hands in her lap and doesn't say anything for a while. She's no longer Megan. She's turned into Valerie. Jack realizes he is holding his breath.

When Megan/Valerie speaks again, she talks about the funeral and how awful it was. And then one morning when her husband Daniel had gone to work, the phone rang.

"'So I went down and answered it. And. The line was very faint. There were voices, but I couldn't hear what they were saying. And then I heard Niamh. She said, "Mammy?" And I…just said, you know, "Yes." And she said…she wanted me to come and collect her. I mean, I wasn't sure whether this was a dream or her leaving us had been a dream. I just said, "Where are you?" And she said she thought she was at Nana's. And would I come and get her? And I said I would, of course I would. And I dropped the phone and I ran out to the car in just a T-shirt I slept in. And I drove to Daniel's mother's house. I could hardly see, I was crying so much. I knew she wasn't going to be there. I knew she was gone.'"

The storm outside makes the windows shake. Megan wraps her sweater closer around her.

Jack doesn't know what to say. Megan has tears in her eyes. He had no idea she was so good. She looks up at Jack. "Was I horrible?"

"You're great. I mean—wow."

"My accent was probably all over the place, I might as well just go back to saying *boyo* all the time."

"No, your accent was amazing. I felt like you were another person. How did you do that?"

"That's one of the cool things about acting, learning to be somebody else. I don't have her a hundred percent yet, but I think I'm getting closer. It's so sad, Valerie's story," Megan says. "Losing a child, can you imagine anything worse?"

Losing a child. Jack is having a child. He lets that settle over him. And it feels good when Megan snuggles beside him and rests her head against his.

"Thank God we're years and years away from worrying about anything like that," Megan says. "Because there's enough stuff in the world to worry about already."

Like Normandie. Who's been texting him at least ten times a day. It's time to end things with her. She's too controlling, and she is *definitely* freaking him out. And he's tired of being dishonest to her and to Megan. No more running away from things. If he's going to be a parent—even if he won't be in Buddy's life every day—he still needs to face things head on. So instead of ignoring Normandie's texts, he replies to one and suggests they get together.

They meet at a bar in Westwood.

"How's your new place working out?" She kisses his cheek and he realizes she knows where he lives.

"It's fine."

"You and Megan are back together?"

"We're not together. I have my own bedroom."

Normandie nods. She doesn't believe him. She orders another glass of red wine and seems unhappy when Jack gets a Diet Coke. "So who else are you seeing?"

"Nobody," Jack says.

"You drive over the hill a lot." Oh my God, she *is* following him.

"I have a friend in the Valley."

"It's okay, Jack. You can tell me about your other girlfriend." Normandie gulps at her wine.

"I don't have another girlfriend."

"With the Audi?"

Audi? Who has an Audi? *Laurie.*

"She's not a girlfriend."

"Who is she?"

"You know—I'm kind of sick of you being suspicious all the time. I can't do this anymore. We need to take a break from each other, okay?" Good, he's said it.

"She looks old. The Audi woman," Normandie says. "But she's pretty. Where did you meet her?"

"Did you hear what I said? She's not my girlfriend. She's..." Hmmm, how to describe his relationship with Laurie? "My friend."

Normandie laughs. A little too loudly.

Jack stands up. "I better go. I have a class."

Normandie puts her hand on his arm. "This is Wednesday. You don't have a night class. Only on Tuesdays and Thursdays."

She is a psycho.

"You need to stop following me, Normandie. I mean it."

"Okay. If you tell me about your new girlfriend."

"She's *not* my new girlfriend."

Normandie laughs again. It sounds like a bark. And before Jack can say anything else, she's reaching in his pocket. Jack thinks, *She's going to pull off my balls*, but instead she grabs his cell phone.

"Is her picture on here?" She scrolls quickly through the photos on his phone and Jack's thinking, *oh no, what do I have on there*, but he's always been super safe about what he keeps on his phone, ever since the guys at the fraternity got Carter's phone and posted half his videos on YouTube.

Jack reaches for his phone. "Give it back."

Normandie moves away from him. "You shit," she says quietly.

"What?"

"You shitty shit." She flings the phone at his head. It makes a cracking sound and Jack hopes that's the phone and not the side of his skull.

"You said she wasn't your girlfriend. Then why is she having your baby?"

Normandie's voice is growing louder. She snatches the phone from the floor and holds it in front of Jack and there is Laurie's ultrasound. Baby Buddy.

"Shitty shit *shit*," Normandie says as she picks up her wineglass and throws the contents at him. He tries to duck, but he's too late and now Normandie is swinging at him, again and again, not viciously, more like angry little slaps. She pulls at his sleeve and he hears something rip. Jack can feel blood on his face. He picks up his phone. It makes a *click click* sound. Not a good sign.

"I'm sorry," Normandie says. She sits at the table and taps her empty wineglass. She seems calm now. "I shouldn't drink red wine. Something about the sulfites—I get this nutty chemical reaction in my brain." She looks as if she's about to cry. "I feel awful. A relationship shouldn't end in a bar with somebody throwing things. I don't blame you if you hate me."

Jack sighs. "I don't hate you."

Normandie nods. "Good. Maybe we could go to a movie sometime."

"Maybe." Yeah, when hell freezes over.

"Well. I hope you and your girlfriend and your baby have a nice life," Normandie says.

"Sure. Thanks." He's wondering how you take out a restraining order against somebody. But he might not have to—hopefully Normandie is gone for good. And even though his face has blood on it and his shirt is ripped and his phone is broken and he smells like wine, yeah, life could be a lot worse.

He looks at his watch. Oh. He's supposed to be at Laurie's house in an hour to meet Alan.

Laurie

What is the ideal menu for a dinner to introduce your husband to your baby's father for the first time? There doesn't seem much point in trying to find the answer to that on Google.

Laurie decides the meal should be simple; everything needs to feel down-home and comfortable. Jack will be nervous, Alan will be nervous, and Laurie will be nervous about *them* being nervous.

No, no one will be nervous. The evening is about coming together. What do Alan and Jack have in common? Men like baseball—they can watch a Dodgers game. Perfect.

Except Jack is from the Bay Area and probably a Giants fan. Alan and Jack will start to watch the game, and it's okay at first but soon falls apart with shouting and name-calling, and it will end like that game in 1965 where Giants pitcher Juan Marichal hit Dodgers catcher Johnny Roseboro in the head with his bat.

So they won't watch baseball. Or have serious cocktails on the menu either. Cocktails could send the wrong message—Jack might think they're alcoholics. Wine and beer. She'll get a six-pack of Red Trolley. Chips and salsa. The good salsa, with mango.

She considered asking Alan to grill. It would keep him busy. On the other hand, it would also give him an excuse to only care about grilling. "Sorry, honey, too busy. Have to keep an eye on the coals." Laurie wants Alan to be engaged tonight, part of the conversation.

She's found a spinach lasagna recipe in *Cooking Light*. The photo looks spectacular, something every starving college boy will want to gobble up. She'll get a nice loaf of La Brea Bakery bread from the market, crush garlic, mix it with butter, and make her own garlic spread. Simple and much better than the frozen kind.

Dessert? Pregnancy has tipped Laurie's chocolate addiction into the danger zone. If she and Alan took a trip to the Hershey's chocolate factory in Pennsylvania and she were allowed near a giant vat of steaming chocolate, she'd jump in before anyone could stop her.

Fruit would be more sensible for dessert, something to complement the lasagna. She settles on a fruit tart with a light (*ha-ha, we'll see how light it ends up*) chocolate drizzle on top. She realizes if she makes the drizzle, she'll have an entire saucepan of warm chocolate sauce. The thought of that makes her want to skip making lasagna and move straight to dessert.

She begins her dinner preparations. What will making dinner be like once the baby comes? Laurie sees herself pureeing vegetables and fruit, making her own yogurt. Baby Buddy will eat like a king. But when will Laurie have time to make dinner? Will Laurie and Alan be forced to live off microwaved food and takeout? Will they learn to like pureed chicken and peas?

The lasagna's in the oven; the garlic bread spread is ready. She'll make a salad, but that can wait. She looks around, readjusts rugs, books in the bookshelf, makes sure nothing is dusty. The chances of Jack noticing her clean, orderly house are slim to none, but it feels like the right thing to do. The baby's room is almost done. Alan still hasn't put the crib together, but he's brought it inside from the garage. Sometimes at night she sits in the rocking chair/glider and imagines herself with baby Buddy on her shoulder. She's singing to him, rocking him to sleep. "He's Got the Whole World in His Hands," that's what her mother used to sing to her. It's funny she remembers that. Has the sensation of rocking brought the memory back? Generations of mothers rocking and singing to their babies, different but still the same. What song did Jack's mother sing to him? She'll have to ask Jack. She wonders if he remembers.

Laurie wants to make sure Jack thinks her house is the right place for Buddy to grow up—safe and full of love. Alan and I might appear to be a bit tense around each other, but ignore that. Concentrate on the lack of dust bunnies on the floor and check out the moderately sized backyard with a fence. No way will Buddy escape and chase his ball into the street where he'll be run over by a UPS truck.

Did you see? We don't have a hot tub. And if we did, we'd lock it up with a gigantic chain so baby Buddy couldn't get in it unless he had an acetylene torch.

We plan to buy a swing set eventually—naturally one made out of nonasbestos-laced wood. We've talked about putting in a pool, but we'll wait until the baby's older. And if we do, we'll hire a full-time lifeguard. Just in case Buddy figures out how to break through the super triple-locked French doors or back kitchen door or babyproofed windows. Did you notice the windows only open three inches?

Perfect for keeping a baby from falling out, not so great when you're trying to keep your house cool in the summer without using air-conditioning.

We're going to be good parents, Jack. Really. We promise.

Alan comes home late. Terrible traffic, he has a headache and he's afraid it will turn into a migraine. Some warning light went off in his car and he can't find the car instruction manual. Does Laurie know where it is? If it's not in the car, it might be in the kitchen cabinet, she tells him. Alan opens the cabinet door but can only find instructions for the new baby monitor, the new baby gate, and the new baby seat. "What the *hell*?" he says as he tosses everything back inside.

Laurie wonders if she should make a pitcher of Manhattans.

"I don't have time to handle this right now." Alan looks at Laurie. She's smiling at him, her most gentle, nonconfrontational smile.

Alan takes a deep breath. Smiles back. "Okay. I'm going to go outside and walk in again. Start over."

"You don't have to do that. Want something to drink?"

Alan opens the refrigerator. "You got Red Trolley. My favorite." He takes out a beer and opens it.

"Glass?"

"Bottle's fine." He takes a big sip, and his eyes roll back in his head in mock ecstasy. "And I can't find my BlackBerry—I probably left it here. You know, one of those days where everything goes wrong."

"That never happens to me," Laurie says. "My days start out perfectly and only get more and more perfect as they go on."

Alan laughs and holds up his beer. "How about I have a couple of these babies, we get into bed, and catch up on all the *Modern Family* episodes we missed?"

"Jack's coming." Laurie keeps the gentle smile on her face.

"Tonight?" Alan looks around, notices the dining room table is set for three. Nice linens, candles, wineglasses.

"He should be here any minute. We're having lasagna."

"I had lasagna for lunch." Alan sighs. "I better look for that BlackBerry." He walks out of the room. Laurie could run after him. Or start the salad.

She's chopping tomatoes. Is it wrong to imagine Alan's face on them as she slices them sharply down the middle? He's *known* about Jack coming to dinner. She saw him put it in his BlackBerry. Oh, but his BlackBerry is missing. She can hear him in the office, the sound of drawers opening and closing, an occasional, "Shit."

They've only been to two Lamaze classes so far, and she's not perfect with her breathing yet, but she takes a couple cleansing breaths and feels herself calming down.

When the doorbell rings, she runs to the door. *Breathe, breathe.* Jack is standing on the front porch. Does he have a black eye? And is the side of his face bloody?

"It's a long story," he says as he holds out a bouquet of flowers. It *used* to be a bouquet; now it's more like a dozen flowers bent over and twisted and held together by crumpled plastic paper.

"Come in. Are you okay?"

She takes him to the kitchen where she can get a better look at his face. It's swollen and there's a cut above his left eye.

"Sorry I'm late, I wanted to call. But my phone…it's not working anymore."

"Did you get in a fight? Were you robbed?"

"It's my own fault. Sort of."

"This is going to sting." Laurie wets a paper towel and wipes the blood off Jack's face. As she bends in close, she realizes he smells like wine. Was he so worried about tonight he stopped to get a drink before he came to the house? But got in a fight? That doesn't sound like Jack.

"Ow," he says.

"I think it looks worse than it is. But you're going to have a shiner."

Jack makes a face, grimaces again when he realizes that makes his face hurt more.

"I need another beer." Alan has appeared from his office. He looks at Laurie hovering over Jack's face. He opens his mouth to say something, chooses not to, and goes to the fridge instead.

"Alan. This is Jack." Laurie steps away from Jack; she's gotten off most of the blood. Jack looks better, but she notices the front of his shirt is stained with…blood? No, wine. And one sleeve is ripped.

Alan takes in Jack's shirt, his face. "I'd hate to see the other guy."

"Jack ran into a light post," Laurie says. And the minute the words are out of her mouth, she realizes how lame that sounds. Why do people say they ran into a light post instead of saying something that might sound moderately realistic? Car accident. Tripped over the cat in the dark and fell down the stairs. Who runs into a light post, Buster Keaton?

"Would you like a beer, Jack?" Alan asks. "Although it appears you've got a head start on me." He laughs. Jack laughs back, a deer in the headlights look in his eyes.

"Let me get some ice for your face," Laurie says.

Alan pops open a beer for Jack and gets another one for himself.

"Thank you, Mr. Gaines," Jack says.

"Alan. We're family, aren't we? One big happy."

Laurie goes to the freezer and finds an ice pack, wraps it in a dish towel, and gives it to Jack. "This'll make you feel better." She looks on the counter and sees the flowers. "And I'll get a vase for these. Aren't they pretty, Alan?"

Alan looks at the flowers, at Jack. "Is this the part where I'm supposed to say that everything is great and we're all incredibly lucky to be having a baby together?"

Alan has gone back in his office to look for the missing BlackBerry. Laurie watches Jack sip nervously at his beer.

"Alan's in a terrible mood. He's not usually like this," she says. "The missing BlackBerry and he had car problems."

"I should come back another time."

"No. Once we find the BlackBerry, everything will be super." She hopes.

Jack is eating chips and salsa as if he hasn't had a meal in days. "Oops," he says as he drops a wad of salsa on his shirt.

"Want me to get a paper towel?"

Jack shakes his head. "I think I'm going have to throw away this shirt anyway. Maybe I can use it as a napkin." He smiles, but it makes his face hurt again and the dark under his eye is getting more purple. "Thanks for telling your husband I ran into a light post."

"If you want to tell me what happened—you're not in trouble, are you?"

Jack sighs. "Women. I was dumb. I didn't break up with one before I started going out with the other one."

"So one of them attacked you?"

"Sort of. And she threw my phone at me."

"But it's done now? She's out of your life?"

"Oh, yeah. All done." He puts more chips in his mouth, sips his beer, looks at Laurie's stomach. "How do you feel?"

"Good. I'm getting bigger. Third trimester. Packing on the baby weight."

"Yeah, you do look bigger," Jack says. "I don't mean that in a bad way. You look great. Really." He blushes bright red.

"Thank you," Laurie says.

In the office, Laurie finds Alan on his hands and knees looking under the guest bed. "You still haven't found it?"

"No," he says.

"Let me look. Go out there and talk to Jack."

"He's been in a fight. Is he in a gang?"

"I forgot to tell you, he's the leader of the UCLA Crips. His crew is waiting outside. You didn't see his gang tattoos?"

"Funny," Alan says. He finishes his beer and Laurie can't remember if that's his first or second one.

"Don't be mean," she calls out to him, but he's gone and she's not sure he's heard her.

He's managed to make a mess of the desk. Drawers are open, papers scattered on the floor. Laurie tries to think where Alan could have left his BlackBerry. She retraces his daily routine—shower, breakfast, checks his emails… She looks over at the computer. It's on. She should turn it off, hits a key to make sure there isn't something to save, just in case.

Alan's on Facebook. They've always joked about Facebook, how it's a waste of time and invades your privacy. But naturally they both ended up with Facebook accounts.

Alan's wall is up and filled with posts from some of his college friends, Dodgers updates from Peter, several funny fake headlines from *The Onion*. A chat message pops up at the bottom of the screen.

"Missing U," it says. Laurie clicks on the name and sees a picture of an attractive woman with silvery blond hair. Nancy F. Campbell. Studied at William and Mary. Lives in Dallas, Texas. A row of photos underneath. Nancy and her husband in a sailboat. Two young children wearing snow skis.

Nancy of the Christmas letters. Alan's old college girlfriend. Nancy F. for Futterman.

It would be stupid to click on Alan's messages. Not to mention an invasion of his privacy. She shouldn't do it. Instead, she'll walk out into the living room, join Jack and Alan.

Missing U.

What, Nancy can't type "you"?

Unless it's a mistake. Laurie is jumping to conclusions. After dinner, when Jack is gone, she'll ask Alan about Nancy. Tell him when she was looking for the BlackBerry, she went to turn off the computer and there was Alan's Facebook page and a message from Nancy appeared. Naturally Laurie is curious. Not in a nasty, suspicious way, but in a regular, "You're chatting with Nancy, your old college girlfriend" way. And Alan will say, "Yeah, we found each other on Facebook. She's happily married with two kids. I told her I'm happily married and my gorgeous beloved perfect-in-every-way wife is pregnant. That's it."

That's it.

That's not it. Laurie clicks on messages. There are dozens from Nancy, complaining how Bob is never home, how they've talked about divorce. Alan's response to that, "I know what you mean."

What do you mean you know what she means? You've been thinking about divorce?

"Do you ever feel like you made a mistake?" Nancy asks. "Wouldn't it be nice if life could give you a do-over?" That's what Alan has written.

Another message. This one from Alan. "When is Bob going out of town again? I go out of town for business sometimes."

Alan and Nancy are going to have an affair. Laurie can feel her throat closing; she can hear her heart beating over the hum of the computer. What does she do? Does she confront him? She'll walk out to the living room—*sorry, Jack, it's time you learn about the bitter reality of marriage. You think getting hit in the head with a cell phone is bad? My husband is having an* affair. *Instead of being with me, supporting me through our pregnancy, he's planning on running away with his college sweetheart.*

She's too angry to cry. But she has to make it through the evening, so she'll try to push Alan's infidelity to the back of her brain, at least for now. "It'll be okay," she says to Buddy. "We'll get through this. We've got each other."

She clicks off the computer, not looking to see if Alan had anything else he needed to be saved. Tough titty.

On the desk she notices several crumpled up tissues. Alan has an annoying habit of blowing his nose and forgetting to throw the tissues away. Germ factory, Laurie has pointed out. But Alan (the cheating rat bastard) forgets. Laurie picks up the tissues, ick, and tosses them in the trash can. She sees something silvery at the bottom and—voila, there is Alan's BlackBerry.

Alan

His skin is dark—not a deep, mahogany brown like the dresser in the bedroom, but a creamy, lightish milk chocolate color. It's a beautiful color, warm with pigment, like the color skin should be instead of beige. Jack's eyes are large and dark brown. And when he speaks, his smile is movie-star perfect.

He needs a haircut. Or maybe he likes wearing it long, the edges brushing his shoulders. It could be the way college kids wear their hair these days and Alan doesn't know any better.

He can't take his eyes off Jack. Because he's not seeing Jack—he's seeing Buddy. Buddy grown up at twenty-one, Buddy who won't have blond hair and green eyes like Alan. Buddy with brown skin and black hair and a smile to make girls swoon. *I bet girls swoon when they see you, Jack*, Alan thinks. Then wonders why he's thinking of the word *swoon*; it sounds like something his parents would say. Hair too long, swoon. Alan is a thousand years old. He shouldn't be having his first child; he should be a grandfather. He should be put away in an assisted-living facility.

Jack is handsome. Not aggressively handsome like a male model or most of the waiters in L.A. who aren't really waiters, they're actors passing time until they get their big break. But Jack isn't aware he's handsome. No wonder Laurie liked him when she met him—Jack projects innocence and vulnerability.

It's obvious he's scared to death of Alan. And if Alan were in a better mood, he'd try harder. But he needs to find his BlackBerry. He can't function without it; he's got meetings tomorrow for the Choc-O project, and yeah, it's important to meet Jack, but couldn't they put it off, do it another time? And Laurie, Laurie standing there smiling and pretending everything's okay when it's clearly not and seriously, nobody's going to say *anything* about Jack's black eye and the blood on his face?

And why does Jack smell like wine? Did Laurie leave out that tidbit? "Oh, Jack has the tiniest problem with alcohol, but he's been in treatment and he's fine now"? Except he's not fine, he's drunk. First on wine, now he's drinking Alan's beer. How's he going to get home? They can't let him get behind the wheel of his car. Suppose he smashes into somebody. Who's going to be liable? The people who gave him the beer, that's who. And Laurie, über happy, like she's had a bottle of Xanax, which she wouldn't do because of the pregnancy—but she's acting as if she had a stop-and-shop lobotomy at lunchtime.

Alan watches as Jack devours the last of the chips. Oh—Jack's not just drunk; he's *stoned*. He's got the munchies.

"Looks like you need a refill on the chips," Alan says. He takes a deep breath. Okay, he will force himself to be nice. He promised Laurie.

But Jack jumps up as if he's been caught doing something he shouldn't. "Sorry," he says. "I didn't have lunch."

"That's okay. Come on, we'll get some more." Alan picks up the empty bowl and heads into the kitchen, nodding at Jack to follow him.

"What do you think of the house?" Alan says, trying to make conversation.

"Nice. I thought it would be. Laurie—Mrs. Gaines—your wife, she told me about it. I like the Valley. Some people don't; they like the Westside better. But I think the Valley's fine. I think it's great."

"How's that beer? Need another one?"

"I'm good." Jack raises his half empty beer. Alan looks down at his own bottle and realizes it's empty. "Don't mind if I do." He takes another Red Trolley from the fridge. How many has he had? Is this his third? No, probably his second.

"That lasagna smells good. Especially when you're starving, I bet." Alan smiles at Jack. It's supposed to be a friendly smile, but Jack looks more alarmed than relieved.

"It smells great."

Alan opens the cabinet to get more chips, but the baby lock is stuck in place. "I hate these things," he says. "My parents didn't have baby locks or gates and I turned out okay." He tugs at the cabinet door and it still won't open so he yanks it, hard, and the lock cracks as the cabinet door swings open and smacks Alan in the head. "Whoa. That's a pain that's gonna linger," Alan says.

"Yeah." Jack looks like he wants to flee.

"So, let's go back in the den. Maybe there's a game on. I bet you're a Dodgers fan."

It figures Jack would like the Giants. One more dose of poison in Buddy's genes. Jack tells Alan about growing up in Menlo Park, about his sister who went to Princeton and is in med school at Johns Hopkins.

Alan nods. Jack is obviously bright. Good-natured. All the

things Laurie said about him. Alan was wrong to not want to meet Jack before. Everything is going to be *hunky-dory*. And naturally there's a reasonable explanation for the blood and torn shirt and wine smell.

Jack takes a deep breath and looks down at his shoes. He's ready to say something important. Alan isn't sure he wants to hear this. Jack clears his throat and finally looks up. "Mr. Gaines, I'm sorry about what happened. If I could change it, I would."

"Call me Alan. You won't be insulted if I draw up a few legal documents for you to sign?" Alan is making a joke, but Jack doesn't get it.

"Laurie didn't say anything about legal documents."

"Well, she wouldn't. Because she's not as suspicious as I am." Alan is making another joke, but Jack doesn't get this one either.

"I don't know about signing anything," Jack says. "I'd have to have somebody look at it first. My father always told me to be careful about stuff like that."

"Is your father an attorney? Because if he's not, what would he know about legal documents? Jack, I'm making a joke; obviously it's not a very good one."

Jack laughs. "I get it." It's obvious he doesn't get it at all. "Maybe I should check on Mrs. Gaines," he says. "Make sure she's okay."

"She's fine. Hon?" Alan calls. "When's dinner? We're ready to *eat* each other out here."

When Laurie appears, she's still wearing the fake smile, but Alan senses something sinister behind it. "Look what I found," she says and she tosses him his BlackBerry.

"Wow. That's incredible. Where was it?"

"In the trash can. Under your desk. Isn't that funny? It must've fallen off. When you were looking at Facebook."

"I didn't think of looking in the trash can." His BlackBerry is beeping; he has unread messages. Good, he'll check them later, after dinner. And something else starts beeping in the back of his head. Laurie said, "Looking at Facebook." The way she said it, what did it mean, "Looking at Facebook?" And he realizes—his computer was on, he was checking Facebook while he was looking for his BlackBerry. And if Facebook was on—no, Nancy Futterman wouldn't have sent him an IM. Would she? Alan looks up at Laurie.

He knows Nancy Futterman sent an IM. Laurie saw it. And probably checked his other messages from Nancy. Oh boy. *It wasn't anything*, he wants to say. *The Albuquerque trip never happened. Nothing to worry about.*

"I'll get dinner going," Laurie says and she walks into the kitchen. She takes the lasagna out of the oven and puts in on top of the stove. "I've got salad in the fridge. Jack, do you want to help me serve? And there's garlic bread in the oven too." Jack joins Laurie in the kitchen. Alan stays where he is; he can hear the refrigerator door open.

"Oh," Laurie says. "Who drank all the beer?"

Jack

Something's changed. It happened after Laurie found the BlackBerry, but Jack isn't sure what's going on. He looks over at the droopy flowers on the table. There didn't seem to be any point in explaining to Laurie how after apologizing for throwing the cell phone, Normandie followed him to his car and watched as he got inside. She seemed fine, almost normal. Until she saw the flowers on the front seat.

"Flowers? For *her*?" she yelled and reached across Jack to grab them and she smashed them over and over against the car window. Then apologized again. Jack told her not to worry. He's definitely going to get that restraining order.

Laurie's husband is pounding down the beer. It's like being back at the SAE house, watching Carter timing himself to see how long before he passes out. When they finally sit down to dinner, Alan switches to wine. He insists on filling Jack's glass, and Jack lets him, but just to be polite. Somehow it seems important to keep a clear head.

No one says much as they eat their salads. "This is delicious," Jack tells Laurie.

"Thank you, Jack. It's nice to feel appreciated."

Why does her comment seem more directed at Alan than at Jack? He watches as Alan separates the tomatoes and green peppers and mushrooms and arranges them into little piles on his plate.

"Do you go on Facebook much, Jack?" Laurie asks.

Alan drops his fork. "Shit," he mutters and bends down to pick it up.

"Sometimes," Jack says.

"It's such a great way of keeping in touch with people," Laurie says. "Back in the dark ages, when I was growing up, people wrote letters. Or talked on the phone. Now there's email and texting. Isn't it interesting how communication has evolved over the years? What's next? Too bad we can't figure that out or we'd be as rich as Mark Zuckerberg."

"Yeah," Jack says. He looks over and sees Alan eating his mushrooms. When the mushrooms are done, Alan moves on to the tomatoes.

"Facebook's nice when you want to find old high school friends." Laurie winks at Jack. "Or exes. You know, see what they look like now. Are they fat? Or bald? Married?"

"I don't use it as much for that. Not yet."

"Just wait. It's sort of like having your very own private detective. Isn't that right, Alan?"

Alan doesn't answer. He's eating his green peppers.

"Of course Facebook has a dangerous side too," Laurie says. "What about all the people out there you *don't* want to have contact with again? You didn't like them in high school; why would you like them now? What happens if they track you down?"

"You don't have to friend them," Jack says. "Or if you do you can unfriend them later. Or block them so you don't see their posts."

"I guess I'm not too Facebook savvy. I only have about a hundred friends; you probably have thousands, Jack."

"Eight hundred," Jack says. He feels bad for Alan. Why isn't he part of this conversation? Jack turns to him. "What about you, Mr. Gaines? Are you on Facebook?"

Alan looks at Jack. At Laurie. His eyes are sad. "The salad was terrific. Let's have some lasagna."

Laurie's lasagna is excellent; she explains she's been getting a lot of recipes from the web, healthy foods mostly. "For the baby, but also for Alan and me," Laurie says. "We need to set a good example."

"Are you going to let the baby have McDonald's?" Jack asks.

"We'll try to limit fast food, but I think it's almost impossible to eliminate it completely. Plus there's the 'if you can't have it, it'll just make you want it more' thing. Like saying to your child you can never have McDonald's french fries, that's the only thing they'll think about. They'll *kill* for french fries."

"McDonald's is the worst," Jack says. "I like In-N-Out. Fresh beef and potatoes, real lettuce."

Laurie nods and turns to Alan. "Alan and I used to go to In-N-Out all the time."

After lasagna, Laurie asks Jack if he'd like a tour of the house. Alan volunteers to clean the table and load the dishwasher. Laurie says to Alan, "You can get the fruit tart out of the fridge and serve that up. Make some coffee too."

The way she says "make some coffee" sounds as if Alan doesn't make coffee, he'll be in big trouble. Jack thinks Alan is already in big trouble. He and Alan seem to have a lot in common, besides the baby. Neither one is having an especially good night. And Jack's face is starting to throb again and his eye feels puffy and sore.

"So you've seen the dining room and the kitchen and the den," Laurie says. "I guess one of the good things about living in California is you've already earthquake-proofed everything so babyproofing is almost redundant." Jack nods, but he's lived his whole life in California and never thought about earthquake proofing, not once.

Laurie leads Jack outside to the patio. "There's no pool. Maybe in our next house," Laurie says. "But we'll make sure we have a yard too. I hate backyards where you step out and all you see is pool. Zero yard." She looks around. "I said 'our next house,' didn't I?" Jack nods at her. "Huh," Laurie says. And she's back to describing the yard. "That's a lemon tree and our neighbors have an avocado tree. Sometimes living in California is great."

"Yeah," Jack agrees. He wonders where he'll be living next week. Life with Megan and the roommates isn't going to work out much longer. Florence, the girl whose room he's in, is breaking up with her boyfriend, so she's moving back and Megan says Jack is welcome to stay in her bedroom, but it can't be permanent because of the roommate policy, but hopefully freakish Jeff will leave soon—except he's filed some petition to stay on for six additional months, although no one understands why he wants to stay with people who don't like him.

So Jack's about to be homeless. Will Laurie let him set up a tent in the backyard? He can live off lemons and avocados and drink water out of Laurie's garden hose.

"It's a one-car garage," Laurie explains. She's waving her arm like one of the models on *The Price is Right*. "Of course we keep so much junk in the garage there's no room for a car. In the imaginary next house we'll have room for two cars. Plus storage."

Good. Jack won't have to sleep in the yard when it's cold; Laurie will let him stay in the garage with the extra suitcases and Christmas decorations and bikes and boogie boards.

They step back inside the house. "I bet you'd like to see the baby's room," Laurie says, and Jack nods. He's not exactly sure why Laurie is giving him a tour. In a way, he thinks it's more for Laurie—she wants to prove how the baby is going to have a nice place to live. Jack's never doubted that. But if it makes her feel better, he'll let her show him around.

The baby's room isn't huge, but he likes the color. It's a cheerful yellow, not too orangey. At the top of the room is an alphabet border with animals illustrating the letters. "Nice," he says, pointing to the border.

Laurie nods. "We put that up ages ago. Back when I was pregnant the first time. I told you about that, didn't I?"

Jack shakes his head.

"I had two miscarriages. Early ones. People say it could've been worse. I'm sure they're right." She is silent for a minute. "But it was still awful. Because they felt like babies, like my children. And then…they weren't there."

He's not sure what to say. "But now you've got Buddy."

"I do. I have baby Buddy." She looks down at the pieces of crib on the ground. "Alan's going to put it together this weekend. And my mother sent the chair. Try it out."

Jack sits in the glider and moves back and forth. It's comfortable, and he wonders if people other than new mothers buy gliders like this.

"How much does a baby remember about their first

room?" Laurie says. "I think I remember my room, but it might be from seeing pictures of it. My room had wallpaper with roses on it. Big red roses. Did I look at them when I was in my crib, falling asleep at night? Did I try to count them? Touch them? Do you remember your room?"

Jack thinks. "I'm like you; I mostly remember the photos. My walls and ceiling were blue. And my father painted constellations on the ceiling with glow-in-the-dark paint. I sort of remember looking up at my ceiling and thinking, *Is that the sky?* And then when my parents would take me outside, I was totally confused. The black sky, the stars? Why was that different than my room?" He smiles. "Who knows what babies think?"

"Did your mother sing to you?"

"I doubt it."

Laurie smiles. "Of course she did. You don't remember any songs?"

Jack shakes his head.

"You could ask her."

"Yeah." Knowing he never will because what's the point? He looks at Laurie's stomach. He reaches over and stops. Looks at Laurie.

"It's okay," she says.

He touches Laurie's stomach, very lightly, his fingers barely touching the fabric. "Can he hear us? Does he know we're talking about him?" Jack asks. As if baby Buddy wants to answer him, he kicks.

"Oh," Laurie says. "Did you feel that?"

Jack nods. "It doesn't hurt?"

"No. It's kind of nice, him reminding me he's in there."

Jack keeps his hand on her stomach. It feels as if baby Buddy is trying to rearrange himself, make himself more comfortable.

"Should I talk to him?" Jack asks.

"If you'd like to."

Jack hesitates, bends down closer to Laurie's tummy. "Hey there, Buddy. This is Jack. How it's going? Does it feel kind of crowded? Imagine if you had a twin." Jack looks up at Laurie. Is he doing okay? She nods.

"You're probably getting impatient, that's why you're moving around," he says. "'Let me out,' is that what you'd tell everybody? I get it, man. Trust me. Hey, I'm standing in your room right now and you're going to like it a lot. It's pretty cool, even if you don't have stars on your ceiling. Your parents are excited for you to get here too. Although I guess you're already here, sort of. What your parents want is for you to be on the *outside*. Your mom especially." Jack smiles at Laurie. He's surprised to see she has tears in her eyes. He looks back at her tummy. "Hang in there, Buddy. It's almost time."

Jack straightens himself up. "That was weird."

"No," Laurie says. "It was amazing."

They go back in the dining room and Alan has served up the fruit tart, although a third of it is missing. Alan swipes at crumbs on his chin and smiles at Laurie. "It's good, honey. Especially the chocolate part."

"Did you pick off the chocolate drizzle?" Laurie asks him.

"I can get some Hershey's syrup from the fridge. It's the same thing—"

"It's not the same thing at all. I melted Ghirardelli semisweet chocolate chips and condensed milk and butter—I can't believe you picked off the drizzle."

Jack sits and begins to eat his slice. He pretends not to

notice the finger impressions on the top. "Yum," he says. "I don't think you need the drizzle."

"Of course you do," Laurie says. She's not looking at Jack; she's staring at Alan. "The drizzle is the most important part. It isn't a real fruit tart without the drizzle and you know that, Alan. Can't you be honest about anything?"

Jack takes a bite of the tart. "Yum," he says again.

But no one is paying attention to him. Laurie goes into the kitchen and comes back with coffee mugs and a pot of coffee. She pours coffee for herself and Jack, leaves the pot and empty mug on the table in front of Alan.

Jack eats his slice of fruit tart as quickly as he can; he wants to get out of here. Even the drama back at Megan's or the thought of Normandie waiting in the shadows pales in comparison to the creepy vibe in Laurie's house.

He stands up. "Um—I don't mean to be rude, but I have an early class tomorrow."

Alan pushes the fruit tart toward Jack. "Have some more."

"No, thank you. Dinner was great."

"Are you sure you have to go?" Laurie puts a hand on his arm.

Jack nods and turns to Alan. "Nice to meet you—" He's ready to say Mr. Gaines again, but remembers in time. "Alan."

"Same here, Jack." Alan looks tired. "I'm not usually such a rotten host. And I'm sorry I was suspicious about how you got your black eye."

Jack hesitates. "I lied, Alan. I didn't run into a light post. My ex-girlfriend threw my cell phone at me because she saw a picture of baby Buddy's ultrasound, and she thinks I'm having an affair with your wife."

Alan doesn't say anything.

"That's ironic," Laurie says, and Jack doesn't understand

what she means. She has her hands on her stomach, and he'd like to feel the baby kick again but isn't sure he wants to do it with Alan watching him.

"How about another beer?" Alan asks Jack.

"I think you drank all the beer, Alan," Laurie says and turns to Jack. "Thank you for coming."

Why does Jack get the feeling there are going to be fireworks when the door closes behind him? Should he say something, tell them not to fight? Wish them good luck? Hope you don't throw things at each other once I'm gone.

"Maybe we can do it again," Jack says as he steps outside.

"I hope so." And Laurie closes the door.

Laurie

Alan explained. Or tried to explain. "It's a mistake. Nothing happened with Nancy Futterman."

"But you wanted it to?"

"No, of course I didn't. It was—I don't even know what it was. It was nothing."

"It was something."

Alan sighs. "There's no good answer here."

"The good answer would be that you shouldn't have started a Facebook flirtation with your old girlfriend in the first place."

"It wasn't a flirtation."

"Really? Because it looked like a pretty excellent imitation of flirtation to me." She can tell Alan is trying to think of the right thing to say. Something, *anything* to make things better. Good luck with that, Alan.

"I'm sorry," Alan says.

Laurie shakes her head. "That's not enough."

Alan sleeps in the guest room/office that night. He takes a bottle of Advil with him and says he wishes he hadn't had so much beer. Laurie is unsympathetic. At least she'll have the bed to herself and she can enjoy that. But when she tries to go to sleep, she can't. The bed is empty without Alan in it. And Buddy decides to practice his soccer kicks, so Laurie lies in bed sleepless and angry and exhausted. She can hear Alan snoring from the other room, deep and beer-y. She should go in and wake him up. If she can't sleep, why should he? Guilt alone should keep him awake for weeks.

Life is always full of surprises. But hit me in the head with a waffle iron, hasn't Laurie filled up her surprise quota by now? Miscarriages, mixed-up sperm, her husband is having an affair.

Only he didn't have an affair. Not exactly. It was an online flirtation. He was trying to reconnect with his past, *recherche du temps perdu* or whatever it's called. Nothing serious.

Wait a minute. Why should Laurie cut him slack? *She's* the pregnant one; she didn't sit down and go on Facebook to hook up with old boyfriends.

She is never going to fall asleep tonight. There's a good chance she'll never fall asleep again. Alan's snores grow louder. "Shut up," she yells at him, but he doesn't hear her.

She could forgive him. People make mistakes; marriage isn't always easy. The switched sperm has been a nightmare, especially for Alan. Has she been selfish? Not given enough consideration to his feelings about the pregnancy?

And yet she thinks back to Alan not getting in bed at night because he had "work" to do. Work, aka chatting with Nancy. He lied. He betrayed her.

Laurie could post something on Alan's Facebook wall. She knows his password; he used the same one for years: *password*, because he thought that was so clever until she pointed out that it was on the list of one of the most frequently used passwords. Like *123456* or *696969*. Alan promised Laurie he'd change it to something tricky and complex. He chose *password6969*. So Laurie is able to get into his computer any time she wants. Right now she could go to his Facebook page and post a heartfelt apology to Laurie. Attach a photo of a cute puppy and Alan's wall post will say, "Uh-oh! Somebody goofed up BIG time. Thought about cheating on my devoted wife with a skanky hose bag named Nancy Futterman."

She looks at the clock and realizes it's almost two in the morning and she hasn't been able to go to sleep yet and this is no fun at all, imagining fake Facebook posts when your husband is thinking about cheating on you and you're pregnant and he's sleeping in a different room and you have no idea what will happen next.

Except tomorrow night is Lamaze. She can't bear the idea of going to class with Alan, sitting on the floor between his legs, practicing relaxation exercises, and listening to Kathy's soft voice, "Depend on your partner. It's about trust. You trust him ultimately." No, she has a tiny problem with that now. She doesn't trust her husband. Not ultimately. Not at all. Will she ever be able to trust him again?

She checks the clock. Will it hurt the baby if she stays awake? "Oh, Buddy. What a mess," she says to him. "Buddy, and I promise to *never* call you Buddy once you're born, I do not regret you. Please believe me. In spite of your what-the-hell genetics, I adore you. And you're the only good thing in my life right now."

What will happen with Jack after the baby is born? Is Laurie expecting too much from him? That's her biggest mistake—making contact with sperm donor number 296.

She should have read his information and stopped there. But she got too greedy, needed to know more.

Will Jack be around to see baby Buddy? Shouldn't Buddy be able to meet his birth father? Know what it feels like to be held in Jack's arms? Or should Jack fade into the background? Laurie will keep in touch with him by email, by Facebook (ha), send him occasional Buddy photos. And when Buddy is old enough, they can meet in person. By then Jack will be married and have children. He's told his wife about Buddy, and Jack's wife, unlike obstinate intolerant Alan, will understand and want Buddy to be part of her family—not take him away from Laurie, of course, but make sure Buddy always feels included.

Laurie is crying now, her face pressed into the pillow because she doesn't want Alan to hear her. Not that he could hear anything over the sound of his snoring. It's too late. She can't do anything to stop him. She should let him run off with Nancy Futterman; they'll be happy together, make a wonderful couple.

And Jack will graduate from college, take the next steps in his life, go to graduate school, get a job, get married. He will have his own life, his own children.

Laurie will be alone. Raising Buddy by herself.

In the morning, Alan asks if taking five Advil is too many and Laurie suggests twenty-five and he doesn't laugh.

They don't talk about last night. The breakfast table seems crowded with people who aren't there—like Jack and Nancy Futterman.

"I have to work late," Alan says.

"Lamaze class."

"I forgot."

Laurie doesn't say anything. Does he really have to work late? Was he planning another Internet rendezvous with Nancy Futterman? She's too tired to ask him any of these questions.

"The Choc-O project, I told you about it," Alan says.

Alan forgets Lamaze and Jack coming for dinner. Laurie remembers everything about Alan's work. "I know. Chocolate water," she says. "It sounds sort of odd."

"The Belgians are anticipating big Choc-O sales in North America, so the repackaging for the North American market is a big deal."

Labels for chocolate water, more important than having a baby. "I can go to Lamaze by myself," Laurie says.

"Once Choc-O is out of the way—we need to hit a home run on this one. There are more downsizing rumors going around."

"Maybe you could live at your office. Would that be easier for you?"

Alan looks at her. She realizes she's crossed some kind of Rubicon. And because she knows him so well, she realizes he's not going to back down.

"Sure, I could live at my office. It wouldn't be very comfortable. No shower, no bed."

This is her chance, the exact moment where she could apologize. Yes, she's entitled to be angry but being bitchy won't help anything. She stays silent.

He looks at her for a long time. "The company has the apartment at Oakwood Toluca Hills. I could stay there for a couple days. Until Choc-O is done."

When did Alan get this idea? When did he look into moving out? Was this part of his plan with Nancy Futterman? *We'll rendezvous at the Oakwood Apartments,*

Nancy. My company keeps a place there for clients visiting from out of town.

Laurie can tell Alan wants her to protest. Beg him—no, don't go. You can't move out. I want you to stay here. I need you. It's crazy for you to leave. We're having a baby; we shouldn't be living apart. Don't be ridiculous.

"I think you're right," Laurie says. "It'll be easier for both of us."

Alan looks surprised. But he nods. "Okay. If that's what you want. I'll figure it out with the office, let you know the details." He gets up from the table, checks his watch. "Late already." For a moment Laurie thinks he's going to kiss her; instead, he puts his hand on her shoulder and gives her a small squeeze.

"I'm sorry," he says. "I know I keep saying that, but it's true. I am. The Nancy Futterman thing was stupid. I don't blame you if you can't forgive me." He waits for her to say something. "You have Buddy. And Jack," he says. "And me? What do I have? I don't know what I have. Nancy just offered some kind of escape." He hesitates. "I wish I could fix this. Make it better."

After Alan is gone, Laurie cleans the kitchen. Alan ran the dishwasher last night, but he forgot to put in detergent, so she has to run it again. It might be a good idea to clean out the refrigerator, so she does that too. While she's feeling super productive, she changes the shelf liners in the cupboards, sharpens the knives, decides the kitchen curtains look dirty, and throws them in the wash. Calls Grace and says she'll be in the office after lunch. She goes into her bedroom and cries for half an hour. Turns on the TV and watches a young couple win a trip to Bali on *Let's Make a Deal* and that makes her cry all over again.

When she's finally stopped crying, she heads into the baby's room and begins to put the crib together. Alan has left copious notes, but at least one page has gone missing, so instead of an easy job like the first time they did it, this time it's impossible.

How long will Alan be gone? A few days? Until the Choc-O project is finished? Until Nancy Futterman's divorce is final? No, he won't be gone long. Just long enough for them both to cool off. They are smart, logical people who love each other very much. They are having a *baby*. A grown-up time-out might be exactly what they need. Years from now they'll laugh at this; they'll tell Buddy about it. "Wow, pregnancy is hard, much harder than we thought. We even had a *time-out*, Buddy, isn't that funny? A time-out like we used to give you." And grown-up Buddy will laugh and this will be at Laurie and Alan's thirty-year wedding anniversary and Buddy will raise a glass and announce to the crowd, "To my parents. Who have the greatest marriage ever."

Still feeling industrious, Laurie begins to assemble her birthing bag. She needs to make a labor playlist for her iPod, pack a charger, and an *extra* charger—Grace warned her about that. A favorite nightgown, a toothbrush—one of her pregnancy books suggests "a reassuring photo." What kind of photo would she find reassuring these days? A photo of her holding Buddy in her arms after he's born? She can't very well take a photo of that, can she? A photo of someone you love. Would that be Alan? Any photo with Alan in it would depress her right now. She'll cut a photo of Daniel Craig from a magazine and bring that with her. A photo where he's not wearing a shirt.

What else to bring? Your labor partner/birth coach. Oops, another problem. Has Alan abdicated that duty? Oh, well. Maybe Daniel Craig is available.

She's thinking about calling her mother to tell her about Alan. Except her mother will want to drop everything and come to L.A. and that's the last thing Laurie needs right now. It's only going to be a couple of days, she tells herself again. She'll finish the birthing kit, make a pan of brownies, and eat the whole thing.

As she's cracking eggs for the brownies, she drops one on the floor. When she squats down to clean it up, the phone rings. Damn, she left the phone in the bedroom. It's not as easy to move around as it used to be. Suppose she falls over? She grips the counter for support and almost slips on the egg. Oh, great. Now she'll be on one of those "I've fallen and I can't get up" commercials. Right now they're about elderly people, but they'll add alerts for pregnant women living on their own. She could be their poster child. The phone keeps ringing. Alan? He's already realized what a stupid move he's made and he's ready to come home. "I forgive you. You forgive me, let's start over," that's what she'll say to him. She runs to the bedroom with the grace of a hippo from *Fantasia* and picks up the phone.

"Hello?"

It's Jack. "Hey. I just wanted to know if you were okay."

"Oh," Laurie says, trying to hide the disappointment in her voice. "I'm fine."

"I hope you don't think I'm too—like in your face or anything."

"No, not at all. I was just doing some baby things. The birthing kit for the hospital, trying to put the crib together."

"I thought Alan was going to do it."

Uh-oh. Should she tell Jack about Alan moving out?

"He's hasn't gotten around to it yet. Lazy bones."

"He'll do it soon. I could tell, he's really excited about the baby. As much as you are."

Laurie doesn't answer.

"Laurie? Are you there?"

I can do this by myself, she thinks. *I don't need anybody.* Somewhere in her head she can hear her mother ready to offer advice.

"Are you busy later today, Jack?" she asks him.

Alan

He has Facebook messages from Nancy Futterman, but he ignores them. If he were less cowardly, he'd email her and say they can't communicate anymore. "Sorry, Nancy, I was using you to avoid dealing with the absurdity of my life. I'm IMing you from the Palmer-Boone corporate apartment. Does that give you any idea of how well it went over when Laurie saw the messages we'd been sending each other on Facebook? Yeah, exactly. Lead fucking balloon."

He thought when he mentioned the apartment to Laurie she'd laugh and talk him out of it. But she didn't. Instead, she helped him pack his suitcase—he assumed he'd use his favorite Ed Hardy carry-on bag she'd given him as a joke birthday present ("An Ed Hardy suitcase? Really?" she said), but she told him she was using it for her birthing bag.

Even when he was standing at the front door, he was ready for her to grab the suitcase from his hand and say, "Enough already. We both know you're not going anywhere." But she was silent.

The first night he was sure she'd call. He kept his phone close by, just in case. But the only time his BlackBerry buzzed is when it announced a new email—from someone in Nigeria telling him he'd won $1.6 million. Nothing from Laurie.

He decided to allow for one night. One night for both of them to sulk, for him to beat himself up over his rotten behavior, one night for Laurie to hate him—not that he blames her. Who made this stupid bed? *He* did and now he's got to lie in it—and it isn't even his bed. It's the queen-sized bed at the Oakwood Apartments, fully furnished, with linens and housewares. Convenient for Palmer-Boone employees coming in from out of town, cheaper than a hotel. And also available to Palmer-Boone employees in case of emergencies—like the time Alan and Laurie had a power outage during a heat wave.

"I feel like I'm in somebody's fuck pad," Laurie said when they walked in. "It reminds me of that movie with Jack Lemmon where he pimps out his place to people at work."

"This isn't like that," Alan told her.

"*The Apartment*, that's the name of the movie."

"I've never heard about anybody using it for affairs," Alan said. Not true. Grayson, a VP in Specialty Materials, used it to meet his secretary here for years.

"I guess they don't have a problem with theft because everything is so ugly. And *brown*," Laurie said as she examined the brown carpet, brown cabinets, and brown plates. "And—gross, the people who've used the glasses and the silverware, do they really clean them?"

"That's part of the agreement, you have to." Alan pointed out a small dishwasher. When Laurie opened it, the door creaked and something black and oily dripped on the floor. "Lovely," she said. "It's haunted."

Laurie insisted they put the comforter cover on the other side of the room—"They *never* clean comforter covers. In hotels or in places like this." And when Alan tried to pull up the blanket, Laurie shook her head. "Just imagine Indians. And smallpox."

Alan is thinking of Laurie and the smallpox blanket and the haunted dishwasher. He wishes Laurie was here with him. They could laugh about the brown plates and the microwave that looks as if it's one of the first ever invented. Laurie appreciates things like that; it's one of the reasons he loves her. One of the many reasons. Her wicked sense of humor. Her crooked smile. Her legs, her breasts, her body. He realizes he is writing out a list in his head. He closes his eyes, and Laurie is in the apartment making haunted *whoo whoo* dishwasher sounds. Who knows how Nancy Futterman would react to a room like this? She probably wouldn't make a joke. She would *never* make *whoo whoo* sounds. "Alan, why aren't we staying at the Four Seasons?" Nancy would say. "I need room service."

It's much better that things didn't progress with Nancy. For a million reasons. Although poor Bob was probably thrilled at the thought of Nancy running off to L.A. with another man. And now Bob's looking at Nancy, her face splotchy and red from crying—she's hunched over her computer and typing frantically, "Why won't Alan answer me?" And Bob will tell her encouragingly, "Keep trying, Nancy. He'll write back."

Alan will email her soon. Apologize. Tell her he and Laurie have worked out their issues. And by the way, Laurie's pregnant. Thanks, Nancy, for your support. Can't wait until your next Christmas letter.

Laurie doesn't call in the morning. Alan thinks about trying her before he goes to work, decides texting might be better. "Miss U." But the minute he sends the message he regrets it. It sounds too casual; he should have spelled out *you*. He could send her another message, but he has to get to the office to work on Choc-O.

Maybe Laurie's called him at Palmer-Boone. When he gets in, he asks Wendy, his secretary, but she says no. "I'll track her down," Alan says with a smile he hopes comes off as casual. And then he begins to worry. Laurie is eight months pregnant. Of course he should track her down. Suppose something's happened, a medical emergency and she can't get to a phone? He calls again. When she doesn't pick up, he leaves a message. "Just want to make sure you're okay. Let me know."

He'll drive by the house at lunch.

Only Charlie, his fellow Choc-O VP, wants to work through lunch so Alan doesn't get a chance. Laurie hasn't emailed or phoned or sent a text; he thinks about calling one of the neighbors and having them check on her. Except then he'll have to explain the fight and why he's staying at the Oakwood Apartments—too complicated.

Will Laurie go to Lamaze without him? He could show up and surprise her. With flowers. Unless she decides to skip class. And that nosy woman who always wants to sit beside them at Lamaze, Victoria Martinez, she'll ask him why he has flowers and by the way, where is Laurie?

At lunch in the conference room Charlie asks how Laurie's pregnancy is going. Pretty typical, Alan says. The first one's the hardest, Charlie says. Because you don't know. You don't know *anything*.

Charlie has three kids. My life was incomplete without them, he tells Alan. Although sometimes...how many are you and Laurie going to have? That's a trick question, Alan wants to say. Because even though it seems like we're having one, we're not really. We're sort of having half of one. Or one and a half if you count Jack. Impossible to explain. "We'll have as many as we can," that's what Alan says.

After lunch, Wendy tells him Laurie called. "She said everything's fine."

What does that mean? How can everything be fine when Alan isn't living at home?

He works until eight since there's no reason to hurry home. On the way back to the apartment, he goes to the drive-through at In-N-Out. It was a Friday night ritual when Alan and Laurie were dating. Stop by In-N-Out, eat french fries on the way home. Alan likes extra salt, hates ketchup; Laurie likes ketchup, hates salt. So Laurie had the responsibility of seasoning the fries in the takeout box. Half with salt and no ketchup for Alan, half with no salt and ketchup for Laurie. And as Alan would drive, Laurie would put fries in his mouth. "Perfect," he'd say when she'd hand him fries, sharp and salty. Occasionally she'd touch one of her ketchup-y fries by mistake—"*Ah,*" Alan would yell. "I'm tasting *ketchup.*" By the time they'd get home, there were never any fries left.

Tonight it's just Alan and it's hard to salt the fries while he's driving, and he decides to eat them anyway, but they don't taste the same. He might as well be eating the box.

He walks through the parking lot to his apartment, past a group of kids playing touch football. One of the disadvantages to this complex is because it's so close to movie and TV studios, it's crowded with parents who've brought their children here to audition for TV pilots and movies and commercials. Once when Alan was staying at the apartment to work on a project, he was sitting by the pool and a five-year-old girl mistook him for a producer and handed him her headshot.

"I'm not—" Alan started to say, but the child gave him a rehearsed grin and pointed to her résumé.

"I take horseback riding lessons. And gymnastics and I can do a full split," which she demonstrated on the pool deck.

Back in his apartment, he sits on the brown sofa eating his cold burger and fries and watches a documentary about *Hitler's Other Family Members* on the History Channel. He checks his phone for messages—nothing from Laurie. No emails either, but his mother has sent a link to her Ancestry.com account. "You'll find this interesting!" she's typed.

She's already come up with a huge list of potential baby names, all based on past family members she's tracked down through the web. "Lawrence is nice, it's an old Gaines family name, I've traced it back to Cornwall in 1618!!" She emailed him a few weeks ago to explain how she'd found a family connection to William Henry Harrison—their family is related to a U.S. president! Days later, another email with more exclamation points—this connection linked up to the Churchill family, yes, *that* Churchill family. And if they were linked to Winston Churchill, that meant they were also linked to Princess Diana and her family. Princess Diana! A U.S. president *and* royalty.

Several days later, another email. She'd made a mistake.

No connection to Churchills or Spencers or William Henry Harrison. But a hint that *might* link to Abraham Lincoln. Which would be a thousand times better, since William Henry Harrison only served thirty-two days in office.

He hasn't told his mother about Jack. Genealogy means so much to her—if she finds out that the baby isn't Alan's, will she see it as the end of Alan's line?

Where is Laurie? Shouldn't she be calling so he knows how she's doing? Unless she's at Lamaze. He checks his watch. No, she should be home from Lamaze by now. He could call her. But she'll think he's being a pest. A little room, that's what they both need.

He knows it's a bad idea to drive by the house, but he wants to reassure himself that Laurie is okay. Suppose he sees her through the window and she's crying? That would be an excuse to go inside. "I'm sorry, honey. Let me stay here with you," that's what he'll tell her. And she'll forgive him and say she knows the only way they can get through this is if they have each other.

The lights are on in the house, that's a good sign. Laurie didn't come home from Lamaze tired and depressed and crawl into bed. He's guessing she's curled up on the sofa in the den watching TV. He parks in front and wonders if he should go inside. Or drive around the block again.

Is this a terrible idea? He thinks about heading back to his apartment—no, he's come all this way. He gets out of his car and starts up the walk, notices a car in the driveway behind Laurie's. An old Honda Civic. It looks familiar, but he can't put his finger on it—remembers it belongs to Jack.

Oh. Jack is at his house. Why? Alan looks in Jack's

car—it's packed with boxes and suitcases. T-shirts and tennis shoes on the floor. Jack's living out of his car? Great, that bodes well for baby Buddy. Homeless dad. Super.

Alan walks up to the front door. He has his key and he doubts Laurie has changed the locks. He *hopes* she hasn't changed the locks. Should he ring the bell? But if Laurie and Jack are in the middle of something, he shouldn't disturb them.

In the middle of *what*? He peeks in the living room window—the curtains are drawn, but they're sheer enough so you can see people if they're in the room. There's no one there.

He'll just look in the kitchen window. They could be at the kitchen table drinking hot chocolate. As he makes his way to the side of the house, he stumbles against the recycling bin. Damn, is it garbage day tomorrow? That must be why Jack is here. Laurie called him to help take out the trash. He has to stand on his tiptoes to look in the kitchen window.

The lights are on, no sign of anybody. He sees a saucepan on the stove and a bottle of Hershey's syrup on the counter. He was right about the hot chocolate. They could be in the den—but to check he'd have to go in the backyard and the gate is hard to open and probably locked.

On the other side of the house, he has to move past bushes that slap at his face and he wishes he'd gotten the gardeners to trim them back the last time they were here. He'll make a note. Assuming he sees the gardeners again. The front bedroom light is off, but the lights in the middle bedroom, the baby's room, are on.

He pushes his way through more bushes—when did his yard turn into a fucking forest? He hopes the next-door neighbors don't see him and think he's someone trying to break into the house. A dog begins barking and Alan *really* hopes the next-door neighbors don't have a gun and a shoot-first mentality. He crouches below the window and raises his head slowly to look in the baby's room.

Laurie and Jack are sitting on the floor, the pieces of the crib around them. Most of the frame has been assembled. Laurie holds up two long screws and makes a face like, "Uh-oh, did we forget these?" Jack takes them and shakes his head. Points to another spot on the crib where they should go.

Laurie picks up a baby mobile. Alan hasn't seen it before. Where did it come from? Marine animals dangle from a blue plastic circle. Whales and jellyfish and sea horses. Jack nods at Laurie; he seems to approve.

Alan notices two mugs on the floor beside Laurie and Jack. And a plate of cookies. Did Laurie make Jack cookies?

He could still go inside. Ring the bell, not use his key. Laurie would make him a mug of hot chocolate, offer him a cookie.

Unless she's happier putting the crib together with Jack. He watches her as she takes a sip of her hot chocolate. Jack holds the mobile in his hand and pushes a button. It begins to spin slowly and Alan can hear the faint sound of music.

Jack

Jack wonders if his life would have turned out differently if he'd had a mother like Laurie. Not that he's exactly sure what kind of mother she'll be since the baby isn't born yet, but he can already tell she won't be a "my child must be a genius *or else*" mother. "I want the baby to be happy," Laurie says when they're putting the crib together. "Maybe that sounds shallow, Jack, but after going through all this—not the *you* part of this, the miscarriages part—it makes you realize happiness is severely underrated."

He doesn't disagree with her. He thinks about the times he's been happy lately—when he listens to Megan recite lines from her play, for example. He is so proud of Megan—it's like a kind of wonder that somebody could be so good. And that somebody like Megan could like *him*.

Happiness is feeling baby Buddy kicking away in Laurie's belly. "He really wants out, doesn't he?"

"Wouldn't you?" Laurie says.

And being the father of a baby…he can't even explain how that makes him feel. Although once the baby is born, everything could change. But now it seems right, being with Laurie, feeling Buddy wiggling around. Even if Jack ends up living on the street in a cardboard box and begging for change at freeway exits, he has still managed to do one amazing thing.

"Would you like me to get you more hot chocolate?" he asks Laurie.

"Maybe later." She frowns. "I wish I could remember where I put the crib linens. It's funny—you spend so much time picking out a crib and linens, and when you bring the baby home, he'll sleep in a bassinet."

"You don't put him in the crib? Isn't that what it's for?"

"You want him close. In some cultures, babies share a family bed for weeks, for months. Or years. One of the reasons is because of breast-feeding—babies eat a lot more frequently in the beginning."

Jack hadn't thought about breast-feeding. "You're sure you're going to do that?" he asks Laurie, trying not to look at her breasts.

"Yeah, it'll be nice. All this hormonal stuff happens when you're pregnant—not just your body changing, emotional things too. In a good way. You're suddenly anxious to do it all. Be a mother, a mama bear." She growls. "See?" She growls again.

"I'd be clueless," Jack says. "I didn't know about the bassinet. Or how breast-feeding works. What happens if you're not around? How does he eat?"

"You rent a breast pump and express the extra milk and save it. In the fridge. A lot of people think breast milk is better for a baby. Did your mother breast-feed you?"

Jack has no idea. He can't imagine his mother taking time off from her busy schedule to breast-feed him. Of course, he can't imagine his mother taking time to get pregnant. "I don't know," he says.

"You still haven't told them?"

Jack shakes his head. "Too scary."

"They might surprise you. Be excited. They're going to be grandparents."

Jack tries to picture the look on his mother's face when he tells her she's going to be a grandparent. *You're too young, you're not married, she's married to another man, you donated your* sperm*?*

"I think it's better they don't know. It's enough for them to realize I'm finally going to graduate. Graduate *and* be a father? Their heads might explode. What about you? Did you tell people?"

"I told my mother and she's okay with it. She's somebody who likes things a little off-center. My dad was the same way; they were perfect for each other. He died when I was a little younger than you."

"Sorry," Jack says.

"He was a cool guy. He taught high school English. He always said he felt his goal was to teach kids to like reading. Hemingway or Jane Austen or *MAD magazine*—it didn't matter. Liking it, that was the important part. You two would've gotten along. The sperm switch, he would think that was crazy, in a good way. Alan's family, they're more—conventional. He hasn't told them yet, but he will eventually."

"Maybe when the baby's born and looks like me—unless you could tell them you had an affair." Jack's trying to make a joke, but when Laurie doesn't smile he remembers Laurie talking to Alan about old girlfriends on Facebook. "Oops," he says.

"That's okay."

Jack isn't sure how to ask about Alan. Laurie told him Alan was going to live somewhere else for a couple of days.

"Alan isn't mad at you," Laurie says, as if she knows what he's thinking. "He's not mad at me either. He's sort of mad at everything else. He's somebody who likes his life to go a certain way. He's very orderly. He doesn't like surprises."

"But he wants to have a baby, doesn't he?"

"Yes. But not exactly this particular baby." Laurie gives Jack a sad smile.

"He should be here though. With you."

"Don't worry about Alan and me. It'll work out. You'll see."

Jack nods. He hopes she's right.

Laurie tries to get to her feet—it's not a pretty sight. "Come help," she says to Jack, "and if you laugh at a pregnant woman trying to stand up, I will kick you in the shin. And a mad pregnant woman kicking you is not something you'll forget."

They have more hot chocolate in the kitchen and she asks him if he's excited about graduation. He says he is, but he'll mostly be glad when it's over. He only has one final that worries him. "The professor hates me," he tells Laurie.

"I've heard that excuse before," she says. "What's the class?"

"Medieval Literature of Devotion and Dissent."

Laurie makes a face. "An elective?"

"For my religious studies minor. I thought it sounded fun."

"Nothing about that sounds fun. What's the final?"

"Orthodoxy, Heterodoxy, and Heresy."

"If I were you, I wouldn't be drinking hot chocolate. I'd be drinking gin from a bottle."

"The final's fifty percent of my grade and Mr. Bryant told me unless I make an A, he's not passing me."

"So you're studying hard."

Jack shrugs. "I'm trying. But studying in my apartment…" He explains his living situation, the distraction of Jeff, how

Casey the monochromatic dresser has suddenly decided to be in a band, and she's taking drum lessons and there's a drum set in the dining room now. How Florence is coming back since she broke up with her boyfriend, and as much as he'd like to stay in Megan's room, he can't because of the stupid roommate rule.

"Megan is your girlfriend?" Laurie asks. "Not the one who threw the phone."

"Normandie threw the phone. Megan is my real girlfriend." He shakes his head. "I wasn't sure at first. Which I guess is why I had *two* girlfriends, you know, because it was easier than picking one over the other. I didn't do it to be an asshole, I swear. But the whole time—I kept thinking about Megan. Even when I was with Normandie. It sounds completely lame."

"But I understand. You were taking Megan for granted. So when you saw you could possibly lose her—"

"That seems obvious now. But it didn't at the time. Sometimes I feel like I'm never going to figure anything out."

"You're too hard on yourself." Laurie's smiling at Jack. She's got a hot chocolate mustache.

Jack looks around the kitchen. He's not sure if he should say anything or not. But what the hell. "I have a confession," he says. "About why I donated my sperm."

"You don't have to tell me."

"I want to." He takes a deep breath. "I took money from my fraternity party fund. Not for drugs or anything like that—my parents cut my allowance and I needed money for gas and food. And beer. So the sperm donation, it was to pay back the money I borrowed." He corrects himself. "The money I stole. It wasn't about doing something to help infertile couples. It was for money. For me."

Laurie looks at him. She hates him now. He doesn't blame her; he hates himself.

"Did you think I'd be mad about that?" she asks him.

"Yeah."

"I don't care why you did it. That was never what this is about." She laughs. "Who knows what it's about? I don't understand it. I don't understand a lot of things—big issues, like…fate. Like was I was meant to have miscarriages and learn from the experience? So they were ultimately a *good* thing? Because they weren't. They sucked. But I guess if some woman had to get pissed off at the fertility clinic where she worked, fate must've been working that day when she switched Alan's sperm with yours because—no offense—I would've preferred Alan. But you know what? Buddy is going to be pretty spectacular."

He doesn't know what to say.

"Everybody screws up, Jack. That's why we get second chances," Laurie says.

"I think I'm on my third and fourth and fifth chances. How many do we get?"

"As many as we need."

"Good," Jack says. He sighs. "Life is bizarrely bizarre. Like how mostly I try to do the right thing, but then it blows up in my face. And then stuff that *shouldn't* be okay turns out fine." He pauses. "Wow. That was either super deep or total bullshit."

Laurie grins at him. "Do you think Buddy is going to be like you? Because that would be okay with me."

Jack thinks that over. "Maybe. But I hope nobody ever throws a phone at his head."

Laurie insists on walking him to his car. She looks inside and sees the clutter. "I'll clean it after I move," he says. "Megan has a friend who's looking for a roommate. It's a house and I'd have my own bedroom. The only negative is the house is in Lancaster."

"Lancaster? That's a million miles away from UCLA."

"I know, kind of a schlep."

"You should stay here. In the guest room."

Jack isn't sure he's heard right. "At your house?"

"Why not? I don't make a lot of noise, no drum set."

"I don't have much money for rent."

"You wouldn't have to pay rent. Just help around the house—dishes, take out the garbage, pick me up when I fall over. You need a place where you can concentrate on your finals."

He thinks it over. "What happens when your husband comes back?"

"There's plenty of room. You don't have to decide right now. Think it over. Thanks for helping me with the crib." She smiles at him.

It takes him almost forty-five minutes to get back to Megan's apartment because there's an accident on the freeway. Jack imagines commuting from Lancaster and there must be more advantages than your own bedroom, but he can't think of any because the thought of being trapped in a car for four hours every day pretty much negates anything positive.

He pulls up to the apartment just as Megan is getting home from rehearsal, and she's so excited she's practically bouncing out of her shoes. "It went fabulously tonight, like this *thing* that happens when it's not about memorizing lines, you sort of *become* the person. All of us, we *were* our characters. Abso-fucking-lutely magical."

This is a girl to spend the rest of your life with, he thinks. Her uninhibited joy, how she attacks everything with a take no prisoners attitude. How did he get so lucky?

"What?" she is saying to him. "Why are you looking at me like that?"

Casey is playing her drums, Florence is in her old bedroom, and she's very attentive to Jack—if anything *too* attentive, like she's ready for a rebound relationship. "Lance told me he couldn't be faithful," Florence says to Jack, touching Jack's hand and looking into his eyes. "He said he could never promise me anything, but I didn't believe him. So who's the stupid one here, Lance? I mean Jack." She squeezes his fingers and giggles. "That's funny," she says. "I called you Lance." She squeezes his fingers again.

Jack stays in Megan's room; they lie on the bed like spoons. She's telling him details about the play and he can tell how happy she is because she's not doing her Irish accent.

"I haven't asked about you," she says suddenly. "I'm such a selfish cow. Are you okay?"

"I found another place to live," he says.

"Not in Lancaster?"

"No, just over the hill. In Sherman Oaks." He's looking at Megan. He feels as if he's about to make the best or worst decision of his life.

"Can I show you something?" he says.

"Sure."

Jack gets out his cell phone. It's chipped on the edges and the volume control comes and goes, but at least it's working again. He scrolls to the ultrasound photo and holds it out to Megan.

"Whoa," she says. "Ultrasounds are cool. It's crazy that's a baby. Did your sister get married? Is this her baby?"

Jack looks at Megan. Okay, here goes. "It's sort of a long story."

He's not sure how Megan will react. The phone is back in his pocket, so at least she can't throw it at him. "I can't believe you told me all that," she finally says. And Jack sighs. Yeah, he knew honesty would bite him in the ass. Again. But Megan is kissing him. And grinning. "I am so *honored* you would reveal this to me. I wish you'd told me before. I could have helped you; it must've been horrible, dealing with this by yourself."

"Yeah."

"It's wild, isn't it? How many people it takes to make a baby?" Megan says. "Sometimes family isn't as simple as you think. Can I see the ultrasound again? Does the baby look like you? I can't believe you don't know the sex. I'd want to know immediately."

She talks about how they have to think about names and when can she meet Laurie and Jack starts to laugh because Megan is talking so quickly and he finally puts his finger to her lips. She smiles and kisses the tip of his finger.

"I think I could kind of love you," she says, and she kisses him for real this time.

Laurie

She tries to convince herself she doesn't miss Alan. It's not as if she sees him that much during the week; they both have jobs. And sure, they're married, but does that mean they're together all the time? Of course not. Alan living somewhere else? She barely notices he's gone.

Bullshit. She misses making coffee for him in the morning, picking up his socks from beside the hamper—why they don't make it *into* the hamper drives her insane. But who would have thought she'd miss Alan's dirty socks?

She misses his laugh, the touch of his hand on the small of her back. His presence.

One day without Alan has turned into two. Then three, now a week. Now longer. They've spoken on the phone; Alan tells her Choc-O is coming along and the Belgians are pleased with everything so far. He asks how she's feeling and says he misses going to Lamaze. Laurie knows that's not true—he felt uncomfortable at the Lamaze classes he attended. "I feel like I should be wearing Birkenstocks and smoking pot," he said.

"Tell Buddy hi from me," he tells her on the phone.

"I will," she says. He doesn't mention coming home. Neither does Laurie. She's told him about Jack moving in—is that the reason for Alan's chilliness? Laurie thinks

Alan is using Jack's visit at the house as an excuse—it makes it easier for him to stay away. Out of sight, out of mind. In Alan's Oakwood apartment, Laurie isn't pregnant at all.

Jack has been the perfect houseguest. He's quiet and seems happy to handle chores like rolling the trash cans to the curb for garbage day or unloading the dishwasher. Laurie tries to make sure he has his space and time to study. "You don't have to entertain me," she says to him. He asks if he could look at one of her baby books, just to learn a little more about what's going on. She gives him one but makes him promise to focus on his schoolwork.

When Jack goes to class, Laurie does a quick clean sweep of the house before she heads into the Hidden Valley office. She's surprised how orderly Jack is, almost like Alan. In the bathroom, he hangs his towel on the towel rack and wipes the bathroom sink so she can't see a trace of soap or toothpaste. Jack's toothbrush and comb and hair gel are arranged neatly on the counter.

The other morning, as Jack was getting into his car, Laurie called out to him, "You need a jacket. It's a little nippy."

Is there an exact moment where you turn into a parent? At conception? When the baby is born? When the young man who donated sperm for your baby is living in your guest room?

"I've got a hoodie in the car," Jack shouts back at Laurie. "Thanks."

As he drives away, Laurie waves. She doesn't need Alan. Who? That's right, she can barely remember his name.

Grace has been traveling with Hal and Emilie, so Hidden Valley is running at half speed. "Perfect timing," Grace told Laurie. "So we'll really boogie after baby Buddy makes his appearance." Laurie tried to explain she'll need to work *less* after Buddy arrives, but Grace pretended not to hear her. "Don't worry. I'll be back for the baby shower," Grace said. And maybe the timing is perfect since Laurie still hasn't gotten up the courage to tell Grace about Buddy's paternity, and she's also unsure how to explain Alan's absence. And Jack living at the house. Conundrum/clusterfuck indeed.

Laurie only has one Lamaze class left and she could skip it, but Jack has been studying all afternoon and needs a break and thinks Lamaze would be interesting, so he asks Laurie if he could come along. "Unless it's weird if they ask who I am," he says. "What do I do?"

"Wing it," Laurie tells him.

When Laurie was young, her grandmother gave her a subscription to *Highlights* magazine. The magazine had a squeaky clean, too-good-to-be-true quality. The riddles and jokes were okay, but her favorite page was the Goofus and Gallant cartoon. In each issue, two boys are faced with a decision. Should I eat that last piece of pie? Goofus—and you know he's a goofus because he has that unfortunate name and also because he wears sloppy clothes—always, *always* makes the wrong decision. "I'll eat the pie," he says. Gallant (another loser name) dresses like a prig; he clearly has a stick up his ass. "I won't eat the pie," Gallant says. "Perhaps someone else might like it."

Jack hasn't heard of Goofus and Gallant, and Laurie tells him he should be grateful his parents never made him read *Highlights*. But he understands the concept, so when Jack and Laurie arrive for the final Lamaze class and Laurie points out Victoria Martinez and says she and Alan refer to her as "Gallant," Jack understands.

Victoria Martinez is slim, her baby weight concentrated in her pregnancy bump (an expression Laurie loathes) and her maternity clothes are superstylish, clearly expensive. Her purse is a huge Prada satchel she tosses casually on the floor, and Laurie is certain Victoria will buy (if she hasn't already) a matching Prada diaper bag. The diamond in her engagement ring is the size of a gum ball, and she moves her hand to her face constantly, allowing it to reflect the light so other women will notice and comment, "Oh, what a *gorgeous* ring."

Mr. Victoria Martinez is small with a dark unibrow; he wears a gold watch so large it looks fake, like if you get too close a spray of water will squirt you in the face. Laurie has never heard him speak.

Victoria never stops talking. She is always complimenting everyone. To Miranda, who is wearing a hideous red-and-white checked maternity blouse that looks like a restaurant tablecloth, "Miranda, I *adore* that top. Where did you get it? No, *Target*? Impossible." Victoria's next victim is Shea, a gorgeous, shy black woman. "You're so flexible, Shea. Bet that comes in handy in the *boudoir*." Shea knows Victoria is full of shit and occasionally looks over at Laurie and smiles.

Victoria saves her most Gallant behavior for Kathy, the teacher. "I don't know what I would do if I'd gotten another Lamaze teacher. You're the best, Kath. I'm going to write a personal letter to the head of Lamaze to let them know what a *prize* they've got in you."

Victoria tried to suck up to Laurie when class started, but Laurie refused to play along. "Cute jeans. Isabella Oliver?" Victoria said, and Laurie knew immediately something was up because Laurie's jeans look cheap and the pregnancy panel has stretched out so far it droops almost below her waist and the legs are too wide, like clown pants. But they're her most comfortable jeans, so she wears them anyway.

Victoria is the only one who comments when Alan stops coming to Lamaze. "Where's your cute husband?" she asks the first time Alan misses a class.

"Work," Laurie says, hoping that will be enough to shut her up. No such luck.

"Evan would *die* if he couldn't be here. He wants the full pregnancy experience. He says he'd go through labor with me if he could. I wish," Victoria says and she reaches back to pat her husband's hand.

"Work again?" Victoria says the second time Alan is absent.

"Big project. Waiting on the Belgians," Laurie answers and moves to the other side of the room to practice her breathing. Laurie notices Victoria watching her and whispering to the other mothers. Poor Laurie.

"I'm nervous," Jack says as they walk into the class.

"I told you. You could be back at the house studying."

"I can't read any more Middle English. It makes my eyes bleed."

This last Lamaze class is more of a review—they practice their comfort measures and progressive relaxation. When Laurie sits between Jack's legs, she can feel him hesitate before he puts his hands on her stomach. But he breathes along with her, "Hunh, hunh, hunh," and seems to get into it.

"Don't worry about how your vocalization sounds," Kathy says. "If grunting makes you uncomfortable, pick a word or a song lyric instead, whatever works for you."

We sound like a demented chorus, Laurie thinks. A roomful of pregnant women making strange sounds, practicing to have a baby.

At the end of class, Kathy tells them they've done a great job and they'll do a great job in the delivery room as well. Most of the moms have brought Kathy gifts. Laurie found a mini Grow Your Own Herbs kit she thinks Kathy will like. Victoria gives Kathy something in a Tiffany bag.

As Laurie and Jack are walking out to the parking lot, Victoria approaches them. "Your husband is still busy with his project? He must be working very hard," she says.

"That's the kind of man he is," Laurie says.

Victoria turns to Jack, waits for him to say something. He doesn't.

"At least you didn't have to come alone tonight, especially for the last class." Victoria addresses this to Laurie.

"I know. It's great Jack could join me." Laurie puts her arm around Jack's waist. She lowers her voice and moves in close to Victoria. "Don't tell anybody, but Jack is my lover."

Victoria's mouth opens—she doesn't close it right away. Laurie gives Jack a small squeeze and Jack, bless his heart, rolls with it, gives Laurie a squeeze back.

"Laurie's smokin' hot," Jack says to Victoria and he squeezes Laurie again.

Laurie and Jack are laughing so hard in the car they have tears running down their faces.

"Maybe you shouldn't laugh so much," Jack says. "It could be bad for the baby."

"No," Laurie says. "I think we're guaranteeing that Buddy will have an excellent sense of humor."

Jack likes that. Laurie can see him smile in the dark of the car. "As long as he's a Goofus." He starts to laugh again.

At the house, Jack heads straight to the guest room. Laurie promises him a hot chocolate break later. She thinks about calling Alan. Reconsiders. Reconsiders again and picks up the phone.

He's not there. Or he's not picking up. "Hi," she says. "It's me. Just wanted to let you know everything's okay. Last Lamaze class tonight, all rockets are firing, awaiting countdown. Let me know how you're doing."

She clicks off, wonders if Alan is sitting in his apartment looking at the caller ID and deliberately not picking up. She should go over there, knock on the door, and tell him it's time to come home.

Why are we so stubborn? she wonders. *Neither one of us will make the first move.* It's turned into a contest—who can hold a grudge the longest? Life would be easier if they were the kind of people who yelled at each other instead of retreating into some stupid monastery-like silence. How long is this going to last?

Baby Buddy gives her a sharp kick. When he is born, he will be one giant elbow. Maybe Alan will call back tonight. And if he doesn't, Laurie will try him again tomorrow. But right now she'll make hot chocolate.

Alan

He would like to show up for the final Lamaze class. He's seen the reminder notice on his BlackBerry. *I could go,* he thinks. *That would make Laurie happy. There's probably some sort of review and I could get caught up. Make fun of Victoria/Gallant.* He leaves work early—maybe after Lamaze he and Laurie can get something to eat. Have a mini-date.

He misses her. It's not just living in the crappy brown apartment; it's not having her around. The other morning, he woke up, and as he was walking into the kitchen, he called out her name. At first he thought he was losing his mind. And he supposes he is in a way, living apart from his pregnant wife. He's met a few people in the Oakwood complex—a woman named Janet who's come to L.A. with her two children to "try and make it in the biz." She's left her husband back home in St. Paul ("He'll come out when the kids hit," she told him) and her full-time job is driving the kids to dance and voice lessons, proofing their new headshots, trips to the orthodontist ("Heather's got a wicked overbite"), casting calls, and trying to get meetings at the top talent agencies.

"What about school?" Alan asked her.

"Homeschooling is the only way to go. And once Heather or Oliver land a show, the studio will hire an on-set tutor."

Alan watches Heather and Oliver at the pool. They are eight-year-old twins, slight like their mother with wide grins, and Janet is being truthful about Heather's overbite. Poor Heather is eat-an-apple-through-a-picket-fence material.

Janet invited Alan for dinner one night. ("No funny business. I'm a *very* married woman.") Her apartment is a mirror image of his own, but Janet has brightened things up by putting posters on the wall of Lindsay Lohan and Justin Bieber. "I want to inspire them, show them what to shoot for." Heather and Oliver are polite; they take their plates to the sink when they're done, they ask Alan ("Mr. Gaines") if he'd like more water, another napkin, leftovers. After dinner, they head to their bedroom to do homework.

Alan has told Janet he's living here while he works on a project for his job—he was driving his wife *insane* at the house.

"You don't have to explain anything to me," Janet says. "My husband thinks life in L.A. is crazy. And Hollywood—he calls it 'nonsense.' He won't say nonsense when the checks start coming in. Somebody's got to be aggressive about their careers. They only have so much time—it's brutal out there."

Alan agrees. Sort of. Subjecting children to agents and casting calls, that seems pretty brutal too.

"I wasn't sure I wanted to have kids," Janet is saying as she pours Alan another glass of wine. "I'd done some acting, local stuff in St. Paul. A little modeling. And getting pregnant—did I want to do that to my body and then have the responsibility of children? I mean, that's a big step."

Alan agrees.

"Your whole life changes. It's not about *you* anymore. And that's fine. I don't want to sound selfish because I don't consider myself a selfish person. I'm practical. You'll see. It's obvious you don't have children yet. Or you wouldn't be staying here, would you?"

Alan considers telling her about Buddy and Jack and why he's staying in the apartment and how even though his life is screwed up these days, his life will *never* be as screwed up as the lives of Heather and Oliver. At dinner, he watches them practice lines for a breakfast cereal commercial. Both children are trying out, but only one child will be chosen.

"It tastes like bubble gum, the most yummy kind!" Heather says with a ghastly fake smile, her retainer smacking against the roof of her mouth.

"Take out your retainer. You sound like you have a speech impediment," her mother tells her.

"It tastes like bubble gum, the most yummy kind!" says Oliver. His reading doesn't sound as false, but the way he pronounces "yummy" is too chirpy and enthusiastic.

"Well, that was better than Heather's. But you've got to step it up. Do you know how good the kids you're going to be competing with are? One of you has got to get this and I know it'll be hard on the other one. But if neither of you get it, do you think I want to drive back here with a car full of losers?"

Heather clicks the retainer in her mouth.

Janet turns to Oliver. "The way you said yummy, it sounded like a gay person would say it. Say it more *manly*."

Alan would love to stay, but he's got work. Janet knows what that's like. "Come back anytime. Hopefully you'll catch us on TV soon."

Alan goes straight to his car and drives to Lamaze. "Us." You need a license to drive a car but not to have children. He bets Janet didn't have any trouble conceiving—no switched sperm for her. She'll probably continue to give birth to siblings for Heather and Oliver, at least until she finds a child who can make her money.

Alan is tired and sad and wants to tell Laurie the Janet

story. She'd love it, in a horrified sort of way. He checks his watch and realizes he'll be late for Lamaze, but hopefully just the fact he's showed up will make Laurie feel better. When he hears the sound of a helicopter overhead, he knows that's bad news. And sure enough, traffic slows to a crawl and he realizes he'll never make it in time.

As he pulls into the Lamaze class parking lot, he can see cars driving away. Damn. At least he had good intentions. He's ready to head back to the apartment when he notices Laurie's Audi. So he won't get full credit, but partial credit will be better than nothing.

As he turns, his headlights sweep past Laurie's car and he sees two profiles. Laurie's and Jack's. Their heads are thrown back and they're laughing. Laughing hysterically. Laurie reaches over and grabs Jack's shoulder.

It would be easier if Laurie and Jack were having some sort of fling, some escape—say, like his imaginary Albuquerque adventure with Nancy Futterman. What Laurie and Jack are sharing is deeper—more profound and disturbing. They're sharing the love of their unborn child. And how does Alan fit in?

He doesn't.

Back in his apartment, he looks in his refrigerator for something to drink. A beer would be great. But all he has is a half carton of milk and a Red Bull. He can't even give himself a good pity party.

In the morning, he sees that Laurie has left a message on his cell. He should call her back. Maybe on his lunch break.

He and Charlie are supposed to be working on Choc-O, but Charlie calls in sick. Alan could work on Choc-O by himself, but he's thinking about Jack. Laurie's told him Jack is studying for finals. Religious studies—that sounds rough. Alan wonders if he could check out Jack's classes online, see what they're like. And he has another idea—if he has lunch in Westwood, he could stop by UCLA. He hasn't been there in years. Who knows? What are the chances he could run into Jack?

The UCLA campus is beautiful, and he's surprised at how young the students look. He sits outside Bunche Hall and eats a Subway sandwich. When he's done, he picks at a bag of barbecue Ruffles. He's about to give up when he sees Jack walking out of the building. A pretty girl with blond hair and a lot of eye makeup runs up to Jack, grabs him by the front of his T-shirt, and pulls him toward her. Jack almost loses his balance—the backpack on his shoulder slips down to his elbow and the girl laughs. Pulls him harder. He gives up, allows the backpack to fall to the ground and kisses the girl. She puts his arms around his neck and, still laughing, twirls him around until they fall on the grass. The kiss goes on a long time and Alan tries to remember the last time he kissed Laurie like that, in public, not caring if anybody saw them or not. When the kiss ends, they are still on the ground and the girl throws her legs over Jack's. They sit there, grinning at each other. They're not talking; they don't have to.

The pain in Alan's chest is so intense for a moment he thinks he's having a heart attack. He wants to kiss Laurie like that. He wants to go back to the beginning, fall in love with her again. See their relationship as infinite. He wants his family. The two of them—no, the *three* of them.

He's driving back to his office. Charlie has emailed to let him know he's feeling better and they can motor on Choc-O tomorrow. Alan is thinking about Buddy—Buddy who hasn't heard Alan's voice in a while because he's listening to Jack. Will he be confused when he's born, not recognize Alan? Will Alan look at Buddy's life as some kind of constant competition with Jack? Who will give Buddy the best birthday present? "I taught him how to tie his shoes," Alan will tell Jack. "Oh yeah?" Jack will say. "I taught him how to send his first text message."

Maybe after Jack graduates, he'll get a job out of state. Or in a different country. Alan could suggest that to Jack. "I've heard the Peace Corps is incredible. Have you thought about looking into that? They have some excellent programs in the Ukraine. And it's only a two-year commitment. You'll be back home in no time."

Why couldn't Jack have stayed number 296? A piece of paper. A specimen in a vial. That's when the big problem started. When Jack became flesh and blood.

Jack

The first time he notices Alan is when he's eating lunch at Falafel King. Alan is standing across the street wearing a baseball cap, and as Jack turns to make sure it's him, Alan pulls down the brim of his cap so it covers his eyes, which only makes him look more conspicuous. Maybe he'll come over and say hello. But when Jack's getting an iced tea refill, he looks across the street again and Alan is gone.

Jack has seen Alan drive by Laurie's house at night. Sometimes Alan turns off his car lights, which Jack thinks is strange because how many normal people who don't want to attract attention to themselves go driving around neighborhoods in Sherman Oaks with their headlights off?

On a trip to a car wash (Jack thought it would be a nice surprise for Laurie if he cleaned her Audi), Alan's car was parked across the street. Jack almost waved, but realized Alan imagines he is being discreet.

Jack and Megan are having coffee at Kerckhoff and she asks him if he knows a middle-aged preppyish blond man, because she's seen him around campus a few times and he seems to be interested in Jack. "Do you have a stalker?" she says. Jack debates telling Megan about Alan, but it might be worse for Alan if Megan knows because she'd confront him. "Yo, *yo*? Are you stalking my boyfriend?"

And Laurie doesn't need anything else to worry about—she's got so much going on with work and baby-related things, like brunches or showers, and Laurie's mother was going to come to one but fell while running to get on her treadmill and cracked her knee, so she'll be on crutches for at least four weeks. "Don't you *dare* have that baby before I get there," she told Laurie.

Laurie assures Jack she has everything under control. But because she says that so many times, Jack suspects she is feeling less in control as each day passes and her due date gets closer.

"Did you know in China sometimes they breast-feed their children until they're six?" she says at dinner one night.

"Huh." Jack hasn't figured out how he feels about watching Laurie breast-feed. He definitely doesn't want to see her breasts. Ever.

Does he want to be in the delivery room when the baby is born? Laurie tells Jack it's his decision. He remembers the sex-ed movies they showed in middle school—women screaming as giant baby heads squeezed their way out of vaginas. It was upsetting back then. What would it be like watching in person?

"I have two birth coaches," Laurie says. "And I'm not sure either one of them wants to be with me when the baby is born." She's joking, but Jack suspects she's afraid she won't have anybody with her when she has the baby.

"If you want me there, sure, I'll be there," he says. "I might pass out though."

"That's okay. You're in a hospital. Is there a better place to pass out?"

It still makes him nervous. He asks Megan her advice, and naturally, Megan volunteers to be Laurie's birth coach. "I'd be amazing," Megan says to Jack. "I'd hold her hand, help her with her breathing. I love the idea I could share part of Laurie's birth experience; we would empower each other. Don't you think?"

Jack nods. But he knows Laurie will be more comfortable with him, even though she likes Megan. The first time he brought Megan over to Laurie's house, Megan fussed over Laurie. Made her sit down, fixed herbal tea. Would Laurie like Megan to whip her up some fresh bread? How about a foot massage? Jack had never seen that side of Megan before, the supernurturing caregiver. "Would you like me to wash your hair?" Megan asked Laurie.

"I'm having a baby. I'm not an invalid," Laurie said. "But a foot massage might be nice sometime."

So everything is good. Except for studying for finals and worrying about what it will be like in a delivery room. Why is he acting like such a wimp? What is he afraid of? Babies get born all the time. He can handle it. He's never fainted in his life. What makes him think he'd faint now?

"I think I'm nesting," Laurie says as she washes another load of towels and sheets, folds them carefully, and puts them back in the linen closet.

"Were they dirty?"

"I don't think so. See? I'm forgetting things. Does that mean I'll forget the baby after he's born? Am I going to be one of those mothers on the news who leave their baby in the car while they shop in the mall for five hours and when they come out there's a crowd and they're broken the windows, but it's too late—" She looks worried.

"You won't be like that. You're way too..." Jack tries to think of the right word without offending her. She's complained about Alan being anal and compulsive. But that's how *she's* been acting lately. He decides on, "You're going to be great."

Laurie nods, exhales. "Did you know the average length of a newborn's umbilical cord is two feet?"

"Huh," Jack says.

She doesn't talk about missing Alan, but Jack knows she does. They speak on the phone, but the calls are short. "I'm fine," she says to Alan. "You're fine?" As far as Jack knows, Alan will be there when the baby is born. "But you never know," Laurie says to Jack. "It's always a good idea to have a backup plan."

Jack's immediate plan is to move back in with Megan once finals are done, so when his parents come down for graduation, they'll see his place and he'll have his own room. (Florence has gotten back with her boyfriend Lance *again*, but she's going to keep paying rent because she has the feeling it might not work out. You think?) His parents will meet Megan and he's sure (hopefully) they'll like her, and she'll like them (probably) and they'll go to graduation and since Laurie's baby is due the week after graduation, his parents will be back up north and never know anything about it.

Is the baby going to look like Jack? Sometimes he thinks that would be cool. A baby version of himself. And then he freaks out—will the baby look enough like him so people would *know*? Like his parents? Suppose his parents come to visit L.A. and they see him with Laurie and the baby? And his mother says, "That's funny. Laurie's baby looks *exactly* like you looked when you were a baby, Jack."

Unless the baby looks like Laurie. Alan would probably—no, *absolutely* prefer that. Why wouldn't he? Jack is anxious for Alan to move back home and he suggested it to Laurie, but she said neither of them were ready for it yet. But when? When the time is right, Laurie says and Jack says that's kind of a bullshitty answer, and Laurie laughs and says that's the best answer she can come up with right now.

Sometimes Jack wonders what would happen if Alan never comes home, if Laurie has the baby and Jack doesn't move out. He'll graduate but go to graduate school in Los Angeles. Laurie won't need a nanny. Jack can be a kind of nanny. A manny. How hard could that be?

Probably really hard. When he looks through Laurie's baby book, he's shocked at how complicated it is to take care of a baby—feeding times and when to introduce solid food and what about colic and diaper rash. How do you ever know the right thing to do? He's asked Megan, who tells him it's no big deal. "Instinct kicks in. Nature. You know, that survival of the fittest shit."

Megan drops by Laurie's house every now and then with care packages for Jack and an occasional baby gift for Laurie. "Sorry, I didn't wrap this," Megan says to Laurie as she pulls a black KISS onesie out of a bag. "Is this insanely adorable or what?"

"I love it." Laurie holds up the onesie and Jack imagines baby Buddy and Laurie at a KISS reunion concert singing along to "Rock and Roll All Nite."

Laurie comes with Jack to see Megan in *The Weir* and afterward tells Megan how good she was. "The play is great, amazing. And you were wonderful. It was sad, but beautiful… I thought they were going to throw me out of the theater I was crying so hard," Laurie says. Megan, who knows about Laurie's miscarriages, gives Laurie a hug.

"If you can't make people cry, what's the point?" Megan says to her.

Laurie is working on a Hidden Valley story she thinks Jack will like, so they drive to a cul-de-sac in a residential neighborhood in Encino where Laurie tells Jack the street is named for Edward Everett Horton, a famous character actor who built a large house here in the '20s called Belleigh Acres. She spells it for him.

"Belly Acres, get it?" Laurie says, and Jack nods. Funny. But he doesn't see anything resembling a big house.

"The house was gorgeous. F. Scott Fitzgerald stayed in the guesthouse for a while. But they tore everything down to build the freeway," Laurie tells him. "Isn't that sad? At least they named the street after him."

Jack looks around at the condos and apartment buildings; he can hear and see the freeway traffic below them.

"I've driven by here a million times. I saw the street sign, but I never knew about the house," Laurie says. "We found some black-and-white photos; they'll be in the next Hidden Valley. You should check out Edward Everett Horton's films or go to YouTube and find *Fractured Fairy Tales*; they're hilarious. He's the narrator. He has the most incredible voice." She looks around again. "And now other people are going to know about this place. That's pretty cool, to take something forgotten and bring it back."

"Very cool," Jack says. He has no idea what *Fractured*

Fairy Tales are, but if Laurie says they're good, he'll check them out.

He is studying on the steps in front of Royce Hall waiting for Megan when he notices Alan standing nearby. Not spying on him from a distance this time. Jack wonders what to do. Pretend he doesn't see him? Before he can decide, Alan walks over. "Nice campus," Alan says as if this is his first visit to UCLA.

"Yeah."

Alan clears his throat. "Laurie doesn't know I'm here. Is she okay?"

"You talk to her. She would've told you if she wasn't."

"I thought because you see her all the time…I wanted to make sure." Alan looks as if he hasn't shaved in a few days and he must not be sleeping well either. Jack doesn't remember bags under Alan's eyes before. "I love her," Alan says. "I know it doesn't seem like it—she's having a baby and I move out. The Facebook thing—that was my fault. But Laurie's reaction… you wouldn't understand how crazy women get."

Jack could tell Alan about Normandie, how he ran into her a week ago on campus and she introduced him to her new boyfriend, Jeb. Jeb is short with a thick neck and freckles. "Jeb's a wrestler," Normandie says, "and he's teaching me all kinds of moves. Want us to show you the double-leg takedown?" She grins at Jeb and he grins back. "Or the cement mixer?" Normandie leans close to Jack and whispers, "You let a good one get away, Jack. Never forget that."

"My loss," he says to her, trying to imagine what the cement mixer looks like.

"It's not as if I'm jealous of you," Alan tells Jack. "It's more about the baby."

"That makes sense," Jack says.

"Sometimes I think it does. But sometimes…not so much." Alan looks at the campus. "I grew up sharing everything—a bedroom, clothes, bikes, ice skates…my parents' attention. Big family, five kids. *Five*. I was the youngest. And that was fine. It's the way it was. Only now, I'm done with that. I want something of my own. Like a child. My child should be mine. Shouldn't it?"

"But it is. Yours and Laurie's."

"Yours too."

"No, I was just the—" Jack's not sure what to say. Sperm or specimen or donor, none of those sound right. "Like when you make cookies, I was the butter." Oh man, *what* did he just say?

Alan seems to weigh that. "But I wanted to be the butter. And the flour and the vanilla. I wanted to be all of it."

They're comparing the baby to *baking*? "But in the end, you still get the cookies," Jack says.

"The cookies." Alan nods, doesn't say anything for a while. "Buddy's going to grow up confused."

"Everybody grows up confused," Jack says. "I'm more worried about changing diapers."

Alan shakes his head. "I don't care about diapers." He looks at Jack. "Are you going to be around? After?"

"I don't know."

"Does Laurie want you to be?"

"She says I should decide what's best for me. And I don't know what that is right now. I mean, I'm a kid. I'm not ready to be a father. Trust me, the last thing I want is to get in your way."

"I'm glad you're taking care of her," Alan says.

"She misses you."

"She told you that?"

"She doesn't have to say anything. I can tell."

Alan runs his hands over his stubby almost beard. "She's never going to forgive me."

"You could give her a chance."

"I miss her so much."

"So let her know. Look, I'm not any kind of expert in relationships—I sort of suck at them, but you and Laurie...it's stupid the way you're acting. When you both love each other and you're having a baby, it's kind of—duh, get over yourselves."

Alan thinks that over and nods at Jack. "What happens after you graduate?"

"I don't know yet," Jack says.

Alan smiles. "Have you ever thought about joining the Peace Corps?"

Laurie

Elephants are pregnant for almost two years. Their babies can weigh 250 pounds at birth. Baby Buddy must weigh at least 250 pounds already. *My marriage might fail*, Laurie tells herself, *but at least I'll make it into the* Guinness Book of World Records. *That's something Buddy can always be proud of.*

Her due date is a week away, and she is impatient and short-tempered, and impatient at being short-tempered. Jack is studying all the time; Alan is calling, but the conversations remain short. Yes, he'll be at the hospital. He hopes she's doing well. Does she need anything? *For us to be living in the same house again*, she'd like to say to him. He is doing the best he can. She knows he is, but honestly, at nine months pregnant, her back constantly aching, her feet too fat for her shoes, sometimes doing the best you can isn't remotely close to being good enough.

Are elephants smart enough to be depressed and impatient during their long pregnancies? She bets there's no Lamaze for elephants. No *pant pant pant*, deep, cleansing breath bullshit. No epidurals either. That must suck. Of course, female elephants probably have supportive male elephants with them during their pregnancy and labor—no, of course they don't. They have mates like Alan—selfish and plotting affairs with other elephants.

Alan tells Laurie he's watched Lamaze videos online so he's caught up. It's exciting; he can't wait. And she believes him, but what will it be like in the delivery room, the two of them together again? Awkward. Will they be cool toward each other?

It feels like years ago, a lifetime ago when she and Alan made the decision. They were traveling, taking advantage of being young and married and eager to go anywhere and try anything. They'd found themselves at the top of a small waterfall in Costa Rica and everything around them was bright green and lush and sauna warm, and they looked down at the bottom of the falls, to a small green/blue circle of water. A few other people were jumping, but Laurie hesitated.

"I'm scared," she said.

"Me too." Alan smiled at her. "You know what? I think we should go to another country."

"What? Are you saying that so I don't have to jump?"

"I'm saying that because I think it's time." He paused. "For a *metaphorical* another country."

Laurie didn't say anything.

"Traveling with you is fantastic," Alan said. "But we need a new adventure."

"All these metaphors, my head can't keep track of them. Are you talking about what I think you're talking about?"

Alan nodded. "A baby."

"A baby."

"You and me. Our baby. It's the next step, right? Part two of our lives?"

Laurie looked down to the pool at the base of the waterfall. It seemed so far away. "Our baby. Yeah, that's some adventure." She grinned at Alan. "I don't know what's scarier—this waterfall or…" She trailed off. "I would love to have a baby," she said.

"So? Are you ready?"

"We have to get pregnant? Right now? Here?"

"No, silly. After. Assuming we survive the fall."

At that moment, Laurie couldn't imagine being married to anyone else. Alan was the man she loved, in spite of his invisible eyebrows. And soon he would be the father of their child.

"The jump part, you can go first," she said.

"No way. We're in this together." He took her hand.

They closed their eyes. And jumped.

Baby Buddy kicks twice—little taps as if he's preparing for one big kick.

"Be patient, Buddy. Like me. Well, not like me. But be patient anyway."

She has to go to Trader Joe's. What should she make for dinner? Jack likes pizza, and it's easy to buy Trader Joe's ready-made pizza dough and add fresh veggies and cheese. The pizza stone in the oven helps too. Of course, that's probably some babyproof kitchen no-no—hasn't she heard about all the children who are knocked unconscious when hot pizza stones fall out of the oven and land on their heads?

She writes down a shopping list for Trader Joe's: dark-chocolate-covered pretzels—she'll only get one bag this time. And not vegetable pizza tonight. Prosciutto and mozzarella. She'll be good and have one slice. Or two. Buddy kicks again, and she takes that as a sign. *Yes, Buddy. I'll have two slices of pizza. After all, you're a growing boy.*

Alan

The lady at the Safe-Tee Baby store shows him the choke tube tester. "Babies put everything in their mouths," she explains. "*Everything.*" She drops two marbles inside the plastic tube where they fit easily. "See?" She nods ominously.

Alan wonders how children ever survived without a choke tube tester. *Shouldn't our planet be extinct?*

"This is our most popular newborn toy," she says as she holds up a brightly colored stuffed horse and rider. "Sir Prance-a-lot." She makes the horse gallop on the counter. Alan reads the attached tag:

> *Sir Prance-a-lot to the rescue! Clip this whimsical activity toy to your stroller or car seat, and it will keep baby busy wherever you go. Crinkle, jingle, clack, squeak, touch… we're off on a learning adventure! This darling baby horse toy features a vibrant mix of colors, textures, teethers, ribbons, knots, and activities, all carefully designed to stimulate baby's senses.*

"And you want to make sure to stimulate your baby's senses, don't you?" the clerk says.

No, he'll let baby Buddy grow up in a room with no

light, no music, no physical touch, no crinkle, jingle, clack, or squeak sounds. Buddy's life will be an interesting social experiment. He's sure Laurie will go along with the idea.

"You've got all your baby gates and knob guards and toilet locks? Because an accident can happen like *that*." The clerk snaps her fingers.

"How many children do you have?" Alan asks her.

"None. Not yet," she says. "Do you need anything gift wrapped?"

Alan declines; he'll wrap everything himself. Laurie has always accused him of being inept at wrapping presents. He'll look for online tips, wrap the baby gifts so cleverly she'll think he's had them done professionally, and when he tells her *he's* done it, she won't believe him. She'll fall in his arms and the past few weeks will be forgotten.

Unless Jack is there and wants to watch Laurie open presents and Jack will sit close to her and laugh at Sir Prance-a-lot and the choke tube tester—who would choose dumb baby presents like that?

Friends at work talk about buying their wives "push presents" to reward them for giving birth—pearl necklaces, diamond tennis bracelets. Laurie isn't a big jewelry person, but Alan found a silver necklace with a tiny diamond cross. Very subtle, elegant, and pretty. A push present or a "forgive me for screwing up big time" present? Both? He'll wrap up the baby presents, keep the diamond cross necklace in his pocket, and give it to her after the baby is born. But tonight he'll stop by a florist and Laurie's favorite Thai food place. Show up at the house and surprise her.

Back at his apartment, he wraps presents using a "Wrap the Perfect Gift" site he's found on the web. *Laurie will be impressed*, he thinks as he makes perfect flaps for one end of the box. He wonders if Laurie's called today, and he reaches in his pocket for his BlackBerry, but it's not there and he has a flash of seeing it on the counter at the Safe-Tee Baby store. Damn. He could call, but the store is probably closed. He'll stop by in the morning.

He returns to his wrapping. The other end of the box looks as good as the first.

He can't wait to see the look on Laurie's face.

Jack

It's time to tell them," Subhra says on the phone. "They're going to be grandparents. They have a right to know."

"No, they don't. And you promised—"

"But I'm excited. I'm almost an aunt. Do you feel like a father?" Subhra asks him.

"Not really. Maybe a little." He's explained how Alan moved out and Subhra asks what kind of man would desert his wife when she's about to have a baby. Jack defends Alan—he didn't desert Laurie. It was sort of a mutual decision.

Subhra remains skeptical. "So now Laurie is depending on *you* for emotional support?"

"I shouldn't have told you any of this," he says.

"Sorry—I didn't mean that about the emotional support. I'm sure you've been terrific. And I'm sorry I'm missing your graduation. Mom's promised to take tons of pictures. Dad bought a new video camera. Hey, maybe they could stay in L.A. until the baby is born."

"You're starting to make me crazy. I have to study now. It would suck if Mom and Dad show up and I don't graduate."

"Yeah," Subhra says. "I can hear Mom screaming from here. I think I'm going to tell them about the you-know-what. Bye."

She hangs up before he can protest.

Heterodoxy and orthodoxy and heresy. Not exactly a jolly good time. But he studies for two hours straight, no breaks. Not for TV or Facebook, and only one visit today to YouTube to watch *Fractured Fairy Tales* ("Leaping Beauty," very funny). But now he's hunkered down, his brain feels sharp, he's focused—he's going to *ace* this, make Mr. Bryant *eat* his A. *Fuck you, Professor Asshat.*

Laurie doesn't interrupt him. She seems to know when he's seriously studying versus when he's studying and desperate for distraction. What's her life going to be like when the baby comes? He's asked her if she's worried about how her life will change.

"Sometimes it feels scary," she says. "The responsibility."

"Yeah. We did that thing in high school, where you carry a sack of flour around for a week like it's a baby, and it was really hard."

"How did you do?"

Jack hesitates. "I left my flour baby in my locker one night."

Laurie looks at Jack. Oh well. Good-bye manny job. "My friend Drew used his flour baby as a football," Jack says. "He failed. I got a B-minus because even though I left it in my locker, I fed it most of the time. Some flour babies starved."

Laurie smiles. "I hope I don't do that. But suppose I feed Buddy *too* much? And how do I sleep at night when I'm worrying about SIDS?" She takes a deep breath. "Or suppose Alan never comes home."

"He's coming home," Jack says.

"How do you know?"

"Because he's having a baby." Simple answer. That seems to satisfy Laurie. A little.

His final is in two days. He maps out his study plan and tacks it to the bulletin board above Alan's desk. Megan texts words of encouragement. "U will ACE this!" "U R a SCHOLAR ROCK STAR!"

He's ordered his graduation gown and tried it on for Laurie. She tells him he looks "quite the professional." He wishes he knew what kind of professional he'll turn out to be.

If he'd known months ago he'd finally be graduating and having a baby, he would've said that was bullshit. But here he is—a soon-to-be graduate and a father. Who knew?

When Laurie goes to Trader Joe's, he loads the dishwasher. Afterward, he walks into the baby's room. The changing table is ready to go, baby wipes and diapers handy. The sea creature mobile is hooked on the crib rail, and Jack pushes the button to make it spin. It plays "Under the Sea" from *The Little Mermaid*. Everything in the room is waiting for the baby—stuffed animals on a shelf on the wall, a diaper pail that smells vaguely sweet, like cherry. The room feels cozy and comfortable—a room version of a womb. The transition won't be too tough for Buddy, Jack hopes.

But Jack is wasting time; he's got studying to do. He'd really like to take a nap, but as Margery Kempe would say, "As for patience, it is worth far more than the working of miracles."

Delivery

Everyone at the hospital is friendly and efficient—*another day at the baby delivery office*, Laurie thinks. It's like working at a car wash—a car pulls in, gets soaped up, a good scrub, a rinse, dried off, the car drives away, another one arrives.

But this is my life, we're not talking about a clean car. I'm having a baby, she wants to say to the nurses. *Do you know what I've gone through? Now something miraculous and extraordinary and impossibly astonishing is about to happen. Look at me, I'm in labor, I'm bringing my child into the world.* I am not a car.

"I know you're not a car," Jack says, and Laurie realizes she's said the last part out loud. "How do you feel?" he asks her.

"Like I'm having a baby. Did Alan call?"

"Not yet." Jack smiles, but she isn't reassured. She looks around the hospital room at the blinking monitors. "I should've done a water birth," she says.

"That's his heartbeat." Jack points to a monitor, and Laurie watches Buddy's EKG line move up and down.

The idea of Buddy being hooked up to a fetal monitor while he's still waiting to make his appearance is disconcerting. They say it doesn't hurt him, but how would they know? What is Buddy thinking about right now? Is he scared of the contractions? Or has he figured it out—"*finally* I'm getting out of here"?

"They told me to take a nap," Jack says. "Like I could sleep." He laughs, his voice higher-pitched than usual. "Do you need anything?"

"My iPod."

"You should've let me do your playlist."

"I'm not sure Viking metal is how I want to bring Buddy into the world." Laurie feels the beginning of another contraction. The contractions are like period cramps, but deeper, more intense.

Jack notices. "Does it hurt a lot?"

"Don't talk about pain in a negative way," Laurie says. "You need to help me embrace it, make it a positive part of the birthing experience."

"Yeah, I heard that in your class, but it sounded like bullshit."

Laurie frowns at Jack. "I *want* to believe it's true, that I can ride these contractions like waves in the ocean, but you might be right. Wait a minute." She remembers something. "Before I passed out, did you say something about your parents? They're on their way?"

Jack sighs. "I was hoping you forgot. I'm hoping they get lost. Or maybe there'll be a gigantic traffic jam and you can have the baby and get home before they show up."

"What are the chances of that?"

Jack forces a smile. "What are the chances of anything?"

Laurie's car is in the driveway, but she doesn't answer the door. Alan is standing on the front porch with flowers, Thai takeout, and the bag of newly wrapped baby gifts. Jack's car isn't here. He could be at class. Unless he's moved out. Oh well, more Thai food for Alan and Laurie.

He looks in the living room window. The last time he was here, he was sneaking around like a criminal. But he is bold now—bold and reformed and soon to be reunited with his wife.

He rings the doorbell again and waits. No sound from inside. She could be asleep, but it's early. He can't hear the TV, so he doesn't think she's in the den. Has something happened? She was reaching for a mixing bowl on the top shelf in the kitchen, and she fell and can't get to her phone? It's not breaking in if it's *his* house.

When he walks inside, everything is quiet—no TV, no music, everything is still.

"Laurie?"

Silence. He checks the kitchen first, but Laurie isn't there. She's not in the den or the bedrooms or the bathrooms. That's good, he tells himself. She isn't hurt; she's fine. She's just not home. Maybe she's having dinner with Grace. Alan could call Grace; he reaches for his cell, remembers he doesn't have it. When he goes back in the kitchen, he notices Laurie's Trader Joe's reusable shopping bag on the kitchen table. It's the one with surfboards and always makes Alan think of mai tais. He glances inside.

Chocolate-covered pretzels, one bag already opened. Some prosciutto, mozzarella cheese, pizza dough. Why aren't the perishables in the refrigerator? Laurie is a maniac about putting away food, whisking leftover cooked chicken from the counter into Tupperware and refrigerating it immediately, "So we don't drop dead of food poisoning." It's not like her to leave food out.

He looks around the kitchen—except for the Trader Joe's bag, everything seems normal.

He goes in the bedroom again. Did she leave behind any clues? There's a printed list on the bedside table. At the top it reads, "Birthing Bag." There's a check mark beside it. Alan opens the closet door—the Ed Hardy carry-on bag is gone.

"You'd think they'd have a TV in your room," Jack says to Laurie.

"You'd think somebody facing a big exam would be studying for it."

"I'm prepared. Plus I've got more adrenaline now because of the baby, so I'm extra confident."

"You don't want to be overconfident."

"If you make me paranoid about being overconfident, I'll flunk."

"No, you're going to make at least an A," she says. "Or something higher than an A, if that exists. Do you want to talk about heresy some more? I can relate, since I feel like I'm being roasted on a spit."

A nurse with bright blue eye shadow opens the door.

"Good news. The grandparents are here," she says to Jack. "They're in the waiting room. I'm sure you want to see them."

Jack looks at Laurie. "I'm being roasted on a spit too," he says.

Alan doesn't like to pray out loud. Except in church. Except now when he's driving over the hill to the hospital. "I made some mistakes, God, I admit it," he says. "Some real whoppers. But I'll change. Please let Laurie be okay. Laurie and the baby."

He's driving badly; if he gets pulled over, he'll be arrested because they'll think he's drunk. Not like those scenes in movies where kindly cops escort sweaty, expectant fathers to the hospital, lights flashing, sirens blaring. No, Alan will be handcuffed, sentenced to life in prison, no chance of parole. He'll never meet baby Buddy and spend the rest of his life as Big Al's bitch.

He called the hospital from the landline in the house to confirm Laurie is there. The nurse says she's doing fine. But is that what she tells everybody? What else would she say? "Your wife's at death's door, the umbilical cord is wrapped around the baby's neck, and the baby's vestigial tail—well, whoops, not so vestigial, it's *three feet long*, but no worries; perhaps he'll grow up to be a gymnast and his tail will come in handy on the high bar"?

Suppose Laurie tells him to go away? She doesn't need him; she's got Jack. Why would she need Alan? Because he is her husband, dammit. And to hell with the genetic component, the specimen switch—he is going to be a father.

He rolls that around in his brain. He's driving to the hospital where his wife is in labor. And in a few hours, he'll be holding his child.

His wife. His child.

"I'm going to be a father," he says. Not noticing the *thunk thunk* sound of his flat tire.

Jack's parents aren't sitting; they're pacing, and Jack has a moment where he thinks about running away—away from his parents, out of the hospital, out of Los Angeles. He could hitch a ride, hop on a train—do people still hop on trains? Is there a train running anywhere near Cedars-Sinai Hospital?

When his parents turn to him, he sees they're not alone. Megan is standing between them. When she notices Jack, she runs over and kisses him.

"You must be scared shitless," she says.

Contractions are about grammar, Laurie thinks. You eliminate one letter, add an apostrophe, and squish the words together. Voila, a contraction. Do not becomes *don't*. They are becomes *they're*. What do they have to do with having a baby? Laurie was taught in Lamaze about contractions and muscle groups, and yes, labor is painful, but women continue to have children over and over again, so how painful could it be?

They left out the part that explains how labor feels like dogs chewing on your entrails. How contractions build slowly, not bad at first, and then they come faster and stronger and you are thinking, *Okay, I can handle this one*, and then there is the peak and Laurie thinks dogs chewing your entrails might feel better. She could ask the nurse her opinion, but she is too busy screaming.

"You're doing great, Laurie," the nurse says.

You are, Laurie wants to correct her. *If I get through this, contractions will never be part of my life again. I won't ever use a contraction again.*

She corrects herself. *I will not.*

When Alan pulls into the hospital parking lot, the attendant shakes his head. "You really screwed up that rim, dude." Alan nods at him. He couldn't be bothered to change the tire. How badly could he screw up his car anyway? He got used to the thunking sound after a mile or so and then when the rubber wore away, the sound of metal on pavement. *I wonder if I'm making sparks*, he thought.

"You got everything?" the attendant calls out to him as he starts to get out of the car.

"Thanks," Alan says, and he reaches back into his car to get Laurie's presents.

"Your parents are fantastic," Megan says to Jack. "Why didn't you tell me how fantastic they are?"

Jack meets his mother's eyes. He's expecting some sort of death ray that will turn him to salt or melting ectoplasm, but she's smiling at him—a gentle smile, nothing insidious behind it. So far.

"Subhra called us," his mother says. She shakes her head. Jack's not sure how to interpret the shake—disappointment? Resignation?

"Subhra called me too. She's really bummed she can't come," Megan tells Jack. "A doctor, *whoa*." Megan squeezes Jack's mother's arm. "Anjali told me all about her."

Megan is calling Jack's mother by her first name. Why does it feel as if the world is about to end?

"Subhra filled us in. On everything. You should have let us know about your situation," his mother says.

Situation. That's what his mother is going to call it? He looks over at his father.

"Your mother's right. We would have been happy to assist in any way." Jack's father nods at Jack.

"I wasn't sure how to explain it."

"You know you can always tell us anything." And before

he can say anything, his mother is throwing her arms around him and hugging him tightly. For a small woman she's strong, and he bets she could crush his ribs if she wanted. "Don't worry," she says. "We're here."

Laurie is in a cave. It is not a friendly Flintstones cave; it is more like the one in the movie where the guy is trapped by a rock and has to cut off his arm. When she saw the movie, she did not understand how anyone could ever be pushed to that point. *Oh, but now I get it, James Franco.* Of course you cut off your arm, you would have cut off your leg or your head and that is probably why they do not have any knives in delivery rooms because they are well aware that women in labor would happily saw away at any body part they could get their hands on, they would do *anything* to lessen the pain.

"How're you doing, Laurie?" the nurse asks. "Would you like some more ice chips?"

An ice pick. That could work. "Yes," she says. "I would very much like an ice pick."

Alan is directed to the waiting room; a nurse will speak with him and take him to Laurie. He's not surprised to see Jack but is surprised to see Jack embracing a petite Indian woman. She has short, black hair and she's wearing khaki pants and a navy turtleneck. A man stands nearby; he's tall, like Jack, slender and handsome, in jeans and a Stanford sweatshirt.

Megan spots Alan first. She pulls Jack away from his mother. She whispers to Jack, but Alan can hear her. "Red alert, creepy stalker husband finally showed."

"Hello." Alan waves, awkward with all the things in his arms. Everyone is looking at him as if he's going to say something profound. "I've got Thai food," he says.

Before anyone responds, a nurse with blue eye shadow appears. "Laurie is getting lonely. She could use her birth coach."

Alan doesn't say anything. Neither does Jack. They look at each other for a minute, not sure what to do.

Alan hands the food and gifts to Megan, reaches for Jack's elbow. "That's us," he says.

Jack looks as if he's about to protest, but instead he follows Alan.

Laurie is thinking about pushing. Thinking about pushing will help her stop thinking about contractions. She is trying to remain positive. Well, as positive as she can possibly be, especially in this delightful position, her legs spread wide, the view on one hand *Penthouse* pornographic, on the other, just another day in the life of Dr. Liu and the nurses. Laurie already is sure she is making medical history and will end up featured on *Inside Edition*. "Go on, Buddy," she says to the baby. "Come out with feathered wings. So far everything else has been extraordinary. You do not want to disappoint anyone with some kind of boring, typical birth, do you?"

She is still not using contractions. Scary.

"Some people are here to see you," Dr. Liu says, and Laurie thinks he means the team from *Inside Edition*. "Pardon me," she will say to the news crew. "I do not usually meet people with my legs wide open."

Alan appears by the hospital bed. He reaches for Laurie's

arm, but it's taped to the side for the IV. He settles for patting her hand. What can he say to make her smile, make her glad to see him? "Pretty funny, running into you in a place like this," he tells her.

A stupid joke, that figures, Laurie thinks. But it is Alan; he is here—beside her. A good thing. And someone else is speaking. Jack.

"Remember that scene in the *Alien* movie?" Jack says.

Laurie sees Alan shake his head at Jack. Do not talk about the *Alien* movie, not a good idea. Laurie wants to tell Alan that is okay, talk about the *Alien* movie. Should she tell him to get out of the way of the *Inside Edition* crew?

"It's time to push," Dr. Liu says.

It *is* time to push. Say it the right way. But pushing is the good part, what she has been waiting for, the part that means the pain is almost over, and when she is done with the pain, she will get the best reward ever.

Alan and Jack are holding her hands. "Hang in there, honey, you're doing great," Alan says.

"Don't forget to breathe," Jack tells her. "And vocalize. Huh huh huh," he says to her.

"Huh, huh, huh," Laurie repeats.

"Two birth coaches, how'd you get so lucky?" Dr. Liu says. "One more big push."

How did *you get so lucky and I do not know if I can push one more time. If I do I am afraid I will push out the baby* and *my spine and all my organs, and that might not be a good thing, except at least Jack will get his* Alien *wish.*

"That's the way, honey." Alan has moved to the foot of the hospital bed. "I can see the head. Jack, come look."

Jack turns to Laurie. "No worries," he says. "I'm fine here." He breathes along with Laurie.

"He has dark hair," Alan announces. "A lot of hair."

"Better than a baldy," Jack says. "I know people say all babies are cute, but not the bald ones."

"Huh huh." Laurie will love the baby if he is bald or if he has a lot of hair or if his head is covered with Bermuda grass.

"Good job, Laurie," Dr. Liu says. He is bent between her legs, and she wonders if the baby will shoot out like a rocket or she will hear a dramatic sound—a balloon popping.

"Oh...there's more of his head. I can see more of the head, oh oh oh." Alan can barely make words.

"Huh huh." *This is crowning*, Laurie thinks. *They should give me a scepter.* She wants to laugh, but she is not in her body; she is hovering above the room, watching Alan at her feet, intent on the delivery, watching Jack, who is pale, a scared smile frozen on his face. They are both in the room. Waiting for the baby.

It does not sound like a balloon popping and Laurie is not sure she hears anything; instead, she feels her body relaxing and the sensation of something slithering, wet and slippery, and she realizes her baby is born.

Alan and Jack are silent, but Laurie isn't worried, and *hallelujah*, she realizes she's using contractions again. Nurses are moving around her and Dr. Liu appears with a tiny pink and purple body, limbs flailing, bigger than a kitten, but making kitten sounds all the same. The baby is shiny and new, and his fists are clenched together close to his chest. His eyes are shut, and he's frowning as if he's annoyed at the fuss.

"Hello, Buddy," Laurie says as Dr. Liu puts the baby into Laurie's arms. He feels warm and small and very wiggly.

"I don't think he's a Buddy," Alan says. He is holding Laurie's hand again.

"Yeah," Jack agrees. "He looks more like a Buddette."

Buddy is a she. A girl. Years from now, will she talk about this in therapy? "Yeah, my parents must have wanted a boy." "No," Laurie will tell her. "We wanted a baby. We wanted *you*."

And will she believe that? She'll probably say something like, "Oh, great. Like it wasn't hard enough growing up with three parents instead of two." And Laurie and Alan will tell her life is full of unexpected things. Their daughter will roll her eyes, her eyes that are a combination of Laurie's and Jack's, but also the attitude of Alan's. She is a combination of all three of them.

Laurie is breast-feeding the baby in her hospital room. Alan and Jack are with her, watching closely, as if they're afraid they'll miss something. "I read somewhere men are able to breast-feed," she tells them. Alan and Jack shudder. "Yeah, exactly the reaction I would have expected. Don't want to give it a try?"

"Nope," says Alan.

"I'll take a pass," says Jack.

After feeding the baby is done, she asks Alan and Jack if they'd like to hold the baby. They glance at each other—who should go first?

"Don't make me flip a coin," Laurie says.

Alan steps forward and takes the baby. He holds her as if she's made of glass. "She's so light," he says. When Alan speaks, her eyes open. Big and brown, she looks right at Alan as if she's heard his voice before. "Hello," he says to her. "Welcome, pretty girl." Everything about her is so perfect, so new. He doesn't think he will ever be able to let her go.

Jack is standing by the window. "I'm not sure I should hold her," he says. "I read all that stuff where you have to support her neck—suppose I don't and her head flops back?" Jack shudders.

Alan looks at Jack. He pulls the baby closer to his chest. Jack is waiting for *his* turn.

"Don't worry," Laurie is saying to Jack. "People know how to hold babies; it's automatic."

Jack shakes his head. He doesn't believe her.

Why does Alan have to give the baby to Jack? Isn't she *his* daughter now? Alan looks down at the baby. Dark eyes and black hair—he has never seen anything so beautiful. Yesterday he was childless. Three hours ago he was childless. And now—he realizes someone will have to teach this baby, this little girl how to ride a bike. Learn to scramble an egg. Drive a car. Go on dates. No, he will never let her go on dates. Unless he comes along as a chaperone.

"Alan?" Laurie says to him. He knows what she's thinking—she's going to tell him to give the baby to Jack. But suppose he doesn't? Suppose he runs out of the hospital room and takes the baby back to his apartment? They'll live there together, the two of them.

Alan sees Jack watching him. *Does Jack know I'm planning an escape? Suppose the baby is more comfortable with Jack than with me? And Laurie will be able to tell and I'll never be able to hold her again.*

He shouldn't have thoughts like this anymore—worrying about Jack is old Alan behavior. New, improved Alan makes the right choices, even if they aren't easy. Gallant, not Goofus.

He walks over to Jack and gently lays the baby in his arms. "Be careful," he says to Jack. "Don't let her float away."

Jack cradles the baby; he wants to make sure she's safe, but he doesn't want to crush her either. Her head seems safe though, not at all floppy. Whew. He breathes out, then in again. He has a baby in his arms. She's making soft sounds, *coo coo*.

"Coo coo," Jack says back to her.

"She likes you," Laurie says.

"She's just waiting to throw up on me," Jack says. He cradles the baby in one arm. Takes his finger and touches her nose. "She's like a miniature person," he says softly.

No one notices when Alan slips out of the room.

The next day, the room is filled with flowers and balloons; Palmer-Boone has sent a fruit basket and bottles of Choc-O. Sir Prance-a-lot sits on the table by Laurie's bed. Jack's parents are here with Jack. Laurie is wearing her new cross necklace and fielding phone calls from various parents and friends. Grace has called twice, texted at least a dozen times, and sent email pictures of Grace, Hal, and Emilie holding up a handwritten sign that says, "Welcome to the world!" Laurie's mother wants more photos of the baby—what about Skype? "Maybe later," Laurie says. "What's the use of technology if you don't embrace it?" Laurie's mother asks her.

Jack's mother produces a plastic bag and begins to pull out cardboard cartons. "I saw what they wanted to give you for lunch," she says to Laurie, "and I thought I could do better."

"I don't know if I should have Indian food," Laurie tells her.

"Indian? It's Thai. Your husband said it was your favorite."

"Thank you," Laurie says. "Where's Alan?"

"We were talking about baseball," Jack's father says. "He's a big Dodgers fan." Jack's father shakes his head and makes a face.

"Rakesh, go find Laurie's husband," Jack's mother says. "He should eat too." Jack's father goes out, and Jack's mother smiles at Laurie. Laurie is suddenly self-conscious about breast-feeding—is she doing something wrong?

"The baby has a good appetite." Jack's mother sits on the bed beside Laurie. "Jack and his sister did too. Jack more than Subhra. I was afraid he was going to weigh forty pounds at six months." Jack's mother grins at Jack and Laurie sees Jack's face—the guileless smile, perfect teeth. Jack blushes and looks down at his feet. "Don't be embarrassed. Breast-feeding is natural, isn't that right, Laurie?"

"Yes, Mrs. Mulani."

"Anjali."

The food smells good, pra ram and chicken satay, tom yum soup. Jack's mother nods at Jack. "Where's your girlfriend? You should see if she's hungry." Jack explains Megan had to leave because she has an audition for *Julius Caesar* and she's told him the girl parts suck and she really wants to be Cassius—"I could have a lean and hungry look," she said to Jack.

Jack's mother turns to Laurie. "It's nice your first is a girl. They're easier. They listen more. But boys—they're more unpredictable. Which isn't a bad thing. Most of the time." She laughs a pretty, musical laugh. "We are so proud of Subhra, and we love her very much. And Jack too, of course." Jack's mother smiles at Jack again. "What Jack does is always so…his journey will never be a dull one."

Jack's mother walks over to Jack and hugs him again—his ribs seem intact, and he's not exactly sure what all the hugging is about, but he'll roll with it. His mother whispers in his ear, "You're still going to graduate, aren't you?"

Alan is in the hallway; his parents called and he couldn't hear them over the noise in the room. They asked about the baby, how much she weighs, how could he forget how long she is, didn't he write it down? And what does she look like? Take a photo and send it right away. We need to see her. "I will," he promises and clicks off, thinking it might be better if he talks to them again *before* he sends the photo so his parents will have some advance knowledge about why the baby doesn't look exactly (or remotely) like him. He's using Laurie's cell and notices she's already taken pictures of the baby. He could send his parents one of these. He scrolls through her photos, back through weeks and weeks, then months and months. The story of two years of their lives, going backward.

For the first photo, Laurie held the phone out, so they'd both be in the shot. They're standing in front of their house, their arms around each other. Except Alan has a piece of ice in his hand, and he's waiting to drop it down the back of Laurie's shirt.

Two years ago. *We were younger, thinner. Life was a glass half full.* He remembers standing at the top of a waterfall in Costa Rica, telling Laurie it was time to start a new adventure. And now…here it is.

Jack's father appears. "My wife sent me to find you. She brought lunch," he says.

"I was on the phone with my parents," Alan says. He's not sure what else to say. What is his relationship with this man—have they become some oddball version of in-laws?

"Your daughter is beautiful. A nice disposition, you can already tell."

"That's good." Alan nods at Jack's father.

"This is certainly a big surprise. For all of us."

"No kidding." The understatement of the century.

Jack's father shrugs. "But—that's life. You never know what you're going to get. Or what will happen. My daughter, a doctor. My son, a father. None of us, we never know. What can you do?"

What can you do?

"I don't have any idea what to do. I'm lost," Alan says.

Jack's father points down the hallway. "Your daughter. She's waiting for you."

The nurse tells them there are too many people in the room and they shouldn't be eating Thai food, but Jack's mother bribes her with coconut ice cream and the nurse says she has some work to do, and when she comes back in ten minutes, wink wink, she hopes Laurie will be resting. Alan is sitting at the foot of the bed eating Thai food and looking at the baby in Laurie's arms.

Jack's mother collects empty plates and cartons and nods at her husband. "We should leave the parents alone," she says. "If you need anything, Laurie, let us know. We'll be at our hotel."

Laurie nods. Jack's mother and father start out, but Jack lingers in the doorway. He's watching the baby.

"Jack. Your final," Laurie says. "Kick ass."

"I will." He still doesn't move—a last look at the baby, at Laurie. "If the baby gets fussy, you could sing that song to her," he says. "You know, the 'World on a String' one."

"That's a great idea. Thank you," Laurie says to him. "For everything."

The nurses have taken the baby away and Laurie sips a Choc-O. "You disappeared," she says to Alan.

He nods at her.

"Were you planning on coming back?" she asks him.

"Did you want me to come back?"

Laurie doesn't answer him. She looks around the room instead. "It already feels empty. Without her in here." She turns to Alan. "She needs to grow up with a father. With you."

"Those aren't necessarily the same things."

"Of course they are. But you have to think they are."

Alan looks over at the empty crib. "My apartment is nice."

"Did you get the one with the haunted dishwasher?"

"They fixed it—or maybe they did an exorcism."

They look at each other for a long time. "Now what?" Alan says.

Laurie shrugs. "It's not just about us anymore. Us used to be only you and me."

"Us got bigger." Alan smiles at Laurie. "You look pretty good for somebody who just popped out a baby."

"'Popped out a baby' isn't remotely close to the reality of labor and delivery. Trust me."

"I do," Alan says, and he kisses her, not on the cheek, but on the lips. His breath is lemony from the tom yum soup.

She pulls him into the bed with her.

"I bet this isn't allowed," he says.

"What are they going to do?"

"You've never heard of hospital jail?" Alan says, and she laughs.

"I missed your jokes," she tells him.

"My jokes? You must have a fever."

"I'm serious. I missed them. And your dirty socks." She hesitates. "I can't do this by myself," she tells him. "Raise a baby."

"Sure you can. You're invincible. One of the strongest, most capable people I know."

"No. I need you. She does too."

Alan is silent.

"By the way, she could also use a name," Laurie says.

"I thought we decided. Jessica Alba Gaines. Works for me."

Laurie shakes her head, leans against Alan. He feels warm and solid and familiar. He feels *right*. "When can we take her home?" she asks him.

Eight-week-old Lee Asha Gaines rests against Laurie's shoulder. The yellow room, now officially the baby's room, is crowded with toys and stuffed animals and baby bathtubs and a bunch of things Jack can't even identify. On a shelf are various stuffed Indian dolls he doesn't remember seeing before.

"They're from my friend Grace," Laurie tells him. "You haven't met her yet, but you will. She's dying to meet you. And furious with me because I didn't tell her what was going on. Aren't they beautiful?" Laurie looks at the dolls. "Grace found them at an antique store in Canoga Park. I like the one with the woman holding a sitar."

"I think it's a sarod, not a sitar," Jack says. He's watching Laurie rock the baby in the glider.

"What am I going to do with you, missy?" Laurie brushes her lips against the top of baby Lee's head and takes a deep breath. Why does a baby's head smell like heaven? "It's time for your nap."

"She doesn't want to miss anything," Jack says.

"But I've run out of verses of 'He's Got the Whole World in His Hands.' I suppose I could make up my own." Laurie begins to sing. "He's got Elmo and diaper rash, in his hands. He's got Big Bird and A&D Ointment, in his hands."

Jack starts to laugh and the baby turns at the sound.

"Great, now she'll never go to sleep. You're distracting her." Laurie sings again, "He's got Beyoncé and poopy diapers, in his hands..."

"What's with the 'he' business? Shouldn't you sing 'she' sometimes?"

"Oh no. Your religious studies minor is rearing its ugly head."

Laurie and Alan have invited Jack and Megan over for dinner. Alan and Megan are in the kitchen cooking—occasionally Laurie hears the sound of a dropped pan then laughter. "Megan's not the greatest cook," Jack has warned Laurie. "She tries though. So cut her some slack."

That sounds ominous, but Laurie nods. "I'm just happy you're both here." After his graduation, Jack and Megan moved into an apartment together. Jack is working as a waiter at an Umami Burger in Santa Monica and taking a GRE prep class. He's still undecided about what he'll do in graduate school. Religious studies might not be the best idea. Maybe psychology. Megan is auditioning for plays and commercials and trying out to be a game-show contestant so she can win a new car or a Vespa. No luck yet.

"My mother sent you a present," Jack says as he hands Laurie a small package. "You wanted to know if she sang to me when I was little, so I asked her and she got you this."

Laurie opens the package to find a CD of Indian lullabies. "Wow. I don't know anything about Indian lullabies."

"In India, a lullaby is called a *lori*. Isn't that weird? Lori. Like Laurie?" Jack nods at Laurie. *Get it?*

Laurie waves the CD. "Maybe if we pop this in the CD player, she'll fall asleep. You think?"

"Can't hurt to try." Jack puts the CD into the CD player on the top of the changing table. The music begins—a woman sings; her voice is high and silvery and beautiful.

"What a gorgeous voice. But I wish I could understand what she's saying." Laurie strokes Lee's dark hair, so much hair for a baby. And it's already curly—no need to dress her in pink to prove she's a girl.

"My mother said there are lots of lullabies about the moon." Jack looks at the liner notes and reads. "*So Ja Chanda. So ja chanda raja so ja, chal sapnon mein chal.*" He reads the translation: "Sleep, my lovely moonchild; sleep, my prince. Come to the world of dreams, come."

"That's pretty," Laurie says. "Although Lee's a princess, not a prince."

"You should learn the song."

Laurie laughs. "Me? I think that's impossible. "

"I bet my mother would help you. Hey, look, she likes it." Jack might be right—baby Lee turns her head to the music as if she's listening.

Dinner is not the disaster Jack has predicted. Megan has made her Famous Mystery Meatballs and Spaghetti.

"What's the mystery?" Laurie asks her.

"If I told you, it wouldn't be a mystery anymore," Megan says.

Laurie turns to Alan. Does he know the secret?

He shrugs. "I just did the salad." He looks over to Lee in the baby swing. Jack and Megan have each tried to make her sleep with zero success. The swing runs on batteries, so it moves back and forth by itself. Lee looks like she'd be happy swinging until the batteries wear out.

"I think she's excited because she has company for dinner," Megan says. "She's pretty incredible."

"Not so much at three in the morning," Alan says. And he winks at Laurie.

"We're taking turns with the feedings," Laurie explains to Megan and Jack. "Alan's a whiz at warming up breast milk."

"Less of a whiz at getting up in the middle of the night. But you adapt." He watches baby Lee.

Laurie takes a bite of the meatball and to her surprise, it's good. Although there's something sweet she can't identify. "I can taste turkey, Megan. And parsley. Onion, maybe a little garlic and oregano."

"Yep." Megan glances over at the baby. "It's crazy how big she is already. And I love her name. The Lee came from you, right, Alan?"

"Alan Lee Gaines," Alan says. "My mother says Lee has been in our family for years. And she insists we might be related to Robert E. Lee." His mother, when he finally told her the truth, was thrilled and couldn't wait to visit California and see the baby. But she also wanted to meet Jack and learn more about his roots. Just what the family tree needed—not only Abraham Lincoln, but a connection to India.

"Where'd Asha come from? Was that your idea, Jack?" Megan asks.

Jack shakes his head. "Not me."

"Alan got a baby book," Laurie explains. "He thought it would be nice for the baby's middle name to be Indian."

"So why'd you pick Asha?"

Alan looks at Laurie. He doesn't say anything right away. "Because it means hope."

When Jack and Megan are leaving, Laurie, with the baby in her arms, whispers to Jack. "What's the mystery ingredient in the meatballs?" Jack makes sure Megan can't hear and whispers quickly to Laurie. "Crushed up Skittles." Laurie makes a face. "I know," Jack says, misinterpreting Laurie's expression. "Isn't that genius?" He leans over to give baby Lee a kiss on the cheek. "See you soon, peanut," he says, and he runs after Megan. Baby Lee watches him go.

Laurie closes the front door and looks at Alan, at the baby. "Suppose she decides to never go to sleep again?"

"I think the chances of that are about a zillion to one. Do you want me to start on dishes?" Alan asks.

"Let's wait. I can do them in the morning."

"Want me to give the sleep thing a try?" Alan holds out his arms for the baby. "Would you like to dance?" he says to baby Lee. The music is still playing from dinner—Laurie picked Frank Sinatra and Jack groaned until Megan shoved him and said Frank Sinatra was an icon and he should appreciate that.

"You won't sleep for your mother, but you'll be good for your old man, won't you?"

"I don't know if dancing with her will put her to sleep," Laurie says.

Alan does a spin, then a dip.

"Alan, stop it, you're going to make her *more* excited." But Laurie can't help herself from grinning at the sight of a grown man dancing with an infant.

"She's having a great time. Maybe when she grows up, she'll be a ballroom dancer." He dips her again and the baby giggles. "We could be a team, father and daughter."

"Good luck with that." Laurie watches the two of them together. And baby Lee does seem as if she's having a great time. Suddenly Laurie draws in her breath. "Did you see that?"

"What?"

"She smiled at you."

"No, she didn't," Alan says. He looks at Lee. "She's not old enough. Babies don't smile for weeks and weeks. Not real smiles."

"It's *been* weeks and weeks. Spin her again. And watch."

Alan holds the baby's arm out as if they're doing the tango. "A tango dancer, that's what you'll be. With a rose between your teeth. When you get teeth." Baby Lee watches Alan closely—she seems very serious. And then her face breaks into a smile. A huge, genuine grin. Toothless. Wide-mouthed. And full of delight.

"Remarkable," Laurie says.

"Awesome," Alan says. He kisses baby Lee on the forehead, spins her again, and they continue to dance.

Reading Group Guide

1. Laurie and Alan's relationship begins to change after the miscarriages. Fertility issues are a huge strain on a marriage. Laurie and Alan both secretly blame themselves, and each other. Is there anything they could have done differently?

2. As a pregnant woman, it's easy for Laurie to accept being a mother. But it's more complicated for Alan and Jack. When Alan finds out he's not the biological father, he feels his parenting role slip away. Jack donated his sperm for financial reasons. What is the definition of a parent? Discuss how Alan and Jack struggle to define their roles as fathers.

3. When Laurie and Alan find out about the sperm switch, Dr. Julian mentions termination as an option. But is it a real consideration for Laurie? For Alan? As a moral choice, should termination ever be an option?

4. All our main characters deal with guilt at some point in the book. Laurie's two miscarriages make her feel she's failed as a woman. Alan feels guilty over his inability to

bond with unborn baby Buddy and about his online flirtation with Nancy Futterman. Jack's got guilt to spare—stealing money, two girlfriends, lying to his parents. Who in the book has the most to feel guilty about? Is there a difference between justified and unjustified guilt?

5. When Alan and Laurie find out their baby is only half genetically related to them, the news is devastating. What would you do in this situation? If you were Laurie? If you were Alan? If you were Jack?

6. Would men and women react differently than portrayed in this book? Would most men sympathize with Alan? Agree with his behavior? Want a do-over? Would women be comfortable with Laurie's decision to have the baby? To insist on meeting Jack and making him part of her life?

7. Laurie meeting Jack makes Alan uncomfortable. Should she have respected his wishes and *not* met Jack? Was she right to allow Jack to move into the house, to take her to Lamaze? How much should Laurie allow Jack to be part of the baby's life afterward? Will that be fair to Alan? And is it fair for Laurie to expect Jack to be involved with the baby?

8. After Laurie and Alan find out about the switched sperm, their relationship becomes more difficult. Alan shuts down and Laurie goes off on her own to track down donor 296. Suppose Laurie hadn't contacted Jack. Would it be better (as Alan says) for them to know nothing about the sperm donor? Keep it a mystery? But what about medical issues? Shouldn't Laurie and Alan know

as much as possible about the donor to ensure the health of the baby?

9. Earlier in their marriage, Laurie and Alan talked about wanting to adopt a child. As Alan says, he doesn't need to replicate himself—but when he finds out he isn't the birth father, suddenly he's very uncomfortable. What makes a child *your* child? Is an adopted child different from a birth child? When do you fall in love with that child? Is Alan's fear a real one? Is it relatable?

10. There are various ways to have a baby when complications arise. Fertility treatments and adoption are two options. Discuss the difference between the time and expense of fertility treatments and adopting in a world filled with unwanted children in orphanages or foster care.

11. Which character changes the most? The least?

12. Discuss Alan's statement: "Families are all kind of different these days." Is that true?

13. What will happen with Laurie, Alan, and Jack after the baby comes home? Where will they be a year from now? Three years from now?

A Conversation with the Author

You've spent most of your career writing film and television. Why did you decide to write fiction?

I've always loved to tell stories in different ways—when I was in middle school, our class performed a play I'd written. For years I drew cartoons and made comic books because my goal was to be an artist and writer for *MAD* magazine. Go figure—I ended up writing film and TV.

A few years ago, I thought about trying fiction and signed up for an online UCLA Extension class.

And was it an easy transition?

No, it was misery. The act of filling up a page with prose—I was shocked at how hard it was. And this is coming from someone who makes a living writing 110-page screenplays or 55-page teleplays. But writing fiction was like learning a new language. I was lucky to have a fantastic teacher, Daniel Jaffe, who was very encouraging. *Expecting* was originally a short story I wrote for his class.

Why did you turn it into a novel?

I showed the short story to a fellow TV writer, and he suggested I expand it. I laughed at him. It took so much effort to write five thousand words, I couldn't imagine writing something at least eighty thousand words. But then I thought—why not?

How was the process?

As hard as I thought it would be. I decided to write it as part of NaNoWriMo, National Novel Writing Month, an Internet creative writing project where every year a group of people attempt to write fifty thousand words during the month of November. With the short story, I had the genesis of a novel, so on November first, I dove in. One of the great things about NaNo is because you're writing so quickly, there's no time to look back. Zoom, you just *go*. When you finally see what you've written in December, naturally some of it is horrible, but it's always a surprise to find gems there as well.

The short story began with Laurie getting the phone call about the switched sperm and ended with her meeting Jack for the first time. Because the story was from Laurie's perspective, there wasn't much about Jack, only what Laurie had read in his donor application. Doing NaNo meant I had to give him a life. I didn't do any other preparation for NaNo besides having the short story. No outline, nothing. That first day I thought—aha—it might be interesting to write the novel from three POVs: Laurie, Alan, and Jack. I had no idea Jack would juggle two girlfriends or struggle with finding a college major; it all sort of tumbled out. (NaNo people—I didn't include the short story in my final page count.)

A science fiction novelist friend told me that when you're writing a book, if you get to page seventy-five, you'll be in love with what you're writing, and suddenly you'll be on page three hundred with no idea how you got there. I was dubious, but he turned out to be right.

How much of the story is from your real life?

No switched sperm, whew. But my husband and I did have fertility issues. Our first pregnancy ended in a miscarriage. Like Laurie's, very early. But it was still devastating.

I remember the insensitivity of some people—one person said to me, "It's just a miscarriage. It's not as if it was a stillbirth." Of course there's a difference, but the loss of an imagined life is still a death. I was lucky to be on staff at *thirtysomething* at the time and was able to write an episode about the experience.

Our second pregnancy resulted in a son, and then we couldn't get pregnant again and started seeing fertility doctors. We looked into adoption too, something we'd always wanted to do. At one point I was pregnant again *and* we had an infant daughter who would be arriving soon from India. But that pregnancy also ended in miscarriage.

I feel lucky and blessed to have both a birth child and an adopted child. And I would encourage anyone to explore adoption.

So where did the idea of switched sperm come from?

We got pregnant the second time through IUI, and my husband made a joke about how he hoped he was the father. I filed that away in the writer part of my brain—"But suppose he's *not*?"

That's one reason I love being a writer. Everything is "what if?" What if Atticus Finch hadn't agreed to take Tom Robinson's case? Suppose Captain Ahab said, "Enough with the whales. I'm going to open a sushi restaurant in Nantucket."

I drove my husband insane writing the book because I wanted to make sure to capture the male perspective—how would a man react? "Honey, what would you do if somebody switched around your sperm?" I see Alan as sympathetic because he's facing a terrible dilemma—his child isn't his child; his wife is becoming friends with the sperm donor. What will be his role in the family once the baby is born?

Your favorite writers?

I love Edith Wharton and Charles Dickens and F. Scott Fitzgerald. John Irving and Kate Atkinson. Colum McCann's *Let the Great World Spin* was so brilliant I couldn't write anything for weeks after reading it. Nick Hornby and Douglas Coupland, Helen Fielding and Sophie Kinsella—I enjoy writers who make me laugh. I wish David Sedaris lived at my house. *Wolf Hall* and *Bring Up the Bodies* were amazing, and I hope Hilary Mantel hurries up and finishes the third book in the series. And I read a lot of mysteries—Ruth Rendell, Ian Rankin, Henning Mankell, and Denise Mina are some of my favorites. Imogen Robertson writes a wonderful series of historical mysteries. I could go on and on.

Any advice to writers starting out?

I hear from a lot of people that they have great ideas for a novel or a screenplay. Ideas are great, but you've got to get it on paper. Then you're a writer, not just somebody who has good ideas. Don't be afraid. Pour it out there. And you'll be surprised.

Acknowledgments

Writing a book feels like the most solitary thing in the world, but it would have been impossible to do by myself.

Thank you to teachers and early readers and people who offered research and encouragement. Barbara Aron, Megan Pratt, Joe Dougherty, Tom and Betsy Hamilton, Brian Wilson Schouweiler, Daniel Jaffe, Barrie Jo Kirby, Ruth Mohanram, Dan Pyne, Seema Malhotra, Christina Friar, Michael Cassutt, Racelle Rosett, Jeff Kline, Ann Kramer Brodsky, Carol Starr Schneider, and Rebecca Harvill.

A special thank-you to Jillian Medoff for her friendship and patience and her excellent advice—so sit down and write a novel already.

Rich Green is more than an agent—we've known each other for years and this book would not be possible without him. Dan Lazar, agent extraordinaire who talked me off many a ledge. Onward! Every first-time novelist should be lucky to have an editor like Shana Drehs and the wonderful team at Sourcebooks.

My children, Max and Lucy, who think the best part of the book is the dedication.

And to John, who wears deck shoes but doesn't tell dumb jokes like Alan. (Most of the time.)

About the Author

Ann Lewis Hamilton has written for film and television. Her credits include *Grey's Anatomy*, Stephen King's *The Dead Zone*, and *thirtysomething,* among others. She lives in Los Angeles.

Expecting is her first novel. Visit her website at: www.AnnLewisHamilton.com.